HARD LIMIT

Meredith W

GUNNISON COUNTY LIBRARY DISTRICT
Ann Zugelder Library
307 N. Wisconsin   Gunnison, CO 81230
970.641.3485
www.gunnisoncountylibraries.org

Paperback ISBN: 978-0-9905056-1-7

PRINTED IN THE UNITED STATES OF AMERICA

For the P.S. team.
For the past ten years…
the good, the bad, and the ugly.

PROLOGUE

E: Meet me at the club in 10 minutes. Please don't be mad.

I reread Erica's text until my brain caught up to her meaning.

Fucking hell.

The club she was referring to could only be one. My knuckles went white, as if gripping the phone on the brink of crushing it might stop her from doing this. Drawing in a deep breath that did nothing to calm me, I pulled up her number and held the phone to my ear. I listened to the endless ring, biting back the string of curses that would fly if she picked up. I knew she wouldn't.

The warm timbre of her voicemail greeted me. I was stung with missing the woman behind the sound, but I couldn't ignore the infuriating fact that she wasn't picking up the fucking phone. I hung up and grabbed my keys. I flew down the stairs to the Tesla and, wasting no time, pushed my way into the rush hour traffic.

Checking the time, I calculated my journey and how long she'd be there without me. Ten or fifteen minutes if I were lucky. My mind spun over what could go down in that span of time in the exclusive underground establishment I'd known for years as *La Perle*.

She'd be prey.

If I were lurking in the shadows there as I'd done more times than I cared to admit, that's all I would see in her. A little blond bombshell with just enough fire to make a Dom want to make her his. A man would have to be fucking blind not to want to bring her to her knees.

I hit the gas and swerved, bypassing a cluster of slowing cars that put precious time between us. As worry plagued my thoughts, so did unwanted memories of the club. I hadn't stepped foot in there since I met Erica months ago. I'd had no reason to go back to that life. My jaw clenched as I thought of everything that had played out there, countless meaningless moments that I'd kept coming back for, years after I left Sophia. Everything about the place was charged with the promise of sex, the darkest kind of possibilities hanging in the air between every bated breath and less-than-innocent exchange.

My chest was painfully tight. Anger was there. The teeth-gnashing frustration that only Erica could elicit. But under all of it was love. Love for Erica that set my desire on fire. Though I wanted her far from all of it, my basest desires painted a fantasy of finding her in the club and being the man to tame her—even as I knew how fucking impossible that task was. In the daylight, she never made it easy, but hell if she didn't submit like a dream at night.

I hit the brake at a red light. I closed my eyes, and there she was, gazing up at me with those hooded blue eyes, endless oceans. All that hellfire spirit tempered in the name of the pleasure I would give her. And I always gave her more than she could handle. I never let her rest until she was sated. Until I saw the wonder in her eyes that only I could put there, having pushed her to a place no one had ever taken her. Until the only word she could form was my name.

We were never short on passion. We couldn't keep our hands off of each other. Adrenaline raced over the fatigue that had settled into my bones after another sleepless night. I could fuck the woman until I was blind, and it wouldn't be enough. She'd promised me a lifetime, and I had every intention of loving her well every day this life would give me.

Love was a small word for what I felt for Erica. Maybe it was an obsession, this never-waning determination to make her mine in every way she'd let me. Heath had noticed, even warned me when he saw how she was changing me. He was no stranger to addiction, and no one could deny that she was my vice. The drug I refused to live without, no matter how many times she pushed me away. I'd fought like hell to keep the upper hand between us to protect her, to keep her out of the path of those who would hurt one to destroy the other. I couldn't lose control and risk losing something more important—the one person who'd come into my life and made it worth living.

Yes, she'd changed me, as much as a man with my particular affinities could change. She'd pushed me. She'd walked into my life, five-feet-three inches of fiery independence. Her mere presence challenged me, getting under my skin, making me habitually hard until I could find the unexplainable peace that being inside her supple little body could bring. Even now, I could barely take a full breath, knowing she was beyond my reach. I clutched the steering wheel tighter. My bloodless fingertips tingled with the need to feel her body under them, loving her, claiming her, restraining her.

Fuck.

I adjusted my inconvenient hard on. Pointless when visions of the night before flooded me now. Her full, swollen lips parting for me and only me. Her nails digging into my thighs as she took all of me in the hot bliss of her mouth.

I released my tense hold, exhaling an uneven breath. My thumb grazed the worn leather of my belt. The hammer of my heart kicked up. The light turned green, and I sped closer to our destination. A flicker of anticipation took over with a rush of blood to my now rock-hard cock.

If nothing else, I'd enjoy punishing her when this was all said and done.

CHAPTER ONE

Two weeks earlier

I slid my cold palms up and down the sides of my dress. I'd dressed up to make a good impression. I knew it was foolish. Especially since this wouldn't exactly be a first impression.

"Coffee?"

Blake walked up to where I stood and held out a steaming cup. He was dressed in dark blue jeans and a white collared shirt that made his skin glow. His skin was tanned from our time at the beach house, the place where we went to escape the city life and recharge. Today, like all the others, Blake took my breath away. He could have stepped out of a catalogue, but there was more to the man than his breathtaking good looks. His entire presence had a way of throwing me off balance. Sometimes—when I wasn't swooning over his perfection—I wondered if I did that to him too.

"Thank you," I murmured. Our hands grazed each other when I took the cup, and I let the heat seep into my fingers.

"Call me crazy, but you look nervous." He sipped his own coffee and cocked his head.

I stared into the creamy liquid, let the rich aroma fill my nose, and tried to imagine what the next half hour would bring. Being here with Blake by my side should have been a small—a great—comfort, but it wasn't. "I can't help it."

He chuckled softly. "You have absolutely no reason to be. You realize that, right?"

Easy for him to say. Across the room, a tall young man was speaking with some of the other investors. I was now on a first-name basis with many of them, but I couldn't get past the fact that they were the makers and breakers of dreams. They were men, more or less, like Blake. Some were self-made, and others had done well in their professional careers and had taken on angel investing as a hobby, dabbling with fresh new ideas.

The young man's jaw was tight, his motions jerky under a tense smile and wide eyes, like he'd consumed all of the coffee in Boston this morning.

"That was me a few months ago," I said. "It's terrifying, and you'll never know what that feels like. Plus I probably have post-traumatic stress disorder from all the shit you put me through in this room. *Twice.*"

Blake's amused expression lacked all the remorse I was trying to elicit from him. Only months ago we'd come face to face in this very room, a meeting that set off an unexpected series of events—our life together as we knew it.

"I can see you're really broken up about that," I added, trying to sound annoyed as I blew a puff of steam off my coffee.

"I was a jerk. I admit it."

"A complete asshole," I corrected.

A cocky grin curved his lips. "Fine, but you couldn't get me to take a single second of it back, because now I have you."

His green-eyed gaze locked to mine as he stood in front of me, his stance wide and casual. He had me all right. As my anxiety slowly melted, I fought the impulse to kiss the smirk off his face in front of all these men in suits. The man drove me wild, in more ways than one.

"What do you think? Any regrets?" he asked.

His eyes darkened as if he could read my thoughts, the amused, cocky man replaced by the lover who held my heart in his hands. I drew in a breath of air through my nose, waiting for the touch that often followed that look. A simple reassuring touch that held in it all the love we shared for each other.

He trailed his fingertips lightly along my jaw, lowering his face to the side of mine. The soft kiss brushed against my cheek could have been mistaken for a quiet exchange between colleagues and filled the air between us with his scent. My breath caught, trapping his essence in my lungs. I wanted to be immersed in it, bathed in that uniquely masculine aroma.

He retreated, returning to his casual stance in front me. His coffee cup occupied his beautiful lips once more when I wanted them against me again. God, the sensual torture I'd endured at the mercy of those lips.

Closing my eyes, I shook my head. There were no words. No regrets. He was right. All the ups and downs, however painful, had been worth it. We'd made mistakes. We'd hurt each other, but somehow we'd come through it stronger. He knew my heart, and I knew his. I couldn't speak for the future, but I couldn't imagine it beside anyone but Blake.

"Still nervous?" he murmured.

I opened my eyes to find his amused smile returned, new warmth in his eyes.

"No," I admitted, too aware of our lack of privacy and conflicted by the sudden shift in the air between us. I tried to ignore the way my heart swelled against the walls of my chest, that nameless reminder of how desperately I loved him. I was a slave to this man and the body that repeatedly shattered my ability to comprehend life beyond our bedroom. I wished now that we were alone, that I could be free to touch him. I ached to touch him.

"Good. This will be fun, I promise." He moved to my side and slid his arm around me, stroking light circles at the small of my back.

Maybe this wasn't casual anymore. Blake had a way of letting the world know I was his no matter where we were. Boardroom or bedroom, he never left much doubt. I can't say I minded. I wanted to lean into him now, breathe him in, and let the world melt away in his arms.

"We're starting in a few minutes. Do you want to eat something? You didn't have breakfast," he murmured, his breath warm against my neck.

I shook my head. "No, thanks." I paused, unable to ignore the little seedling of doubt that grew within me. "Blake..."

"What is it, baby?"

His voice was soft as his pet name for me rolled off his

gorgeous lips. And the way he looked at me... I could ask for the Hope diamond on a silver platter and I had little doubt he would figure out a way to bring it to me.

"Are you sure you want me here?"

He winced, marring his beautiful features with a small frown. "What do you mean? Of course I do. I put you on this board for several reasons, and they weren't all selfish. You deserve to be here as much as any of these guys. "

I rolled my eyes. "I doubt that."

"You have your own experiences—failures and successes—that you're bringing to the table today. You know that."

The reassuring presence of his palm on my back disappeared, replaced by a gentle caress up my arm and back to my cheek. He tilted my chin up until he was all I could see, all I could think about.

"Don't doubt it, Erica. Don't ever doubt your value."

I shook my head slightly. "I guess I'm worried those reasons have more to do with...*us*, than me deserving to be here. What if I don't have anything to contribute? I don't want to embarrass you in front of all these people."

He pivoted his impressive body, squaring with mine. "Listen to me. This is your first pitch as a prospective investor, so it's okay to be a little nervous. Just ask the questions that come to mind. If none do, it probably has a lot more to do with the poor guy over there who's about to toss his breakfast than you. He's the one with his ass on the line, so do yourself a favor. Drink your coffee, waltz over there like you own this fucking place—because in a few weeks, when you're my wife, you will—and do what you do best. Be a boss. Look for talent and decide if this guy's venture is worth a second look."

I swallowed over the emotion that burned in my throat. How he could have that kind of faith in me blew my mind. Then again, not much about Blake wasn't completely overwhelming and mind blowing. "You're incredible, you know that?"

His serious expression softened into a smile that met his eyes. Blake's happiness meant everything to me. I wanted to hold onto it, bind it with my own, and stay that way as long as we could. Hopefully forever.

I closed my eyes, cherishing the brief moment between us. His lips met my forehead with a soft kiss.

"Now, let's go find our seats before I send everyone home and make passionate love to you on that table. I'm having a hard time keeping my hands off of you right now."

I looked up, trying not to let my thoughts run away with the fantasy. "It's a little early in the morning for idle threats," I teased with a half smile.

His tongue slid out, traveling a sensual path across the bottom of his teeth. "Not an idle threat, and I think you know that. Now get your sweet ass over there and impress me."

I waited a second for the heat to fade from my face before I led the way to the long conference table where the others were now taking their seats. We sat down and Blake cleared his throat, glancing down at a paper in front of him.

"Everyone, this is Geoff Wells. He's here to present on his venture, wearable technology applications."

Geoff was young, early twenties. He was thin, his skin pale, and his dark blond hair fell long and untamed on his shoulders. He had all the earmarks of a programmer. His bright blue eyes were wide, darting from face to face, and his Adam's apple worked on a swallow as he waited for all the people seated across from him to get settled. God, did I feel for the man. When our eyes met, I smiled. Maybe I could be a friendly face in the crowd. He smiled back, seeming to relax his posture some.

"Thanks for coming, Geoff," I said. As nervous as I was for him, wanting him to feel more at ease launched me out of my shell. I nodded toward the stack of papers in front of him. "Tell us about your idea."

He straightened and drew in a deep breath. "Thanks for having me. I have been programming most of my life, but the past few years I have been focusing specifically on application development. As many of you might already know, we will be seeing a new market emerging in the technology space over the next year. Software—specifically applications—for wearable technology."

Geoff launched into the details of his project. He spoke animatedly, the way Sid and I sometimes spoke about our business to each other and others. All of us—Sid, Blake, James, and I—lived in another world, our own high-tech bubble. We spoke a different language. I wasn't a codeslinger, but I loved the business side of technology and I reveled in our weird little microcosm. Geoff clearly lived in this world too, and possibly not much outside of it based on his complexion and unkempt hair.

The next fifteen minutes were filled with all the high-level details of Geoff's plan to expand on the applications he'd already created. He hit all the checkpoints I'd drilled into my mind when I was preparing my pitch to Angelcom months ago. As Geoff spoke, I recognized his passion and talent. Beyond that, I thought the idea was pretty neat. I jotted notes down onto the legal pad in front of me, eager for a chance to ask him questions and secretly hoping that Blake was as excited about it as I was.

Blake's phone silently lit up, distracting him from the presentation. I shot him a glare. When he didn't notice, I jabbed him with the toe of my shoe. His frown met my own, and a small knowing smile replaced it. He looked straight ahead, his focus trained on the only person who should have had his attention in that moment.

"What applications have you built so far?" Blake asked when Geoff hit a pause in his presentation.

"I have a handful of apps built for major platforms that will be releasing in a few months."

"How quickly do you think you can bring more apps to the marketplace?"

"It depends on funding. I need a lot more developers who specialize in different platforms working on multiple projects. Right now it's pretty much just me."

"Do you have more ideas already mapped out?" I asked.

"I have several. The technical specifications are ready to go. I just need more hands on deck to build them out so we can release them before someone else does."

I nodded, doing some quick math, matching up his funding request with the timeline in front of us. I glanced to the side, hoping what I saw in Blake's eyes was interest. He looked back to Geoff before I could try to read him.

"Okay, Geoff, I think we've covered all the basics. Do you have anything else?"

Geoff shook his head. "I think that's the gist of it, unless you have more questions."

Blake glanced around, an unspoken last call for questions. When met with silent nods, he prompted the gentlemen on the other side of us to speak. "What do we think, gentlemen? Ready to decide?"

The first man, one who'd sat in on my pitch, quickly passed. He'd passed on mine as well. Geoff worried the inside of his cheek.

The next two investors passed, and I was fully anxious for Geoff now. His gaze landed on Blake, the familiar terror of being unilaterally rejected plain on his features. Blake clicked his pen a few times.

"I will…" He paused, taking another moment to tap the pen to his lips. "I think I will defer to Miss Hathaway on this one."

He gestured to me at his side. My jaw fell open slightly. I loved Geoff's concept, but as the seconds ticked by, I hoped that Blake would be the one to make the move. With his arm over the back of his chair, Blake gave me a crooked smile. Damn him.

Geoff now looked as confused as he was terrified, his face even paler than it had been.

"I like it," I said quickly.

Geoff's face brightened. "You do?"

"I do. I like everything about it so far. I think it has

incredible promise. I'd love to hear more about your specific app ideas."

A broad smile split his face. "Thank you so much. Whatever you need to know—"

"How does next week look for you, Geoff?" Blake interjected, shifting Geoff's attention away from me.

"Next week is perfect. Um, anytime that works for you, of course."

"Great. We'll have Greta set something up in reception." Blake glanced to the other men. "Gentlemen, thank you for coming. I think we're good to wrap up."

Gradually the other investors rose with us.

Geoff gathered his notes and circled the large table to where I stood. "Thank you so much for this opportunity."

"No problem. I'm excited to check out some of the things you've built." I gave him a warm smile and shook his hand. "I'm Erica Hathaway, by the way."

Blake rose by my side and held out his hand next, his palm meeting Geoff's in a firm grasp. "She'll be Erica Landon in a few weeks. I'm Blake, her fiancé."

Geoff's smiled broadened. "Great to meet you, Mr. Landon. I've heard a lot about you."

"Yeah? Well, it's all true." Blake laughed quietly before his attention diverted across the room. "Excuse me. I have to go talk to someone quick. But congrats, Geoff. Erica has very discriminating tastes, so you're lucky to have her in your corner."

I rolled my eyes and nudged Blake's arm, urging him off. "Go away and let us chat."

Blake grinned and left us.

"Sorry. He's… Well, don't feel bad. He horrified me at my first pitch."

"You pitched here?"

I shrugged, in disbelief that I was now sitting on the other side of that table after a matter of months. "Yeah, that's kind of how we met."

"Wow. He must have really liked your idea."

I laughed and fought the blush that I felt certain was coloring my face. *He liked something.*

"Blake is a great person to have on your team. He's taught me a lot." I reached into my purse and handed him my card. "Here's my info if you need to reach out to me for anything. I might contact you with a few more questions before our meeting. I need to let all that information marinate for a bit though."

"Of course." He studied the card closely. "Clozpin?"

"That's my startup." I decided not to mention that Blake refused to print my Angelcom cards until I changed my name. Damn, the man was possessive.

Geoff looked up, his elated smile now a seemingly permanent feature on his face. "Awesome. I can't wait to check it out."

"I'll be in touch, okay?"

"Great, thanks again."

CHAPTER TWO

As Geoff turned to leave with the others, Blake spoke in quiet tones to someone through the open door. I leaned back against the table, waiting for him to return. He closed the door and stalked toward me.

"Alone at last."

I bit my lip. "How did I do?"

He slowed in front of me and wrapped an arm around my waist, drawing me closer to him. "You made me proud. You always do."

"You put me on the spot. Are you going for some sort of record for the number of times you can drive me nuts in this room?"

He smirked. "Would you expect any less from me?"

"No, of course not. Tell me what you really think about his idea though. Am I way off?"

"It has promise. I had a feeling you'd bite."

I skimmed my hands up to his neck, sifting through the hair that fell a little long against the collar of his shirt. "What if you hate something that I love? It's our investment. Shouldn't we agree?"

"I guess, ideally. But if you like something, grab it and go. Just like you did today."

He ran a finger down the front of my dress and back up, cupping my breast through the fabric. I leaned into his touch. The unmistakable proof of his desire was hard against my hip.

"I take it you like when I'm decisive."

He pressed his hips forward, trapping me between the table and his hard body. "I'm not like most men whose dicks go limp at the sight of a woman who has her own mind."

He brought his lips to my neck, trailing down over my collarbone. Goosebumps raced over my skin and my nipples hardened into points that strained against my dress. I arched against him, desperate to give them some relief, but the more our bodies touched, the more out of control I felt of my own.

"You realize that runs in stark contrast to your compulsive need to be in charge of me, right?"

Curving his hand at my nape, he gazed at me. The now serious look in his eye stole my breath.

"I don't want to run your life, Erica. I want to be a part of it, and I want you to be a part of mine. But I won't have you exclusively calling the shots for both of us, especially when it comes to life and death."

I stared, speechless and breathless—from his intoxicating proximity, his possessive hold on me, and the painful knowledge that our relationship hadn't been the only thing in peril over the past few months. At times, our lives had been too. For that, I wasn't entirely blameless.

"That's not too unreasonable, is it?" The tension around his mouth softened.

"No," I whispered.

We'd been to hell and back, negotiating the terms of who held the power in our relationship. He'd made concessions, and in the end, torturous as it had been, so had I. I'd given him more control than I'd ever given anyone.

He relaxed his grasp, roaming over the fabric of my dress, down to where the edge of it met my thighs.

"Good. I'm glad we cleared that up. Now that work's done for the day, I'd like to fuck you on this table, if you don't mind."

I paused, gauging the seriousness of his statement. "I wouldn't mind, but I'm sure no one in the company wants to walk in on that. There's no lock on that door."

"Doesn't matter. I gave Greta explicit instructions not to disturb me in here—under any circumstances."

"Explicit instructions?" I teased.

A small smile broke his earlier seriousness. "Yes, they were filthy. She was appalled when I detailed the things I planned to do to you." He hiked my dress over my hips and effortlessly lifted me onto the table.

"She might be too busy wishing it were her to keep people out." I covered his hands with my own, trying in vain to push my dress back down to a decent place over my thighs. He pushed farther between my legs so I was nearly baring everything.

The reality of what he was proposing crept over me, heating my cheeks and setting a slow burn over my skin. I saw no shred of doubt in his eyes. A second later, he covered my mouth with his, overwhelming me with his hungry kiss. Starving for him too, I let his tongue pass between my parted lips. I sought the warm sweetness of it and gave myself over to it, but where was this really going?

I gasped when he broke away, bringing his mouth

down, kissing me behind my ear and down my neck, drawing a decadent path of desire over my exposed skin.

"Blake... We aren't really doing this, are we?"

Sifting his fingers through my hair, he mangled the twist I'd carefully arranged earlier. "I'm going to be balls deep in you in about thirty seconds. So, yes."

I struggled for my next breath, anticipation and fear robbing me of air.

"Are you wet for me, Erica? Because I'm coming in hard." He pressed his fingertips into the meat of my ass, bringing us closer so our bodies connected through our clothes. "Fast and hard. Is that how you want it?"

Fuck, yes. In time with my mind's silent reply, I gripped his shirt at the shoulders, drawing him closer still.

He kissed me roughly, tugging down the arm of my dress, and spread a torrent of hot, wet kisses over my collarbone and shoulders. I let my head fall back, my mind humming with desire. My breathing became shallow. I spread my legs wider to accommodate him, hugging his hips and welcoming his advance. Lifting my knee, I hooked an ankle around his thigh to urge him against me.

He exhaled sharply, grinding his steely erection against my soaking panties. "Jesus, I want you. Right now." He curled his fingers around the strings of my panties and yanked down.

"Oh, God," I groaned, reeling with the delicious contact and painfully aware of the ache between my legs where my body was more than ready for everything he wanted to give me.

"I've wanted to take you on this table from that first

day. In fact, I have no idea why it's taken this long to get around to it."

"Then get around to it, before someone finds us." I had no idea how or if we'd get away with it, but I knew Blake wouldn't be deterred, and I wasn't about to say no. I unbuttoned his shirt quickly, eager to feel more of him against me.

He wet his lower lip with his tongue, watching me intently as I skimmed over the hard muscles of his chest. "You worried?"

I swallowed, my worry rising to the surface again. "Yes, obviously. I don't want to get caught."

"I think you do. " Mischief flashed behind his eyes. He slid my panties down past my ankles, giving my thigh a quick slap on his journey back to my hips.

"Why would I want that?" My voice was weak and breathy, betraying the physical effect the vision had on me.

He reached for his zipper. Pushing down his boxers, he freed his thick erection, palming the length of it in slow decadent pulls. I bit my lip too hard, suppressing a moan that might go beyond the walls of our precarious location. I desperately wanted him inside me.

"I think you like the idea of it—the chance that someone might catch me fucking you. In public. Where we shouldn't be."

I stared at him, my mind a haze of desire and excitement as I envisioned the possibilities. All of them humiliating but strangely erotic when I imagined a stranger walking in to see Blake fiercely claiming my body the way I knew he would be… soon. My core pulsed, empty and eager to be filled.

"No," I lied.

He threaded his fingers through my hair again, fisting tight enough to make me shiver. That edge, that promise of control, shot a bolt of awareness through me. If I'd been wet before, I was drenched now.

"Yes, you do." The husky words did little for my waning self-control. "Imagine it... you on the brink of coming... so close to the edge that we couldn't stop if we wanted to."

My heart thumped as I imagined the scene he drew. The more we talked about it, the more time we gave someone to find us. "Just fucking do it, Blake, before someone walks in."

He teased his cock against my entrance. "Don't piss me off, Erica. I'll make you scream. Then everyone will know I fucked you on this table."

I closed my eyes and rolled back my head. "Blake, please... I'm begging you. Fuck me now, or..." *Or what? Or... stop?* No. I needed him badly, and I needed him now.

He nudged into me a fraction more. I quivered against him, wishing I could somehow draw him into me, but he held me firmly in place. At his mercy.

"Blake," I pleaded, clawing at his hips. His taut muscles flinched under my fingertips.

Then he bent over me, lowering me so my back rested against the table. He slid his fingertips across my cheek, over my lips, and finally rested on my throat. He caught my hip with his free hand, and without further warning, lunged into me. Our bodies connected with a slap. When an uncontrollable cry left my lips, he covered my mouth, muffling the sound.

Everything inside my core seized around him. My thighs clung to his unmoving body, waiting for more. With trembling hands, I gripped the edge of the table for leverage. Somewhere in the crazy rush of his possession, I wanted him to reach the deepest part of me. On his next thrust, he did. He stoked the burning heat of my needy body, again and again.

I tried to keep quiet, but small gasps and moans crept past my lips into the hot shield of his palm.

The reminder that we could be discovered enflamed all my sensations with prickling fear. My skin heated unbearably. I arched off the table, his name on my lips. I didn't want to get caught, but I couldn't keep quiet to save my life.

Blake did this to me. Turned my body and mind against all reason. His breathing was labored as he fucked me steadily, his silence seemingly locked in the bulging muscle of his jaw. His hand left my mouth, found purchase around my still clothed breast. With a firm squeeze, he taunted the hard nipple underneath. I bit my lip with a groan.

Something right and karmic weighted the air as he pushed us deeper and deeper into our pleasure. This is where we had begun. I closed my eyes, remembering how badly I'd wanted him, against all reason. Now he was mine. Utterly mine.

I'd fantasized so many times about the different ways that first day in his board room could have ended. This was one of them. As much as I'd hated him then, my body still wanted him. I trembled, the beginnings of a climax taking hold. The fantasy coming to life was pushing me to the brink.

"I imagined this... Blake, I wanted this." The confession poured out of me, with all the other forbidden sounds leaving my lips.

Without warning, he pulled out of me, bringing my slow climb to an abrupt halt. My eyes flew open. Before I could speak, he'd pulled me down and flipped me to my belly. My hips pressed against the hard table. Blake bent over me, his erection, slick from my arousal, pressed against my bare bottom. Energy radiated between us—taut and tenuous. My heart beat in a flurry against the table. My hands on either side of me braced me for whatever Blake had planned. His breath kissed my neck. My pussy clenched, desperately empty without him.

"Blake," I whimpered, squirming back against him to be closer.

"This is how I wanted you, Erica. I wanted you bent over this table, screaming my name. I couldn't hear a single fucking word you were saying."

He kneed my legs apart. I fisted my hands into tight balls, my hips pressed back. Then he was inside me again, filling me completely with a hard shove.

I released a small cry before I could stop myself. "Blake!"

My body at his mercy, my cheek against the cool, slick surface of the table, I couldn't imagine anything more intense than what I was currently experiencing. My body buzzed, building with sharp climbing sensations that brought me closer to heaven.

"You're so deep." Shocks of pleasure rocketed through me every time he filled me.

"I haven't shown you deep yet."

Before I could catch a breath and brace myself, he grabbed both my hips. Hauling me back to him, he drove farther into my sensitive tissues. Something between a scream and a groan rumbled through my chest, but before it could escape my lips, Blake's hand was there, silencing the next series of cries as he powered into me.

Hands fisted, toes curling, I came hard and weakened against the table, wasted, but Blake was still hard as ever.

"Come, Blake. Hurry," I whispered. The thought of Greta walking in on us was sobering, and another wave of fear raced through my veins.

He released my hip and stilled inside me. "That was too quick. I think we have time for one more, don't you?"

Blake pulled out slightly. Circling to my front, he found my clit and pressed firmly. I jolted, on edge from having come so recently. Now he was threatening more. With every careful ministration he brought me closer, higher.

This wasn't a quickie. He was destroying me, and I was coming apart.

I cursed repeatedly, not caring about where we were anymore. Mindless, powerless, I lost all sense of propriety and decency as Blake continued to fuck me, rolling his hips with every driving thrust, massaging the tight walls of my pussy from the inside.

My orgasm built like a storm rolling in from a distance, until seconds later it was thundering through me. I could see it, bright flashing pulses of light behind my eyes. And God, could I feel it, a tornado rocketing through my core and shooting out of every limb.

Overwhelmed with sensation, I slapped my hand on the table, drawing a damp path down to my side. I muffled my cries against the table now that Blake's efforts to keep me quiet had seemingly been replaced with the singular task of fucking me as hard as he could.

"Erica!" Blake's tortured groan ripped from his lungs. The only sound that might have been heard beyond the walls of this room echoed off the walls as we both fell limp. Blake's body covered mine as we struggled for breath. His fingers slipped from me, and my pussy fluttered around the hard cock still pulsing inside of me.

Buzzing and deliciously wasted, I faintly registered that we hadn't been caught. The thought flitted away as Blake pulled out of me. A shiver ran over my exposed skin.

"Turn around. Let me clean you up."

I pushed myself up and turned on shaky legs. I feebly held myself up by the table. Blake grabbed my panties from the floor. He cast his gaze down, focused on the task of cleaning my oversensitive flesh with the garment. I stared down at him, wanting to see his eyes but almost afraid to meet them after what we'd done here. If Greta only knew.

A knock at the door had me standing straight and shoving down my dress to cover my nakedness.

"Shit. Blake!" My voice was a panicked whisper.

"Relax. I'll take care of it."

He stuffed my panties into his pocket. He tucked himself away and buttoned his shirt. As he moved toward the door, I pushed away from the table, trying desperately to fix my totally wrecked hair. Frowning, he opened the door only wide enough to greet whoever was knocking, carefully hiding me from anyone's prying eyes.

"Greta, I told you—"

She interrupted his berating tone with a quick apology, but her voice was so low I could barely hear it. Blake glanced back to me, his face revealing his agitation. He stepped out of the room without a word, leaving me to pull myself together.

★ ★ ★

I slumped into one of the chairs. Struggling to still the tremble in my hands, I tried to reason with the promise of danger that had sent my heart speeding and skipping. *Fuck.* Something about this time, apart from the others, had stripped me down in an entirely new way.

My body still hummed and ached where he'd been. Blake was right. Someone could have walked in at any time, and I wouldn't have cared. Sometimes I didn't recognize the person I'd become, the lover so enraptured with Blake's touch, the way he challenged me in every way. He put me on edge, but I didn't want it any other way.

I drew in a deep breath through my nose, determined to pull myself together. I'd triple checked my appearance in one of the room's decorative mirrors. Time stretched on, and when Blake didn't return, I ventured out. Greta sat stiffly typing at her desk. I wanted to ask where Blake had gone, but didn't want to bring attention to anything she might have heard. My cheeks heated. I made my way down the hall to his private office inside the Angelcom building. I approached the door, open only a crack. Reaching to push it open, I stopped abruptly at the sound of a woman's voice.

"When were you going to tell me, Blake?"

My stomach fell, my jaw clenched, and my already worn out nerves stood on edge. I knew that voice. I knew it, and I hated it.

Sophia.

"I told you this time would come. I didn't think it would come as a shock to you," Blake said.

"Then why did I have to hear it from Heath? You couldn't tell me yourself? After everything we've been through."

Blake sighed heavily. "You're closer with him. I figured you'd want to hear it from him."

"I was closer to you before you left me. Having Heath in my life means nothing when you're not in it."

Blake's low tenor filled the momentary silence. "Don't say that, Soph. Your friendship means a lot to him."

"It's about that little bitch, Erica, isn't it?"

"Watch your mouth," he growled.

"She's making you do this, isn't she?"

"I think we both know I don't take orders from anyone, including you. You have all the connections you need. Your business has shown healthy profits for over two years. There's no reason for me to stay invested at this point. We had an agreement, and it's time for us to exit."

"And what about us?"

The sharp edge of Sophia's tirade had softened with these last words, tinged with enough pleading emotion to make my fingers ball into tight fists. I sent up a little prayer that Blake wouldn't back down.

"What about us?"

She hesitated a moment. "She's trying to keep us apart. Can't you see that?"

Silence stretched over several seconds, the truth of her accusation settling into that space with absolute certainty. I wanted Sophia to finally have her claws out of Blake, and his connection to her business was the last thing tying him to her and their romantic history.

"This is the best thing, for everyone." His voice had quieted.

"Don't do this," she begged. "Don't let her do this to you. To us."

"There is no *us*, Sophia. What we had is over. It's been over for a long time, and you know that."

"It doesn't have to be. I'm better now. Just let me show you. I know what you need. This…what you're doing for her…this isn't *you*. You need a sub, someone who can appreciate everything you can give her. She needs a mentor, not a master. I *need* you, Blake. We need each other. Why can't you see it?"

I heard movement and took a step back from the door. My imagination was spinning out of control, filled with wild scenarios of what was taking place beyond my view.

Every vision involved Sophia, her hands on Blake, seducing him into succumbing to her desperate pleas. What if he weakened? She had a habit of touching him like she had a right to. But she didn't. Never again would she have the right to lay hands on the man who would soon be my husband. I harnessed all my willpower not to barge in and tell her so.

"You need to go. It's done."

"What can she do for you that I can't?"

Blake hesitated before saying his next words. "Sophia…we're getting married."

A heavy silence fell. I closed my eyes.

She didn't know.

"When were you going to tell me?" Her voice trembled.

He sighed heavily. "I don't know. Does it matter?"

A short laugh escaped her, a delirious sound that made me worry about what she might do next.

"I guess not. So that's it? She's everything you've ever wanted."

I read his silence as an affirmation. I prayed that it was.

"I imagine she's come a long way since you whipped her then. Does she know about the club?"

"No, and she never will," he shot back.

That soft, ingenuous laugh again. "You're kidding me. You're ready to spend forever with her, and she doesn't even know who you are."

"She does, trust me."

"Don't you think she should know?"

"Enough." The word came out like a threat.

"Blake…" She was pleading again.

I imagined her on her knees, begging him, like the natural submissive she'd been for him. Ready to surrender everything to him if he'd only give in to her.

"You never gave us a chance," she whispered.

"We never had a chance." The low timbre of his voice was barely audible.

"Don't do this to us," she sobbed.

"Leave, Sophia. Don't make this harder than it needs to be."

The movement came closer to the door, and I took a step back, my heart racing in anticipation of seeing Sophia in the flesh.

"Whatever you want, Blake, but I don't think it's this," she snapped. "You're going to regret this. We both know you will."

The door swung open and she gasped. Her shocked eyes narrowed quickly, the bleeding mascara the only imperfection on her flawless face. Her pin-straight brown hair flowed over her shoulders and the top of her designer leather jacket.

"You." The single word seemed to hold inside of it all of her spite. Tears shone in her eyes. Tears of frustration maybe, but whatever I saw there I recognized. A wild and untamed love. A love that breached the barrier of reason. "You're the one he wants."

"Leave, Sophia. Now." Blake gripped the edges of the doorway behind her.

The look of pure disdain on his countenance both satisfied and sickened me. I wanted him to shun her. I wanted her to be the dirt under his feet. But I couldn't deny that to have him look at me the way he was looking at her now would destroy me.

She took a quick step toward me, but I held my ground. As much as her words tore at me, threatening to expose every insecurity I had about belonging with Blake, I couldn't let her see it. The man who could have anyone wanted me, only me. I lifted my chin, grateful for the heels I'd worn that gave me the height to look her in the eye.

"That's right. I'm the one he wants. Now why don't you be a good girl and leave?"

"Fuck you," she spat.

"He just did. Now leave us be. He doesn't want you here."

A sneer marred the perfect planes of her face. "I made him who he is, Erica. The years that he was inside of me will be the years he'll never be able to forget, no matter what you do. Think of that when you're saying your vows."

"Sophia!" Blake's face twisted into an angry grimace as he took an intimidating step toward her.

Without looking back, Sophia disappeared down the hallway, leaving us there alone. I wanted relief, but rage and uncertainty rattled through me, making my hands tremble at my sides.

When Blake turned back into his office, I followed him in. I shut the door and leaned against it, needing its support. I stared at his silhouette as he looked out the window to the sprawling city skyline beyond.

I wanted to talk to him but wondered how I could

possibly keep my emotions from bubbling to the surface afterward. I wanted him to make this right, to erase the terrible things that she'd said. Her words still stung, as if she'd physically hit me with them. The shallow part of me wanted to believe my words had done the same to her.

"I'm sorry," he finally said.

"Why?"

He turned back, pinning me with the same green eyes that had me at his mercy only moments ago. "For her being here. For upsetting you."

"Why was she here?" I had my suspicions, but I wanted him to confirm it. I needed to know they were done, completely and irrevocably.

"I'm pulling my investment from her agency, making her buy me out." He shoved a hand through his hair. "That's what you wanted, right?"

"Yes."

"Well, there you have it."

"Do you wish you hadn't?" I couldn't hide the challenge in my tone. I didn't want to hear regret.

He pinched the bridge of his nose. "It had to be done, sooner or later. Sometimes it's just easier to appease certain people than to face off with them. She's one of those people."

"It's better than being held hostage by her forever, isn't it?"

"We'll see. She's used to getting what she wants."

"What did she mean by..." I let out a breath, questioning how far I wanted to push him after the morning we'd already had. "The club," I said quietly.

His eyes never left me. "What about it?"

I studied him. The twitch in his tightened jaw betrayed everything I'd heard, but he couldn't possibly want to tell me.

"Tell me about it."

He stalked closer, careful steps that brought us face to face. My back was against the door as he placed a flat palm beside my head. He towered over me, wordless empty seconds passing between us. "That place is in the past, and that's where it'll stay. Do you understand me?"

I took a few unsteady breaths. As much as I wanted to know, I questioned whether I should. "You can talk to me, Blake."

His lips fell open a fraction. Filled with a nameless emotion, his gaze darted over me. Before either of us could say a word, he captured my face in his hands and melded our mouths together. His motions were rough, his lips a bruising force against my own, as if he were trying to erase the past twenty minutes. Maybe he was simply trying to erase the past. We could get lost that way sometimes, forgetting everything. But even his fierce passion now couldn't overwhelm what had been said and everything I'd heard.

I pushed him back, ripping us apart. Jagged breaths burned through my lungs and tears threatened, a well of emotion that this morning had brought to the surface.

"Goddamn it, tell me."

Adrenaline and love and the slice of fear that came with facing off with the uncompromising side of Blake pulsed through my veins. He curled his arms around my body, pulling me into a firm embrace that I was powerless to fight. His breath danced over my neck, his lips, softer now, almost resigned as they slid over my pulse. The tender way he moved over me almost demanded that I relax and stop fighting him. I weakened, wanting him to make this all right.

"Let it go. Please." He brushed his cheek against mine. "Just let it go."

I squeezed my eyes closed and held him back, wishing like hell that I could.

CHAPTER THREE

I stared out our bedroom window into the moonlit darkness. I replayed Blake's conversation with Sophia in my head, over and over, like a track on repeat that wouldn't stop no matter how much I wanted it to. I tossed and turned, trying to get comfortable, but I couldn't forget the anger in her voice. Worse, the pain in it—an unsettling reminder that they'd loved each other once. That she still loved him.

And what the hell was the club? I'd thought of little else for the rest of the day but resisted the urge to ask him to tell me more about it. When it came to his past, I had to pry every painful detail from him. I planned to, but tonight I held back. A part of me didn't want to upset him even more than Sophia's visit had, but a deeper part of me worried about what I'd learn with the truth. Did I really want to know about this sliver of history that Sophia shared with him?

Still, I was about to become his wife, and I was haunted by the likely truth that she'd always know a side of him that I didn't. That vast unknown was what kept me from sleep as the minutes and hours ticked by. Blake slept peacefully beside me. Moonlight cast shadows over his face. If I hadn't memorized every beautiful feature, he might have looked like a stranger to me now, from this vantage, in the stark black-and-white of night.

Who was Blake…really? What made a man? What made anyone who they are at any given moment?

Blake was many things to me now. A lover, friend, a healer. A mentor too, yes. I cringed, hating Sophia's derogatory use of the word. Who had he been for her? Had he changed so much for me? Would he resent it as our years together wore on? Forever was a long time.

For the first time in a long time, my visions of happily ever after were tainted with unwelcome possibilities. What if I married the man I thought he was, only to find he was someone else entirely? What would I do then? How on earth could I survive without him, or with him, knowing I wasn't making him happy the way others had?

Blake stirred, momentarily pausing the incessant turning of my thoughts and the torturous barrage of doubt-filled questions assaulting my brain. He turned to his side, curling his body alongside mine. I stilled, hoping I hadn't woken him with my restlessness. His bare arm wrapped around me, coaxing me closer until I could feel his heart beating against me, a slow steady rhythm.

"Love you," he murmured against my neck. Seconds later, his breathing returned to its regular sleeping pattern.

I melted back into the welcome warmth of his chest and breathed out a heavy sigh. I wanted to cry then. I wanted to release all the terrible emotions Sophia had conjured. Why had I given her so much power over me? I had Blake's love. He loved *me*. But…maybe she was right. Doubt resurfaced, making my reassuring affirmations seem childish and inferior.

Maybe I'd never know the man he'd been before or

the feelings he'd harbored while they were together. I tortured myself with the thought until my body simply gave up in the early hours, leaving me barely enough sleep to stay functional the next day.

In the morning, I sat at my desk, rubbing my tired eyes. I thought a new day might help. A fresh start and a clear head, except my head was foggy from lack of sleep. Blake and I had shared our morning coffee, but only a few words passed between us after I told him I didn't sleep well. He hadn't asked why. Perhaps he knew.

I tried to force my thoughts back to work, systematically weeding through the tasks of the day. Emails, meetings, getting everyone up to speed. Thankfully the business had been on track and prospering since our latest partnership. Alex Hutchinson, an accomplished tech CEO whose own e-commerce site dovetailed well with our focus on apparel, had taken a chance on me and the results were paying dividends for both our businesses. Thanks to Sid's urging that we expand our reach and Blake's introduction to Alex, we had been able to work out an arrangement where Clozpin referred more sales to his site and his promotions helped build the membership and traffic of ours. The result was that my business was now more than self-sustaining. I was on track to being able to return Blake's initial investment sooner than I'd anticipated and still hold steady.

I looked up from the stack of papers containing August's financials that I'd been working through. The clock on the wall blurred before coming into focus. Noon was approaching, as was my long-overdue lunch date with

Marie. I'd considered canceling, but we really needed to talk about Richard. He was her boyfriend, but his role in the local press had become unsettling. As much as I wanted to put off our meeting, I couldn't. I startled when the office phone rang.

A moment later, Alli poked her head around the partition. "It's for you, hon."

"Who is it?"

"Someone from the local news. Maybe they want to do a promo for the site? I would have fielded it but they specifically asked for you."

"Okay, thanks." I picked up the phone. "Hello, this is Erica."

"Miss Hathaway, this is Melissa Baker. I'm from local WBGH. I was hoping to ask you a few questions regarding your connection with Daniel Fitzgerald and his campaign for governor."

I was silent a moment, the sound of blood thrumming through my veins loud in my ears. "Okay," I said, tentatively.

"Reports have been released by the local police in connection with the death of his stepson. Some of these reports imply that you are Fitzgerald's biological daughter. We have sources who have also confirmed that you have been working on his campaign. Can you confirm this?"

Yes, all of that was true, but I wasn't about to aid the media in its mission to smear Daniel's campaign or further link him to Mark's death, which was still under investigation.

I stalled. "I'm sorry, but this actually isn't a good

time," I said.

"Perhaps I could stop by your office some time that would be more convenient. I understand you run an Internet business here in Boston."

Jesus, what else did they know? This would be creeping into Blake's arena soon if it wasn't already.

"I'm not inclined to comment at this time. I hope you understand."

"But Miss—"

I hung up the phone quickly and rested my hands on the desk, hoping to still the tremor in them. Shit. It would only be a matter of time before Richard's digging into my personal life would hit the press. As the days passed with no word though, I'd started to hope that Daniel's PR concerns were farfetched.

A little more awake and a lot more frustrated, I left the office to meet Marie. I stepped out of the building stairwell and walked toward the black Escalade that always idled by the curb outside my office. Clay, Blake's hired bodyguard, and most days my personal chauffeur, looked up from the paper he was reading in the driver's side. He unlocked the vehicle. I slid into the back seat.

"Hey, Clay."

"Miss Hathaway," he said, his voice deep and polite.

"You can call me Erica, you know. I won't be Miss Hathaway much longer anyway."

A short nod was his only acknowledgement. "Where to this afternoon?"

"What's your last name?"

Our eyes met in the rearview mirror. "Barker."

"Well, Mr. Barker, I have a lunch date at The Vine on Newbury."

He smiled broadly, revealing his straight white teeth. "Very well, Miss Hathaway."

Ten minutes later, Clay had deposited me in front of the tiny bistro on the busy street. I scanned the dining room for Marie. The eyes of my mother's best friend lit up when I found her. I walked her way and hugged her, relieved to see her but brimming with frustration at the part she'd played in all of this, whether or not she knew it.

"How are you doing, honey? You look tired." Her lips pouted with concern as we settled down across from each other.

"I'm fine. Didn't sleep well last night."

"How's Blake?"

"He's fine. We're fine." I didn't want to get into the real reasons why I'd had a sleepless night. Thoughts of Sophia and their dark past flooded to the forefront of my mind. I pushed them aside when Marie spoke again.

"You must be getting excited about the wedding. I'm sure you can't wait to see Elliot again too. Gosh, I haven't seen him in ages."

I thought back to the last time I'd spoken with my step-father. The conversation had been rushed, and I tried to forget the pangs of disappointment I'd felt learning he wouldn't be coming out to Boston after all.

"He's not coming," I said flatly.

"Why not?

I hesitated. "He reached out to me a while ago to plan a trip out here, to commemorate Mom. It's been ten years."

Her face fell and her lips curled into a sad smile. I closed my eyes, not wanting to think about how Marie had filled my mother's place these past years. Except now we were more friends than anything, and I was absolutely furious with her.

"Anyway, Blake and I want to keep things small. Everything has been happening so fast. I just kept putting off telling Elliot about the wedding, and when we finally talked about him coming out, it sounded like he and Beth were going to be too busy for him to make a quick trip, so I didn't want to put him in an awkward situation by asking about the wedding."

"But he's your..." She sighed softly. "Well, I guess it's your decision, Erica. I'm sure he would make a way to be there, though."

"He offered to fly me out to Chicago, so Blake and I decided to go out this weekend for my birthday. I'll talk to him then and explain everything. It's no big deal, really."

Her eyebrows rose. "That sounds like fun, honey. I bet Blake is going to spoil you rotten." She gave me a girlish smile.

I wanted to return her excitement, but all I could think about was that damn reporter and how this news was threatening to blow up in our faces at any moment.

"Is everything okay?" Marie reached for my hand, feathering her fingers over mine.

I gave her a weak smile and sat back, retreating from her grasp when the waiter filled our waters. We ordered and the silence descended once more.

I cleared my throat quickly. "Are you still seeing Richard?"

"Of course. Why?"

I worried the inside of my lower lip and traced the edge of my cloth napkin on my lap. This wasn't going to be an easy conversation. I didn't want to see Marie upset, but she had to know. I drew in a deep breath, bracing myself. "I have to ask you something, and I need you to be honest with me. I know you care about Richard, but this is important."

"What is it? What's going on?"

"Did you tell him that Daniel Fitzgerald was my father?"

Her lips parted silently, her gaze steady on mine. "Why?"

I wilted, defeated by her reaction. I could have believed her if she'd denied it right off the bat. "Because, somehow, the police know that I'm Daniel's daughter. The investigation regarding his son's death still isn't closed, so they've got his life under a microscope right now. Now the press is latching onto this too. I just dodged a call from a local reporter. I have a sinking feeling there will be more."

"Are you implying that Richard had a part in this?"

I tried not to bristle at her defensive tone. Getting angry with her would go nowhere. I had to make her understand. "The night of the Spirit Gala, Richard was there. Remember, you told me to look out for him because he was covering the event with a photographer. He never introduced himself, but when the police questioned me about Mark's death, they had photos of him dancing with me. Not just one. Dozens of photos. Why would someone spend so much time on me, and how did those specific photos find their way into the police's hands?"

Marie picked up her water with shaky hands and swallowed the liquid down hard. "There has to be some other explanation for this. I don't know why Richard would do this."

"Maybe because he's using you to get information about Daniel. About me."

She shook her head with a frown. "That's impossible."

"He's a reporter, Marie. This is his job."

"He wouldn't do this. I know him." Her calm demeanor had risen to an almost frantic state. The truth hurt. This I knew.

I leaned in. "He said himself that his focus is on political news reporting, right? The controversy around Daniel's campaign—with Mark's death and now an illegitimate daughter helping with his campaign—how could he ignore it? Remember how things were on the rocks between you two, but then he came around after the gala? Everything changed between you two, seemingly out of the blue."

"Stop it, Erica," she snapped. "You don't know what you're talking about."

"How could you tell him about Daniel? You couldn't even tell *me* for a decade, for Christ's sake. And you tell *him*. A reporter? Now I have no idea what this is going to do to my business or Blake's, not to mention Daniel's campaign."

She scoffed. "You're worried about Daniel's campaign? He's given you nothing. He didn't want anything to do with you, Erica. Patty gave him a chance to be a father, and he chose his blue-blood family and his career. You grew up without a father because of that choice, and now you're fighting for his career too?"

My jaw tightened. She wasn't the only person to hold that belief. Blake would rather see Daniel in jail than anywhere else, but I couldn't stomach the thought of his demise because I'd made the mistake of discovering his identity and seeking him out.

"You don't understand what's at stake," I said simply, not wanting to get into the emotional reasons why I needed Daniel a free man. "What else did you tell him?"

"I don't know, Erica." Her head fell into her palm and she closed her eyes. "I had a couple drinks, and we were talking about how accomplished you are. Once I got going about all you've done under the circumstances, I probably went on for a while. Still, knowing what you mean to me, I can't believe he would intend to hurt you by misusing that information."

"Well, I'm nearly positive that he did." And if Daniel ever found out, God help him.

"No one else knows? What about the people you work with?"

I tossed my napkin on the table and shoved my chair back, losing my patience with Marie's obvious unwillingness to accept the truth of the matter. "Think what you want to, Marie. But do me a favor. Next time you see Richard, ask him if he told anyone else what you

48

told him. Look him in the eye when you do, and tell me if you believe him."

I rose to leave, grabbing my purse.

"Erica, wait."

I paused. "You warned me once to be careful around Daniel. If you care for Richard, you might want to pass that advice on to him too."

I turned and walked out, ignoring her calling out my name one last time. I'd already said too much. But hell, if he was already hot on Daniel's trail, he should know Daniel wasn't a man to be trifled with. Maybe Richard already had his suspicions about Mark's apparent suicide. I had no idea who in Daniel's camp knew the truth. But I'd sworn Blake to secrecy, and I wouldn't be the one to put my own father behind bars.

* * *

I came home early and dropped the groceries on the counter. Despite my nagging fatigue, I threw myself into cooking dinner. Blake's family was coming over, and I had been looking forward to hosting since we'd be missing out on this weekend's dinner at his parents'. I lost myself in the task of prepping two large lasagnas, temporarily forgetting the worries that kept threatening to poke through.

I put the pans into the oven to cook and poured myself a full glass of wine, eager for a little mental relief. Alli came through the door after a short knock.

"Hey." She smiled and came to me for a hug. "You didn't come back after lunch. I was worried about you."

"I needed to get some things for the trip this weekend, and I wanted to get a head start on dinner too. Everything going okay?"

"Yeah. Oh, Alex called for you, but I told him you were out and traveling this weekend. He said he would be in town next week so I put him in your calendar for Monday. I hope that's okay."

"Sure."

"Are you excited about Chicago?"

Was I? "I think so. It'll be a little strange. I haven't been back in a while, but I'm looking forward to getting away for a bit."

She went to the counter to pour herself a glass of wine. "I bet Blake has big plans for your birthday. It's your first birthday together!" She smiled broadly and clinked glasses with me.

I laughed and took another sip. I hadn't given the occasion much thought. Between the wedding and the daily flurry of things to do and people to deal with, celebrating was a far away thought.

Alli and I chatted about work and settling into her new apartment with Heath. Things were going well with them—her eyes and the carefree smile that crept over her lips spoke volumes. I was grateful for what they had. They needed each other, I imagined, much the same way Blake and I had grown to rely on each other.

Heath and Blake came through the door several minutes later. Alli went to Heath, and he pulled her into a sweet embrace, kissing her lips gently. My focus went to Blake, who was making casual strides in my direction.

"Hello, beautiful."

I tipped my chin up to meet his chaste kiss. His gaze was warm, but concern lined his eyes.

"How was your day?"

Before I could answer him, Catherine, Greg, and Fiona came through the door, arms full of wine and desserts. They piled into the kitchen, talking over each other and pulling everyone else into hugs. I smiled inwardly, loving all their energy and the lightness they brought into our lives.

"How are my lovebirds?" Catherine asked as she reached up to kiss Blake on the cheek.

He smirked. "We're good, Mom."

She replied with a loving pat on his cheek before turning to me. "Let me help you, sweetheart. Look at this spread. You'll put Greg out of a job."

I laughed. "I doubt it. Greg's lasagna is pretty incredible."

A proud smile lifted Greg's lips. "Why, thank you!"

"Oh!" Fiona's eyes lit up. "I have some things I have to run by you." She winked in Alli's direction.

"Okay." Alli pointed to Blake, Heath, and Greg who were all lingering by the island. "Boys in the living room. The girls need to conference."

Heath rolled his eyes. "Uh-oh."

Alli hushed him and pushed him off with the others.

As the guys got comfortable in the living room, Alli leaned in and spoke quietly. "So, now that Fiona's here, we need to plan your bachelorette party. I just need to know if you want us to surprise you or if you have any specific requests."

"Um, no surprises, I guess. You should invite Simone though."

"Definitely. She's on the list. Do you have anything specific you want to do?"

I shrugged. "Not really."

"Okay, Fiona and I will handle the props." She started typing some notes into her phone.

"Props?"

"Penis straws, blinking tiaras, that type of stuff."

I laughed and refilled my wine glass. "You guys are going to send me off in style, aren't you?"

"Oh, yeah. We're going all out. This will not be a classy affair, I'm afraid," Alli said.

I lifted my eyebrows, almost wishing I had opted for the surprise. "Oh God. I hope there aren't any male strippers. Blake would have a coronary."

Fiona chuckled. "Whatever. We don't need his permission."

"I heard that! And the answer is no fucking way." Blake called in from the living room.

"Blake! Language!" Catherine shot back before putting oven mitts on her hands and pulling the lasagna out of the oven.

Fiona shook her head and leaned over Alli's shoulder to see what she was typing. "We'll figure out a date tonight, and leave the planning—and props—to us. You only get to do this once."

"Okay, just remember I'd like to still be engaged by the end of it," I said. Heaven knew I didn't need Blake barging in on us, having a royal fit about whatever drunken debauchery we were going to get ourselves into.

Catherine rested her hand on my shoulder. "I wouldn't worry about that. I'm not sure anything could shake that man's commitment to marry you. I'm shocked he hasn't whisked you off to Las Vegas yet. You know how he is when he gets a thing in his mind."

"Yes, I do," I mumbled under my breath.

She shot me a knowing look and grabbed up some side dishes from the island. "Dinner's ready!"

We spent the rest of the evening talking about everything—from Heath's work with some new ventures at Blake's office to the details of the impending wedding. By the end of the evening, I was stuffed, and all I could think about was what a crazy future I had in store for me with these wonderful loving people.

After they all left, I retreated to the bedroom to start organizing a few outfits to pack for the trip. Blake came in and gave me a hug from behind.

"Alone at last. I thought they'd never leave."

"I think dinner night here went well. We should do it more often. I had fun." The wine had dulled some of the upset from my day. I was still tired, but more settled than I had been.

"We'll need more space soon."

Our eyes met in the reflection of the mirror.

"We will?"

Blake kissed my cheek. "Eventually Fiona will have someone around and the family will grow. We'll need a better place to host."

I let that thought settle over me for a minute. "Oh," I said softly. Suddenly my body felt too warm.

He released me from his embrace and sat back on the bed. "Have you ever thought about moving?"

"Not really. This place is great. It's certainly nicer than any place I ever expected to have in the city." A part of me had wondered what it might be like to have a place that was *ours,* not just Blake's, but our lives moved too fast to contemplate it much further. He'd given me so much already. I was in no position to ask for more, especially considering the financial inequity between us.

"Maybe we can start looking for places outside the city."

I turned to look at him, confused by this topic coming up so suddenly. "But we both work here. Why would we move?"

He shrugged. "Things change. We might want a change of scenery eventually. We love the Vineyard, but obviously it's too far away for our jobs."

I stared at him, trying to decide if it was something I really wanted. So much was in flux with my life lately. As soon as one part started to seem sure, somehow everything got turned upside down again.

"It's just something I've been thinking about. We don't have to talk about it right now though."

He pulled off his T-shirt and jeans and slipped under the covers. The sight of his beautiful shirtless body effectively deleted any other thoughts from my mind.

"How was your day? You've been quiet." He leaned on his elbow, and the look of concern from earlier softened his expression.

I dropped some clothes into my suitcase on the floor and let my mind return to the less than pleasant run-in with Marie. "I met with Marie for lunch."

"How did that go?"

"She admitted that she let it slip about Daniel to Richard, but she doesn't believe he is the one who leaked the information."

"That's bullshit."

"I know. I'm pretty sure she's in love with him and can't fathom that he'd do this to her." I sighed. "I walked out on our lunch. I feel terrible about it, but I couldn't listen to her defending him anymore."

I ran the conversation over in my mind, no less frustrated by her defense of Richard. I changed into a tank top and joined Blake in bed, switching the lamp off beside me. He drew me up against him.

"I'm sorry you had to deal with that. But at least now you know."

I nodded and rested my head against his chest, skimming my hands down the smooth ridges of his body. "Hopefully she'll come around and realize he's not the man she thinks he is."

I was upset with Marie, but I felt for her too. I knew what it was like to fall hopelessly in love with a man and have that cloud nearly everything else. Without a second thought, I'd defended Blake against every person who'd hurled accusations against his character. Men from his past—Max, Trevor, and even Isaac—had warned me about Blake, trying in vain to sully my vision of the only man I'd ever truly loved. But in the end, no one could shake my belief that he was a good man.

Troubled, maybe, and certainly not always innocent. His history as a hacker wasn't yet safely in the past, and I wasn't sure it ever would be. The man had a way of securing information by any means necessary, a talent I'd never quite been able to wrap my head around.

I searched for his eyes in the near darkness, my heart twisting with the knowledge that so much more lay beyond his words and the experiences we'd shared together. I hadn't mustered up the courage to ask him about the club again, and I wasn't sure I wanted to. Maybe he was right. Maybe I should let it go, but a little voice in my head simply wouldn't.

His brow wrinkled. "What's wrong?"

"Nothing. I'm just a little worried about the business," I said quickly, avoiding what was troubling me more. "I'm worried for Daniel a little bit too I guess. When all this goes public, it's going to affect his campaign. A reporter called me this morning, fishing for information."

He brushed a strand of hair off my forehead. "We knew it would get out eventually."

"I know. I just wish all this was behind us. As long as this investigation is open about Mark's death, I have to live with this lie. I'm scared to death that the police will find out the truth."

"You should have told them the truth when you had the chance, Erica."

I closed my eyes, sensing where this was going. "You know why I couldn't."

"You want to believe that he's someone he's not. That somehow this one act, even though he did it to save his own campaign, redeems him for everything he didn't do for you, all the things he never gave you."

A wave of emotion rushed over me, sending tears prickling behind my eyes. Refusing to give in to the feelings I didn't want to face, I pushed away and tried to face the wall. He turned me back to him quickly.

I opened my mouth to protest but he slanted his lips over mine, silencing me with a slow, commanding kiss. He cupped my cheek while his arm circled me tighter.

I struggled for a breath when he broke the kiss, his eyes dark and intent on me. He traced my lower lip with his thumb. "I'm sorry. I'm not sure that I'll ever be able to forgive Daniel for threatening you and breaking us apart. He and I might always be at odds."

I relented. His resentment sourced from his love for me. "I understand you have your reasons."

"For what it's worth, I hope he doesn't disappoint you again." He caressed my cheek and he lowered, pressing another less demanding kiss to my lips. "I love you, Erica. I only want the best for you."

I closed my eyes. "I know."

"Enough about Daniel."

I nodded with a sigh.

"Don't you want to know what I've cooked up for your birthday?" He cocked an eyebrow.

A small smile curved my lips. "Maybe."

His hands went to my sides, his fingertips wiggling against me. I started laughing, pushing him away to escape.

"You don't seem that excited," he teased.

"I am. Stop!" I couldn't stop laughing as he continued to tickle me. I squirmed until, realizing he was too strong to get away from, I resorted to pinching him.

"Hey!" He flipped me over, caught my hands behind my back, and slapped my ass hard.

I yelped but didn't try to move again now that the tickling torment had stopped. I lay there, letting the burn settle into my skin under his palm. I bit my lip, well aware of how my giddiness was transforming into desire.

"You haven't even asked about your presents," he murmured huskily, sliding his body over mine. Releasing my hands, he caressed up my sides, his erection pressed against my behind.

"You never asked me what I wanted," I replied with equally dark meaning lacing the words.

He exhaled, slipping his hands into the front of my panties. I lifted my hips up to give him space to touch me.

"I know what you want, Erica. I always know, sometimes better than you do."

God, did he ever. I fisted my hands into the pillow above my head, wanting to be taken away by my desire. I wanted to disappear into this darkness, the here and now between us. To hell with the world. I gasped when his fingers slid through the damp folds of my pussy, rubbing gently against my swollen clit.

"How about I give you one of your presents early? Would you like that?"

I nodded, unable to speak without moaning loudly.

"I can't hear you. Say the words."

His fingers slid into me, reminding me of where I wanted him the most. He withdrew, leaving me empty and wanting. I whimpered, lifting my hips back up against him.

"Erica," he sang, a dark taunt ringing in my ear.

"Please, Blake." I struggled to form the words he wanted to hear. By default, I'd resorted to begging.

"Please, what?"

"Please, fuck me. I want my present. Please…"

I lifted my hips, rubbing my ass against him. He cursed and shoved my panties down to my knees. Not bothering to undress either of us completely, he pushed his boxers down just enough. His cock burned hot against my skin. The soft head trailed over my ass and pressed against the opening of my pussy.

"Anything for the birthday girl." The words strained as he drove home with one powerful thrust.

I clenched my jaw around the wordless cry that wanted to escape from my lips when he was inside me completely. I was tight around him. Relief and the sharp need for more washed over me. His hips pushed me forward and down into the mattress, a cushion as he drove into me. Every stroke of his cock into me caused a delicious tingling, down every limb and pulsing where our bodies met. My clit, deep inside me, those secret places where only he could give me pleasure. My arousal drenched us both, making the journey smooth as his pace increased.

Reality was slipping. A new reality where we were the only two players formed as the chase for orgasm took over. I turned my head to the side, gasping for breath as his passionate fucking robbed me of air.

I whimpered as our warm, slick bodies slid over one another. God, this man could do things to me. He pulled out and turned me over, nudging between my legs. He leaned down, catching my lips in his. He sucked them into his mouth, devouring the swollen flesh with lusty swipes of his velvet tongue.

Then lifting my thigh around his waist, he was inside me again in seconds. Going deeper, thrusting harder and faster, he took me to the edge. I ran out of air, gasping, spasming around him, racked with overwhelming pleasure. He caught my cries with one last kiss as he finished. His release burst inside me in rhythmic pulsing thrusts. We shared breath, collapsing together into the soft net of our bed.

"I love you," he whispered.

His body undulated over mine, finding the deepest part of me one last time, drawing out the last ounce of pleasure from our union. I shuddered, feeling stripped, exhausted, and thoroughly loved.

CHAPTER FOUR

Less than twenty-four hours later, Blake and I were in a rental car, letting the GPS guide us toward Elliot's home, a place I'd yet to visit. I looked out the window, noticing all the little ways the outskirts of Chicago were different from Boston, the place I'd called home for years now. I had changed so dramatically since I left. That I'd spent most of my life here seemed suddenly impossible.

I looked over at Blake, who seemed intently focused on getting us to our destination. He took his gaze away from the road a second, catching my lingering stare. He caught my hand and held it in my lap, giving it a gentle squeeze.

"You nervous about seeing Elliot?"

I took a deep breath, hoping to quell the anxious feeling building in my chest.

As long as it had been, this place still held a lot of memories for me. Memories I wasn't sure I was ready to dive into right now. I'd tried to think of the trip mostly as a getaway for us, but for some reason I couldn't quite grasp, I was apprehensive about showing Blake my old world. Maybe because my life in Chicago, with my mother gone, was a shell of what it had been and a far cry from the boisterous and supportive network that he had with his own family.

I'd come a long way from that time. I was all grown

up. Vulnerable at times, but able to navigate my way through the world with more confidence than I had been before. I'd graduated and built a business that was finally stable and prospering. Now Blake and I were getting married and starting our lives together. How could I think about the past when all those days paled in comparison to the days I shared with Blake now? Somehow, with everything we'd been through, he had become my home. I belonged to our life together, and the thought of stepping into my past shook the ground under my feet.

"I'm about to look my past in the face. I'm a little scared, I guess." I looked up, hoping for reassurance. What I found in the depth of his dark eyes was a flash of recognition.

"You'll be fine, baby," he said quietly, squeezing my hand gently.

Suddenly we were the same, two people running from who we were, head first into a new life and a chance to be more together.

The GPS announced we'd found our destination as we pulled up to Elliot's house. I wrapped my cardigan around me tighter, though Blake's hand in mine gave me infinitely more comfort.

Elliot and Beth lived in a charming two-story home a short ride outside of the city. Blue shutters framed the front windows of the house. A few of the windows were lit up. The rooms were brightly colored, and I caught a glimpse of children running inside.

We walked up the wooden steps to the doorway and opened the screen door, which squeaked a little. I pressed the doorbell and stepped back.

Standing on the whitewashed wrap-around porch, I waited, twisting my fingers anxiously. Blake caught my hand again and pulled me against his side. The murmuring of voices inside grew louder, and the door flew open.

"Erica!" Elliot's smile could not have been any wider as he stepped through the doorway and pulled me away from Blake and into a tight hug.

I held him back, and in an instant, I was a little girl all over again, so happy to see him. He looked the same. Aside from a few gray hairs in his dark brown sideburns, he was the same handsome man he'd always been. Of medium height, he stood a little shorter than Blake, but he was fit and lean in the same way. His dark blue eyes brightened. Beside us, Blake cleared his throat.

"Blake." Elliot grinned and pulled back enough to slap Blake's hand in a handshake, keeping his arm around my shoulder. "Great to finally meet you."

"Good to meet you too."

Blake's smile was different. I couldn't place it.

"Come on in," Elliot said quickly.

He led us into the foyer where Beth appeared. She was dressed in casual clothes, and her eyes brightened when we entered. We'd met before a couple times, once at their wedding and for a brief summer visit. She'd always been sweet to me, and I had no reason to resent or dislike her. Elliot had loved my mother, but I wanted him to be happy. Seeing him smile again after my mother had passed away was all I needed to know that Beth was good for him.

Beth had light brown eyes and dark hair swept up into

a messy bun. She brushed her hands off on her pants, leaving behind a white residue that only added to her disheveled look. "Sorry! You caught us in the middle of a major cooking project, so I'm a mess." She leaned in to kiss me on the cheek, careful not to touch me otherwise. "It's wonderful to see you, Erica. I'm so glad you could come out." Her gaze went to Blake who stood beside me. "You must be Blake?"

I warmed. I tried to hide a small smile as I watched them make introductions with the man who would be my husband in a few short weeks. I wanted them to see how happy he made me. I wanted them to like him and see the amazing person he was to me.

As they chatted briefly, I wished even more that Blake could be meeting my mother. I pushed the thought away, shifting my focus to the two brown-haired little girls who were now huddled by their parents' legs, surveying Blake and me with their big brown eyes.

I crouched down, comparing their cherubic little features with the memory I had formed of them through photos I'd seen over the years.

I made eye contact with the younger one. "You must be Clara. Is that right?"

She nodded shyly, and the toe of her bare foot tapped restlessly on the floor.

"How old are you? Oh, wait. Let me guess." I pretended to be thinking. "You seem pretty big. Are you three?"

She smiled and nodded.

"And what is your name?" The girl, who was only a

couple years older than her sister, stood still by Elliot, her eyes intent on me.

"Marissa," she said quietly.

"That's a beautiful name. I'm Erica. I've heard so much about you. It's wonderful to finally meet you."

She stepped away from Elliot after a moment and stood in front of me, her hands covered in flour and dangling at her sides. She cocked her head slightly. "Are you my sister?"

I opened my mouth to speak as I searched for the right answer.

"That's right," Beth chimed in. "You and Erica have the same daddy."

Marissa's brow wrinkled, as if she'd been trying to but couldn't quite make sense of this. "Where is your mommy?"

"Oh," I said quietly. "She's in heaven."

"My fish went to heaven too. Mommy said she would be happy there."

I smiled, charmed by the two beautiful little girls. "I bet she is."

Clara emerged from her spot by Beth and grabbed my hand in her chubby one. "Come...play."

I looked up to see the others smiling.

Beth quickly spoke. "Oh, let's give Erica a chance to get settled before we make her play. She's had a long trip."

I laughed. "It's okay. What are we playing?"

"We make sister cookies," Clara explained, her bright eyes seeming to expect that I knew what that meant.

"Oh?"

She tugged at my arm, and I followed her and Beth into the kitchen.

"Sorry this place is a mess. We started out wanting to make cookies, and then they had to be heart shaped, and then they had to be pink, so..." Beth threw her hands up as we surveyed the counter covered in sugar cookie debris. "This is what we have."

Clara lifted to her tippy toes and grabbed a pink slightly misshapen heart cookie and pressed into my hand.

"Clara calls them sister cookies, since she knew we were making them special for you."

"Oh, thank you." I took a bite and moaned in exaggerated delight. "So good. You made these?"

Both the girls nodded, their eyes bright with pride.

"Oh my God, what is that?"

My eyes widened as Beth caught my hand, bringing my diamond studded ring closer to her face.

"Oh, um." I struggled to come up with the right words, let alone with pink sugar cookie in my mouth. I hadn't thought much about how to break the news to Elliot, but Beth might beat me to it. "We're engaged."

She let out a small squeal. "Elliot, come in here!"

A few seconds later, Elliot and Blake joined us in the kitchen.

"Erica and Blake are engaged!"

"What? When did this happen?" Elliot looked between Blake and me.

"Have you set a date?" Beth interjected before either of us could answer.

"We're just doing a small beachside ceremony in a few

weeks," Blake said.

"You're kidding?" Elliot looked to Beth. They both shook their heads. "Well, shoot, you should have told me, Erica."

I shrugged. "I know you're busy. I didn't want to put any extra pressure on you. Plus everything came together really fast. I can barely keep up with it."

"Well, we'll figure something out. I want to be there," Elliot said without hesitation.

"Seriously, it's going to be really small. I know you guys are swamped." I didn't want him to come because he felt guilty. He had a whole life here and a family who really needed him. That much was obvious as the two little girls padded around the kitchen between us.

"Don't be crazy, Erica. We'll figure it out, one way or the other." Beth came in for a hug.

"Okay, but no pressure. I understand you both have a full plate."

Beth hushed me and we proceeded to work together to get dinner together. Blake and Elliot had retreated to the other room while Beth dove into questions about how Blake and I met. Clara and Marissa took turns feeding me sister cookies and eventually succeeded in tugging me away from their mother and toward another room. Despite Beth's attempts to distract them, I ended up spending the next hour on the floor of their shared room, while the "grownups" prepared dinner and talked downstairs.

I overheard Blake talking about our businesses and some of his contacts in the city. I didn't feel too badly about abandoning him with Elliot and Beth, who were basically complete strangers to him. He could make conversation with almost anyone. When it came to programmers, he was more social than most.

When I was just about full from our pretend tea-party, the whole family settled down for dinner. The girls monopolized the meal with their questions and laughter and generally cute antics. I didn't mind. Their happiness filled up any awkward silences we might have otherwise had, and I was quickly enamored with both of them.

As dinner wound down, Elliot's girls wound up. They were giggling and crawling under the table, interjecting themselves into the grownups' conversation frequently. Elliot's flash of irritation melted in seconds, as he curled an arm around each of them. Collecting them into his arms, he threatened bear hugs and princess kisses.

I smiled, their love as a family evident and infectious.

Beth rose from the table, lifting one of the girls away from Elliot and onto her hip. "I think it's bath time now. Let's say goodnight to Erica and Blake."

"No!" Clara cried, rubbed her eyes, and rested her head on Beth's shoulder.

Beth smiled. "Yes, it's time. Elliot, why don't you and Erica get the fire going in the backyard? I'll put the girls down."

"You sure?"

"Yeah, go ahead," she insisted, shooing him off with a wave of her hand.

He sent her a warm smile, letting Marissa leave his embrace and snuggle up to Beth's leg.

Blake rose quickly. "I'll work on cleaning up dinner.

You two go ahead."

Elliot and I shared a look. Apparently everyone was in on us making the most of our brief reunion. He smiled, grabbed his wine, and stood. "I guess that's our cue. Come on out. It's a nice night."

Elliot's backyard was fenced in, a large play set filling most of the yard and the girls' toys littering the rest of it. I settled down on a chair on the patio while he stoked a small fire to life in the little outdoor fireplace. He sat back, and the fire grew over the next few minutes.

"I can't believe you're getting married."

I laughed. "That makes two of us. I've been trying to wrap my head around it since Blake asked me."

"Blake seems like a great guy. I'm really happy for you both."

I smiled with a nod. "I think so too."

"Is he good enough for you?"

To that I had to laugh. "He's amazing. Completely amazing."

"Just watching out for you. I never got the chance to scare away any of your boyfriends. I feel like I need to make up for lost time," he said, the half smirk on his face telling me he was only half-serious.

"You'll get your chance with Clara and Marissa, I'm sure. They're growing up beautifully."

"Oh, man, don't remind me." He rubbed his forehead.

I stared up at the stars and relaxed into the chair. The night was cool, but the fire was warm at my feet. "I'm glad we could come," I admitted. "It's great to see you all. I can't believe how long it's been."

"I know. It's been too long, really." He sighed and took the last sip of his wine before setting it on the table beside him. "I'm really proud of you, Erica."

Our eyes met briefly before I looked down, feeling suddenly shy. "Thanks, Elliot."

"I watch Marissa and Clara grow up every day, and I see you in them. As much as I cling to these moments with them, knowing they won't last, going through it all over again brings up a lot of memories. A lot of regret that I couldn't be more for you."

"It's okay." I didn't know what to say. I had wanted him to be more too, but I'd come to terms that he couldn't.

"No, it's not okay." He leaned forward, resting his elbows on his knees as he looked into the fire. "I want you to know that I had never loved anyone the way I loved your mother. Up to that point, she really was the most amazing woman I'd ever met. And you were this perfect little extension of her. Cute as hell and smart as a whip. I couldn't help but fall in love with you too. I felt so lucky to be your dad. Then when she got sick..." He shook his head, sadness locking his jaw. "We never saw it coming. My whole world turned upside down. I was young, and Patricia was my life. Then…I was scared to death of doing everything wrong with you. All of a sudden, being a dad seemed like the scariest thing in the world. I was afraid I was going to mess everything up. That I wouldn't do her justice, you know?"

I wanted to comfort him. To reassure him that everything had worked out. It had, hadn't it? I reached out for his hand. He held it tight for a moment and then released it, returning his gaze to the small fire warming our feet.

"I tried calling you so many times," he said quietly. "I wanted to try to explain as time went on, but it's hard to do it over the phone. I wanted to make it out to see you too, but life got in the way. It's no excuse, I know."

"I'm here now. And I understand. I can't imagine what you went through. I missed having you in my life. Both of you. But I managed. I'm a different person for it, I think. More independent than maybe I would have been." I laughed softly, and he looked up. "I mean, poor Blake can't pin me down to save his life."

He smiled, the sadness in his eyes dissipating a little more. "Good. You keep him on his toes."

I do plenty of that. More than I probably should, though Blake would never tire of reminding me of that fact.

I looked up at the sliver of the moon. As far as we'd traveled today, the people in my other life could see the same sky. I wasn't so far away from that world, the life I'd created after all this time. Elliot knew almost nothing about that world—the people who'd become family, the experiences that had brought me to my knees, and the ones that had helped me get back on my feet. How could he?

"I wanted to ask you something," I said quietly. I sat up straighter in my chair, bracing myself for what might come next. "Did Mom...ever talk to you about my father?"

He frowned, hesitation sweeping his features. He was awkwardly silent. I recognized his hesitation. I'd seen that same look when Marie had the chance to tell me the truth about Daniel but didn't. In an effort to respect my mother's wishes, she'd kept silent too.

"I already know who he is. He was in some old college photos that Marie gave me, and I was able to track him down. Marie finally confirmed it. I know Mom didn't really want me to know, but I guess curiosity got the best of me."

He nodded slowly. "I can understand that. Would be hard going all that time not knowing. But she did worry about what kind of influence he'd have in your life if you knew who he was."

"If the way they broke it off was so horrible, I don't understand why her family wasn't more supportive, you know? Having your daughter show up pregnant after college graduation wasn't ideal, but we were never close with her family. They always seemed closer to her siblings and their kids. In retrospect, it was like I was a pariah. We both were."

He grasped his hands together under his chin. "I might as well tell you the whole story while you're here. Who knows when we'll get another chance."

I frowned. "What whole story?"

He ran his hands through his hair and drew in a deep breath through his nose. "According to Patty, when she came home after graduation, she waited to tell them about the pregnancy until she'd heard from Daniel. When it was clear their relationship wasn't going anywhere, she finally broke the news to her parents. Obviously they were upset. But when they found out who your father was, things changed. They weren't as upset about her being pregnant as they were about his decision not to marry her. They wanted her to force him into it, to reach out to his family and expose the truth. They threatened to do it, and that's when she moved out. She needed their help, but she wasn't about to blackmail him into making an honest woman out of her. She wanted you, and she was going to figure out a way to have you and make a life."

Pain tightened my chest. "Why would they do that?"

"Your mom came from a good family. Professionally, anyway. Professors, doctors. Having Patty marry into Daniel's family would have been a coup for them. Patty used to claim that's why they sent her to Harvard to begin with. It wasn't cheap for them, but they thought she'd at least find a husband. A child out of wedlock wasn't their idea of a success."

I shook my head, hating to think of her in that light. Her family had been so cold, and now I knew why. Thinking about all the choices she'd made to keep me, at the expense of keeping her family close, sickened me.

"I'm sorry. All this sounds terrible. It's why I never wanted to tell you and why Patty never wanted you to know. Sometimes you think you want to know the truth, but people can be cruel. Selfish and cruel, and there's no way to tell you the truth without it hurting."

"Not much about discovering Daniel hasn't been hurtful, to be honest. He's... Well, he's a lot like you'd probably imagine."

He stared at me in silence for a moment. "What kind of man is he? She didn't talk about him much."

I inhaled a deep breath. Daniel had more sides than I

wanted to know. "Powerful. Shrewd. Deep into his career and political circles. His way or the highway for the most part, I suppose."

Elliot studied me. "Doesn't sound like much has changed."

"No. But for what it's worth, I believe he did love Mom. I just don't think he had much choice in the matter. If he'd done the right thing, his family might have disowned him."

"And Patty did what she felt was right, and her family disowned *her*."

I sighed, saddened for them both. If things had been different, they could have been together. We could have been a family, with or without their parents' support. Nothing could replace the years that we'd lost, but maybe that didn't matter now.

Beth and Blake joined us on the patio. The heaviness from our conversation lifted a little when I saw Blake. His eyes flashed to mine. I smiled, despite the sadness that filled me.

"The girls go down all right?" Elliot asked.

Beth slumped into one of the chairs, looking drained and in dire need of a stiff drink. "Not without a fight. But they're down."

"Your girls are so precious," I said. "You're doing a great job with them."

Beth managed a smile. "Oh, thank you. I'm trying, but heaven, do they wear me down."

"What about you two? Any plans for kids?" Elliot asked.

My jaw fell open slightly. The question had completely blindsided me.

Beth slapped him on the shoulder. "Quit. You're going to give Blake a heart attack."

Blake looked at me, his eyes more thoughtful than I expected. "We haven't talked about it much. We've got time to figure it out though."

We hadn't talked about it at all, in fact. With the way he was looking at me now, I had a feeling that would be changing soon.

CHAPTER FIVE

We left Elliot's house near midnight. Blake and I drove back to the city and checked into a beautiful five-star hotel overlooking Lake Michigan. We crashed seconds after coming into the room.

My eyes fluttered open. Predawn light seeped into our hotel room, and through the curtains, I caught the glittering shimmer of light across the lake. I sank back down into my pillow. It was barely six o'clock and beside me, Blake slumbered quietly. The late afternoon flight followed by the dinner with Elliot's family had been tiring.

I thought about last night, his first introduction into my world outside of meeting Marie. I was happy he'd met Elliot, and I was proud to come back into their world with Blake by my side. Seeing him and Beth again had been great, but Elliot's words would color the way I thought of my mother's family for the rest of my life. Any hope I'd harbored about having them in my life in the future had been effectively shut down.

Blake stirred and stretched. My recounting of the conversation with Elliot dissolved, and my thoughts circled around Blake. The sheet lay loosely over his hips, putting his amazing body on display. I slid my leg over his thigh and nestled close to him. He was warm from sleep.

"'Morning, sleepyhead," I sang quietly, drawing light circles over his stomach and up his chest.

He groaned and stretched again, scooping me closer to him when he relaxed. "I love waking up next to you."

I hummed my affirmation and pressed a kiss to his chest.

He threaded his fingers through my hair. His eyes were sleepy, his face soft and rested. "Happy birthday, baby."

I smiled. "Thank you. I would have totally forgotten if you hadn't reminded me."

"What do you want to do today? We can do whatever you want."

I raised my eyebrows. "I figured you had everything all planned out. I didn't bother wishing for anything in particular."

He laughed. "All right, guilty as charged. Let's shower and get dressed. We'll get breakfast, and then I'm going to take you shopping."

"Shopping? For what? I have everything I need."

"Honeymoon wardrobe shopping."

I laughed. "I can't imagine that's something you really want to do."

He smirked and rolled me off him as he turned to his side. Propped up on his elbow, he began lazy caresses under the edge of my shirt. "It's your birthday, and I want to spoil you. In all your years living in Chicago, did you ever go shopping on Michigan Avenue?"

I thought of the very few times I'd even walked down the popular street, let alone purchased anything. "No. Not really in the budget."

"Well, this time everything is in the budget."

I smiled teasingly. "Everything?"

Blake cocked an eyebrow. "Do you doubt it? I'm pretty confident I can buy you anything you could ever want."

I planted a playful kiss on his lips. "I don't doubt it. But I'm more interested in your other"—I hooked my finger under the sheet lying precariously over his hip and lowered it slowly—"assets."

"Hmm," he moaned against my lips, shifting his hips up. He was hard, and his erection slid into my eager grasp. "What's mine is yours, sweetheart."

"Then I'll just make myself at home," I murmured, sucking his lower lip between my teeth. I bit down gently.

He groaned and tightened his fingers in my hair. I let my tongue slide over the plump flesh. I pushed his shoulder back until he was flat on the bed.

The smile playing on my lips relaxed as I eased down the length of his toned body. I traced my tongue down the center of his stomach, dipping lightly into his navel. I breathed him in, his musky scent stronger the farther I went, until I was face-to-face with his rigid cock—the thick weight of it heavy in my palms, the veins throbbing as I pumped him gently. I punctuated each stroke with my mouth, swirling my tongue over the head, sucking the salty pre-cum. I wanted to draw more out. I wanted to watch him come apart. I pressed my nails into his hip as I took him fully in my mouth.

"Fuck," he yelled, from the nails or the fact that I'd taken him to the root, I wasn't sure.

I didn't let up on either account.

"Ah," he gasped. "Come here, baby."

I moaned, my core clenching as I imagined taking him fully in other ways. I let him slip from me slowly. "I'm just getting started. Relax."

"As much as I love morning head..." He sucked in a sharp breath as I took him deep into my throat. "Fuck me, it's your birthday. Get your ass up here. You're about to get your first present."

The head of his cock left my lips with a pop. He bent and hauled me up to him before I could argue. I straddled him.

"Hands on the head board," he said, his voice still raspy from sleep.

I placed my hands on the hard wood at the head of the bed and watched him shift down and disappear between my legs.

"Now sit down," he said, his breath gusting against me as the sordid words left him.

"Blake..." I tensed, embarrassed by the position. I didn't know how or why, but he still had the ability to scandalize me. Not giving me the time to refuse, he placed his palms on my ass and guided me down to his face. I lowered tentatively until suddenly his mouth was hot and wet against my sex. I gripped the edge of the headboard and bit my lip, barely stifling a moan.

He lingered at my entrance, teasing the sensitive tissues there. He swept a broad lick down the seam of my pussy. I lowered farther, chasing the hot pleasures of his mouth. He spread me with his fingers and whispered something against my flesh. The air tingled against my clit, making it desperate for his attentions. I shimmied, begging without words. He kissed me there but then moved his attention to the entrance of my pussy. I trembled as his tongue dipped inside me and retreated.

"Blake." When I said his name, I wasn't sure if it was a plea for more or something else. I felt so open, so exposed as he continued fucking me with his tongue. But he'd seen every part of me. I had nothing more to hide.

I itched with the need to touch him. I wanted to run my fingers through the silky strands of his hair while he pleasured me. I wanted to guide him over me, but deep down I knew he'd always give me what I needed, even if it wasn't what I wanted. The position had left me feeling an odd mix of vulnerable and dominant. Perhaps that was what had me unsettled.

"I love your pussy. I want you to come so I can taste more of you. It's never enough."

The movement of his body beyond my view made the bed move, and I knew he must be painfully hard, as desperate to fuck me as I was to be fucked.

"I need you now. Please, Blake…"

My voice was breathy with anticipation. My thoughts scattered with the desire thrumming through me. But he kept on, fucking me with his tongue. When I tried to escape, he only urged me down into his motions. He gripped my ass so firmly there was no escaping.

When I thought I couldn't take a second more, he returned his attentions to my throbbing clit, delivering a series of hard licks and sucks that hurdled me right to the edge of my orgasm. I cried out. I slammed my hand against the headboard, the other clawing its way down the wall. I wanted to touch him. I wanted to take this crazy feeling out on him. I wanted him to feel all of it too.

I was so close. My legs shook as he slid his finger into my greedy pussy. I clenched around the single digit, reminded anew how badly I wanted him inside me. I pivoted my hips, eager for more. I reached down, sifting my fingers through his hair. His mouth left me abruptly.

"Hands on the headboard. That's your last warning."

I put my hand back up and let out a frustrated groan. He pumped in and out of me. I braced for another slow, frustrating climb to release, but instead, he retreated. His broad fingertip, slick from my arousal, began massaging circles over the tight pucker of my anus. I sucked in a sharp breath, launching myself higher, the few inches his grasp would allow.

"Relax," he said quietly, pulling me back down to him.

"Blake, I can't," I insisted, every cell of my body wanting to run suddenly.

"Yes, you can."

I squirmed in a weak effort to escape his clutches, achieving nothing as he held his mark. The battle began between wanting him to finish me and wanting to escape from whatever might ensue from his kinky demands. I gripped the headboard, unable to tear my mind away from his exploring finger. A tight knot formed in my stomach.

He released me and coaxed me down onto the bed so I lay on my back. He leaned over me, his lips glistening. My own trembled. He was unabashed about everything, yet I still clung to my inhibitions as if somehow they could save me from Blake's total lack of them.

He lowered, his body hot against me. "I want inside you, baby. All of you," he whispered.

My heart fluttered. Lust and nerves stole my words. *Goddamnit.*

"I'm—I'm nervous, that's all."

The concern in his eyes faded. He hushed me with a kiss, tinted with my own taste. He moved down my body and lifted my legs over his shoulders, positioning himself between them. I relaxed slightly, my defenses weakening at the sound of his voice and his closeness.

He found his mark, and I tensed, fighting the urge to skirt away from him again. He hushed me. "You have nothing to be nervous about. I love your body. I'm borderline obsessed with it, in fact. Just relax and let me make you come."

He flickered his tongue against me, and then lower, circling the sensitive spot that wanted to tense and release all at once. *Fuck.*

I sucked in a sharp breath and gripped the blankets on either side of me. He kept on, seducing me with his goddamn tongue in ways I never knew were possible. When he stopped, I melted down into the bed, distracted enough to relax. When a slick finger pushed past the tight ring of my ass, I gasped.

"Oh God."

I squeezed my eyes closed, trying like hell to accept this first step toward a level of intimacy that I wasn't entirely ready to give Blake. Despite all the doubts shouting across my brain, a sudden heat rushed to my cheeks and over my skin. The places our bodies met heated, becoming as slick as the finger that was probing deeper inside of me.

I bucked my hips and moaned before I knew what I was doing.

"You like that?"

Do I? Jesus, I didn't know. All I knew was that I was about to come apart—that my body was begging to come apart. I felt everything, everywhere. My body was rioting under the sensations he was giving me. He withdrew from my tight hole only to twist his way back in again. Repeating the motion, he brought me back to the edge with alarming speed. I clenched tightly around his fingers. I hovered, breathless, on the precipice of pleasure and pain, a state that he'd brought me to so many times before.

"I don't think... I can't." I arched my back, my muscles tensing against the penetration.

Blake answered swiftly with a second invasion. His two fingers stretched me, claiming this part of my body as his. I gasped at the discomfort when his mouth covered my pussy again, delivering hot, wet, and tantalizing licks over my flesh.

I went higher and higher until I soared. I couldn't take it anymore. The orgasm crashed over me like a tidal wave. I might have screamed. I might have blacked out. I was trembling when he hovered over me again with lust-filled green eyes.

We were both breathless. He pressed the head of his cock against my pussy and pushed inside of me. Deliciously filled once again, I hurdled toward another toe-curling orgasm. Sensation number three, Blake's ample cock stretching me so wonderfully had my head buzzing. Had I ever been fucked so thoroughly? I wasn't sure.

He pounded into me and my body responded, clutching against his thick penetration. "So tight."

The friction was acute. I clung to him. I was falling again. I was flying. His name left my lips with my helpless cries.

"So fucking tight. Fuck... Come with me, baby. One more time."

I trailed my nails down his back as he drove deeper. My head pressed back into the pillow, and my back bowed off the bed. He was so deep inside of me, and yet I harnessed all my power to fuse us tighter. I spasmed again, harder. I was trembling. A hoarse cry tore from me as he came, spilling warmth into me.

★ ★ ★

We never made it to breakfast. Every muscle in my body was exhausted from what we'd done—what he'd done. We slept a little more, showered, and finally mustered up the energy and willpower to leave the hotel room.

Blake took me to the priciest restaurant in the city he could find for lunch. We had champagne and ate a delicious meal before we headed to the stores. For a while we simply walked, enjoying the fresh air and being together, hand in hand. We passed by a few stores displaying famous brand names I'd never owned and hadn't planned to.

"Let's go in here," he said, halting us in front of a revolving door that was guarded by a man in a suit.

Happy and a little buzzed, I followed him in. I walked along the sparsely stocked shelves, afraid to touch anything, let alone get attached to something. Maybe the bubbly had dulled my senses, because my mind said *Oooh* as we passed a bag that caught my eye. I ran my fingers over the smooth dark brown leather and then down to the clasp where a thick label hung from it. I turned it over and gawked at the hefty price.

Oh shit.

Blake leaned down and whispered in my ear. "Every time I catch you looking at the price tag, I'm paddling your ass when we get home. So just keep that in mind."

I frowned. "What if I accidentally see it?"

"Depends if you decide to buy it."

I took a second glance at the tag to make sure I'd read it right. "This purse is three thousand dollars, Blake."

He shrugged. "Good, get it."

"That is a ridiculous amount of money to spend on a purse," I hissed, not wanting to insult the store staff or reveal that I was woefully out of my element here.

He stood close, lowering his voice. "You worrying about money when I have fucking mountains of it is ridiculous. Pick up the purse and move on. We have a mile of stores to hit today, and I'm buying whatever your eyes land on."

I let out an exasperated sigh. My brain couldn't begin to process spending that kind of money on myself. While I battled over how to convince him that this plan was absurd,

Blake picked up the purse and continued walking through the store without me. I rushed up beside him.

"Blake, stop. I seriously don't need that."

"We're getting it."

"I don't even like it," I lied.

He lifted an eyebrow.

"There are people who have nothing, and you want me to spend an excessive amount of money on something I don't need."

"I want to spend an excessive amount of money on *you*. It's your birthday. I want to spoil my fiancée. I've worked hard for the money I've earned, and that's my right."

We stared at each other a moment, a silent standoff. His jaw set.

"Would it help if I matched the gift with a donation to a charity of your choice?"

I rolled my eyes, my shoulders slumping in defeat.

"Can we buy the fucking purse now?"

I knew I had to pick my battles. This was a war, and Blake wasn't going to let me win it. I sighed in surrender. "Fine."

"Good, because we're hitting the Cartier store next. I'm just breaking you in."

Fresh discomfort rattled over my nerves. *Damnit.* "I might need more champagne for this."

He smirked. "I'm sure that can be arranged."

CHAPTER SIX

Three hours later, we were back in the hotel room. I dropped the few bags that Blake let me carry and collapsed onto the bed. I was shell-shocked, sticker-shocked, and bone tired. Per Blake's request, I refused to look at price tags as much as I was able to. Most of the time, it was irrelevant, because price was never discussed as the salespeople offered their finest wares.

Blake had spoiled me, excessively. Spoiled was an understatement. I had walked away with a new wardrobe, new lingerie for every day of the week, and more designer baubles than I'd ever seen on anyone.

We napped for an hour before showering again and getting dressed for dinner.

I slipped on a long-sleeved black dress that Blake had insisted I get after modeling it for him in the store hours earlier. The hem came mid-thigh, and the back scooped down low—perfect for a late summer night.

I clipped on the large-faced diamond-studded watch that must have been obscenely expensive. The afternoon, draining as it was, had been amazing. I couldn't help but feel special as the salespeople nearly danced around us, vying for every opportunity to slide Blake's credit card through the machine by wowing me with the best of everything.

Blake was dressed in dark gray pants and a black button

down shirt rolled up at the sleeves. His hair was mussed from our nap. His eyes were bright and sparkling. I couldn't help but smile as his reflection came closer to me.

"Thank you."

"For what?"

I rolled my eyes. "Where do I begin?"

He laughed, fondling the sparkling diamonds that dangled from my ears. "You're welcome. And thank you. For agreeing to make me the happiest man on earth. I already am, but getting to share the rest of my life with you is the best gift you could ever give me."

"I feel the same way. I don't need diamonds and handbags to be happy, though."

He cocked his head. "Spoiling you makes me happy. So let me do it a little bit."

"How about we limit the shopping sprees to special occasions?"

"Whatever you say, boss," he muttered, nuzzling my neck.

I couldn't hide my smile when he spun me toward him and captured my lips. What started slow had become a deep and wanton kiss in moments. He pushed past my lips, his tongue plunging gently to meet mine. I moaned, sifting my fingers through his hair as I pulled up to him. Stepping forward, he pressed me carefully against the mirrored dresser where I'd been getting ready. I lifted my thigh up into his grasp. Squeezing me gently, he released my leg and broke the kiss.

His eyes were dark, and the evidence of how much he wanted me strained against his slacks. "I hate to be the voice of reason, but we should probably go. I wouldn't want you to get all dressed up only to have me strip you bare and fuck you mindless before we leave the hotel."

My breath rushed out at his threat. His tongue traveled over his bottom lip, a sensual promise of things to come.

"You can rest assured that will be happening when we get back though. I haven't nearly had my fill of you for the day."

"Are you trying to break a record for the amount of times I can come in a single day?"

A wry smile twisted up his lips. "What can I say? I have a thing for birthday girls."

Already the day had been the best birthday I could remember. Nothing came close to being spoiled and loved well by the man I was about to marry. I pushed him back a little farther and hurried to get ready before we started something we absolutely had to finish.

Blake had chosen a renowned steakhouse in the city. The waiter seated us in a quiet corner of the restaurant. We ordered, and the server poured a bottle of wine into our two glasses. The sun had gone down, leaving a pastel glow over the endless horizon of the lake. I barely heard Blake's voice in the background.

"What are you thinking about?"

I broke out of my trance and picked up my glass. "Let's toast."

"What should we toast to?"

Not the past. The opposite of the past, in fact. "Let's toast to the future."

He touched his glass to mine, the faint clink the only

sound between us for the next few minutes.

"Are you happy we came here?"

I thought about his question, my focus traveling back to the shimmering water. "In a way. I don't know. It's been a lot to take in."

He sat back in his seat as I contemplated everything.

"My family—my mom's family—has a beach house over there." I pointed to the window, to an invisible place across the lake where I'd lived another part of my life. "Across the lake, in Michigan."

Blake's gaze returned to me after a moment. "I didn't know that. When was the last time you were there?"

I took a careful sip of my wine. The robust flavor rolled over my tongue, the aroma coming through my nostrils. I swallowed it, grateful for yet another decadent experience I'd been afforded simply by being in Blake's life. I wasn't sure I would ever get used to being so completely spoiled, but I loved the man and I wasn't about to argue with the things that made him happy. My thoughts skipped back to the lake house and the last time we'd been there as a family.

"A long time ago," I finally said, "before I left for boarding school, we took our yearly vacation there. It was the last summer my mom was alive, actually—the last time I remember feeling like a kid. She wasn't feeling well and couldn't keep up. I had a lot of energy. Elliot's girls reminded me of that. We always had so much fun together, but that summer my mom wasn't up for much. She was always tired. I didn't know it at the time that she was already sick. It's one of those things you don't piece together until you're older."

I closed my eyes, pushing down the emotions that resurfaced with her memory. My mother. The one person who I could always count on to take care of me, to see me through the hard times. God, I still missed her. Her laugh and the way she would hold me tight, with every last ounce of her waning energy. I let out a breath, determined to hold it together.

"After a while, I'd go back in my mind and try to grab my last memories of her. It all made sense one day." I shook my head. "Anyway, her family was always distant. I never had play dates with cousins or visits with Grandma and Grandpa like normal kids. Even then, knowing that she was dying, they didn't change the way they interacted with us. My aunts and uncles would be in town, and they never had room for us there. If the cousins ever bickered, somehow the blame fell on me. After a while I just started to withdraw, do things on my own. Being an only child, that wasn't so hard. Mom, Elliot, and I would go swimming or drive to town. We made our own memories, the three of us."

Blake reached out, feathering a soft touch over the back of my hand. "Why do you think they treated you that way?"

"I used to think it was because of me, that my mom getting pregnant with me disappointed them so much that things were never the same after. But Elliot told me something last night…"

Blake stilled. "What did he say?"

"He told me they had wanted my mom to force

Daniel into a marriage. They wanted her to tell his family and make Daniel do the honorable thing. I guess even after he'd broken things off with her, she refused to push him. She wanted me, and I guess she loved him enough to let him live the life that had been planned for him."

Blake was silent a moment. "She made the right choice. Imagine what your life would have been like growing up in his family."

I traced circles over my glass, fixated on the light reflecting off it. "I don't know. Sometimes I think about it, and I wonder if she could have made him a better person. Or if she'd have ended up like Margo. The perfect wife at the side of her politician husband, consumed with achieving success and looking the part."

Blake laughed softly. "If you're anything like your mother, I'm guessing no."

I smirked. "Are you saying I'm not first lady material?"

"No, you're Madam President material."

I laughed, entertaining that ridiculous thought for a moment. Entrepreneurship was well and good, but I had no political aspirations. I couldn't imagine Blake did either. "And what would that make you?"

He leaned back and lifted his eyebrows suddenly. "Your chief advisor."

I laughed. "Sounds about right."

★ ★ ★

We stepped out of the restaurant and into the cool night air. A few minutes later, we'd wandered to the beach that had darkened now. Lake Michigan stretched out before us like an ocean. We took off our shoes and walked along where the waves lapped up softly on the sand. We wandered for a long time with only the moonlight and the lamps of the promenade lighting our way. I shivered, the cool night seeping into my skin.

"Are you cold?"

"I'm fine."

I started to feel the weight of the day and slowed down. We sat down, and I leaned against Blake's warmth, letting the rhythm of the waves lull me. A little light from a speedboat traveled silently across the horizon.

"Where to now?"

I shrugged, content to be here with Blake, a quiet reprieve from a day full of activities.

"The world is our oyster. Dancing, music, more shopping."

I laughed. "Oh, God. Please no."

"Back to the room?" He raised his eyebrows suggestively. "I have more exploring to do."

I bit my lip and fidgeted nervously. I couldn't stop thinking about what we'd done. I couldn't remember coming that hard with his mouth on me before. The experience had been intense, but I knew where it was taking us.

Blake caught my chin, forcing my eyes on him. "What's going on?"

"Nothing. You're just... You're preoccupied with...*that*."

"Am I? I want full access to your body, including your

ass. I want you everywhere in every conceivable way."

The more I tried to avoid his eyes, the more intently they bore into me.

"Erica... Mark didn't—"

"No," I answered quickly, eager to shut off the topic. "That's not it."

"Then what is it? Something makes you uncomfortable about it. Your body tenses up, and that doesn't happen with us. There's something you're not telling me."

"Do you want to discuss our sexual histories, Blake? I thought you wanted to keep the past in the past."

He released a heavy sigh and stared out to the lake. "I need to know your limits and why you have them. I'm going to be your husband—"

"If you're going to be my husband, you should talk to me and not keep things hidden."

He was silent, and I knew I was walking a fine line with him once more.

"Blake, this trip wasn't about my birthday. It's been so wonderful, but so much of it has been about facing parts of my past that I'd put away a long time ago. Seeing Elliot... I'm glad we did it, but I knew coming here would dredge up old memories, things that hurt. And I'm facing them."

"Are you implying that I'm not?"

"Do you think you are?"

"If this is about what Sophia said, there's nothing there that's worth talking about."

"Was she the only serious relationship you had before me?"

He cursed, staring out at the lake. "I messed around before I met her. I was young. I started to grow up and thought I should try to get serious for once. We met through a mutual friend." He drew circles into the soft sand. "I guess you could say we found a common interest, and I gave it a try with her."

"And after her?"

"I messed around some more. But it was different."

"How?"

He hesitated, shaking his head almost imperceptibly. "Until you, I never wanted another relationship."

The finality of the words made me think the subject had been closed once again. As if someone had opened a door to let in some air and quickly shut it, leaving the space between us stifled and tense again. But at least he'd opened it. As much as I didn't want to explain my reservations, I figured the best way to get him to keep opening up was to set the example.

I fidgeted with my watch, messing with the delicate joints of the band. "I was the same way."

He looked at me, questioning me with his eyes.

"Before Mark, well...there was nothing before him. I was a virgin. I was messed up for a while after that. But as time wore on, I pushed past it. I couldn't let the rape rule my life, and I decided I couldn't swear off men and sex forever, as much as I may have wanted to sometimes. But everything was...emotionless, I guess. It was hard enough for me to get past the physical triggers. I couldn't bring myself to go any deeper and fall for someone."

I winced, not liking the memories that came up. I

didn't like the way it sounded when I said everything out loud either. I sounded like a damaged, cold-hearted tramp. "They weren't all one-nighters. I mean, I dated people, but nothing was ever serious. I never gave anyone a chance to break my heart. I'd already been broken so badly."

He reached up and tucked my hair behind my ear. Fine strands blew in the wind across my cheeks. I inhaled the cool air into my lungs, exhaling the memories that flashed through me.

"So tell me what bothers you so much about anal play. What happened?"

I sighed, feeling anxious suddenly. "I was seeing someone for a little while. I'd had a few beers, I'd agreed to let him...do more. Fuck, you don't want to hear this, do you?"

He reached for my hand and held it in his lap, drawing gentles lines over my skin with his fingertips. "No, but I want you to tell me."

I shook my head listlessly. "He hurt me."

He stopped his caresses, his eyes fixed on me protectively.

"I don't think he meant to. It wasn't like with Mark, but he came before I could get him to stop. I don't really blame him. I guess he was just being an idiot guy, thinking with his...well, whatever. There was something about it that was a little too close to what I'd been through. He never knew why, but I never called him back. And I've never done *that* since."

"You know I would never hurt you."

My heart twisted at the sweet, softly spoken words. "I

know you wouldn't. I just have a hard time imagining that I could enjoy it when it was so *not* enjoyable."

"You would enjoy it."

My face grew warm, and I was grateful for the darkness. I didn't want him to know just yet that I would let him do anything, push me past any limit, including that one. I didn't want to admit tonight that sometimes the things I was most afraid of turned me on as much as they terrified me.

We made love that night. Despite the emotions that had come to the surface between us, we didn't ravage each other the way we'd done so many times before. We didn't talk about our past. We barely said anything, only our names on each other's lips.

Maybe he wanted to remind me that it could be that way between us. Maybe he didn't realize that I already trusted him implicitly with my body, and the slow, passionate way he loved me was proof that he could be whatever I needed, whenever I needed it.

Blake's eyes never left mine, and when he came, the look there destroyed me. I could see into his soul, and what I saw shattered through me.

CHAPTER SEVEN

I returned to work on Monday morning, oddly refreshed considering the hours of travel. I caught up on the email that had built up over the weekend and registered a surprising sense of peace. The weekend had been emotionally intense, but cathartic in many ways. Not seeing Elliot for so long had weighed on me to a degree that I hadn't fully appreciated until we'd reunited. Emotionally I had distanced myself from him, pushing him away over time before I could feel the sting of knowing that I was secondary to his new family now. But the second I walked into his and Beth's home, I knew I couldn't run from away those old feelings.

Elliot held a place in my past, and while it wouldn't always be easy, I knew he wanted a place in my future, however small. Pushing him away wasn't fair to either of us.

We'd parted with promises to see each other again at the wedding.

The wedding. Fiona and Alli were rounding up the final details, and my belly burst into uncontrollable butterflies whenever I imagined it. I smiled inwardly. Slowly but surely, everything seemed to be falling into place around me. After everything Blake and I had been through, we deserved this time.

I lingered on that thought when I heard a familiar

voice enter the office. I rose from my desk and met Alex in the main area. In a flash, I remembered Alli had put him in my schedule for this afternoon.

"Erica, great to see you." We shook hands.

"You too. What brings you to the area?"

"I have family here. My sister just had a baby, so I thought I'd come out for a bit."

"Oh, congratulations. That's great."

"Thanks. Who knows when I'll get around to having kids, so figure I should bask in someone else's joy. Saves me on diaper duty too."

I laughed. "Did you want to just catch up on the numbers?"

"Yeah, hey, let me buy you a coffee and we can chat."

"Sure." A couple minutes later, we were situated at a small table at Mocha, the cafe downstairs.

Simone was busy, so one of her helpers took our order and quickly returned with two iced coffees.

After some small talk about the weather, Alex reached into his blazer pocket and pulled out a check. "I wanted to give you this while I was here."

I took it and tried to mask my satisfaction at the healthy number on it. The partnership between our two companies had become increasingly fruitful, and the financial stability this opportunity had given us was a reward all its own.

"Thanks." I folded the check and waited for him to continue. We usually had our meetings over the phone about routine things, so I was curious what specifically had brought him into the office to speak with me.

"Things have been going well," he said.

"Definitely. I'm so grateful we were able to connect."

He drank from his coffee and set it back down carefully. "I agree. That's actually why I wanted to stop in. I have a proposition for you."

"What is that?"

His lips pursed slightly. "I want to buy Clozpin from you."

My jaw fell, and a satisfied smile turned up the corner of his lip.

"I know this probably comes as a shock. That's why I wanted to talk to you about it in person."

"I can't deny that it is. What spurred this?" I had never seriously considered acquisition as an option. We'd been fledging for so long. Only recently had we had the numbers to really show an upward trajectory.

"Simply, our partnership and the value it's bringing to my company."

"This has been great for us, but obviously your site is way more established. I guess I didn't realize the impact it was having for you."

He leaned forward, resting his elbows on the table. "I am where I am because I see potential on the horizon before most people do. I see potential with this business and with you leading the team here. I have capital. You have Landon, which means you have access to capital too. But I have the infrastructure in place to take your concept to the next level right away. And if I'm going to do that, I want ownership stake."

I nodded. "Wow. I don't really know what to say. I've

never even considered something like this."

He seemed more serious then, as if friendliness were giving way to business now. "I understand. You should take some time to think about it. If it's something you'd like to talk more about, I'd want to see some more detailed financials so we can come up with a valuation. Obviously I want to offer you something more than fair."

"Um, okay." With shaky hands I grabbed my coffee. He'd completely blindsided me with this.

"Do you have any thoughts or questions for me, with this in mind?"

My mind spun as I tried to imagine what this could mean for me and the business, not to mention the people who now relied on it. "I guess my main concern would be the team. What would happen to everyone's jobs? I'd want to make sure everyone was secure."

"Sure, we can work all that verbiage into the sales agreement. In fact I think it's important that you, specifically, stay on and continue to run the business. Basically I want you to keep doing everything you're doing. I'm giving you the opportunity to cash out early but still run operations."

I nodded again, trying to wrap my head around all this new information. "I'll have to think about it, okay?"

He smiled, his business persona softening. "Great. Talk to Landon about it and let me know what questions you might have. If you want to send me some of your financials this week, I can shoot you off an offer. That might help your decision too."

I let out a shocked laugh and rubbed my forehead.

"Okay, sure."

We shook hands and he left me to consider the magnitude of what he'd just proposed.

Stunned, I stared out the windows of the cafe. Alex was right. I had to talk to Blake, because my gut wasn't telling me if this was a good idea or a terrible idea. I was simply stunned.

"Who's the suit?" Simone collected Alex's coffee cup and shot me a curious look.

"Alex," I answered quickly, trying to mask my suddenly off-kilter mood. "We partnered a little while ago. He just wanted to talk business." I was careful not to mention Alex's proposal, lest she mention it to James. I had a lot to think about before bringing the possibility of an acquisition to the team. Though I was eager to get their input on it, I wanted to talk to Blake first. He had the greatest stake in the business, and he also had more experience with all of this than I did.

"I hope you don't mind me using the cafe as an office. I should probably pay you rent for all the work conversations I end up having here."

She laughed, a throaty sound that rang over the steady murmur of the cafe. "Yeah, right. You can pay me back in drinks. Speaking of, when are we going out next? I'm hearing rumblings about a bachelorette party."

I laughed nervously. "Has Alli drafted you into her plans yet?"

"Oh, yeah." She winked, a wicked grin lifting her lips.

I nearly choked on my coffee. "Oh, no. The look on your face is seriously worrying me."

"It should." She laughed again.

I shook my head, and she slapped me playfully on the arm.

"Not to worry, Erica. We'll have a blast."

"I have no doubt." I grinned and grabbed my purse to head out. As worrisome as her playful threats were, I had bigger things on my mind. "All right, I'll catch up with you later."

"No problem, hon. Knock 'em dead." She smiled and gave me a quick hug before I left.

I stepped outside, hesitating in front of the entrance that would take me back up to the office. The aroma of coffee and the promise of fall mingled in the air. I couldn't go back to work with all this news in my head. I glanced up and down the street, unsure which way to go. Clay's black Escalade sat at the end of the block. I walked that way.

I hopped into the back.

"Hi, Clay."

"Miss Hathaway. Would you like me to take you home?"

"No, not yet. Would you mind driving me to Harvard?"

"Of course not."

The financial district disappeared as we made our way to the other side of the city. We crossed the river and wove through the tight streets that surrounded Harvard's historic campus.

"Here is fine, Clay," I said, when we were stopped at a light in an area I knew well.

"Where would you like me to pick you up?"

"I'll give you a ring."

He hesitated.

"I'll be okay, I promise. I'm just taking a walk around campus. I won't wander far." I gave him a crooked smile. He had already taken a lot of grief from Blake for letting me disappear before on his watch. Still, I think Clay sympathized with me a little bit. His presence gave me comfort, but I had to spread my wings from time to time.

"What should I tell Mr. Landon if he asks for you?"

I sighed. "Tell him I went for a walk, and if he's worried, he can call me. I have my phone."

He nodded, and I took that as good enough to leave the car. I wove through the afternoon crowd, a mix of students and tourists. For having only been away a few months, I was surprised I didn't recognize anyone. Harvard was officially in the past, and my, how life had changed.

I walked through the gates that led into the campus. The air changed, and memories of my old life here settled over me. I smiled, grateful that I'd been able to make so many memories here. I walked until my legs started to tire. I found an unoccupied bench under a tree nestled in a fairly quiet courtyard.

People walked, engrossed in their own conversations. The breeze filtered through the old trees overhead. The buildings of brick and stone stood silent and imposing. The faint murmur of the city streets beyond the campus boundaries hummed in the distance.

Everything felt different. The ground under my feet, the air around me, and now too, this place from my past.

Had it been the conversation with Alex? I was used to seeing my world turn upside down with Blake in my life, but this was different. This was my business.

The prospect of selling to Alex thrilled me. And terrified me. A part of me was ready to burst with the promise of going through with it, of being able to say that I did it. After all our struggles trying to stay above water, I could walk away knowing I'd made it a success. I had no idea how much Alex would offer, but based on the already hefty checks his business was paying out to us, I imagined it would be impressive. Blake wouldn't let me accept anything that wasn't more than fair, and Alex had promised just as much.

My mind ran away with the possibilities. Freedom from the daily grind, the kind of freedom that Blake enjoyed being able to pick and choose his projects. Whatever I walked away with from a sale wouldn't come close to Blake's wealth, but I could pay him back and have a little nest egg of my own that I could say I earned. Maybe it would be enough to invest in Geoff's project independently too.

I had worried about how I would make time for his project, with everything else going on. This could be the perfect time to make a change. Troubling little pangs of worry tempered my giddiness. What if life changed more than I wanted it to? The beautiful office Blake had renovated for me, the team with whom I'd grown so close, and the daily routine that drove me forward. None of that would be guaranteed for long once I gave up ownership.

My mind swam back and forth, through every

possibility, until my earlier excitement bordered on anxiety at the prospect of making the wrong decision. My phone rang. It was Alli.

"Hey."

"Hey, is everything all right? You were gone for a while and I didn't see you downstairs."

I sighed, grateful to hear her voice. "I'm fine. I decided to take a walk after meeting with Alex."

"Is everything okay?" Her voice softened with concern.

I closed my eyes. I needed her advice now more than ever. "Everything is fine. I just needed some air. Do you have any plans tonight though? I want to run some things by you."

"Um, sure. Girls' night, or should we invite Heath and Blake?"

Blake would no doubt have an opinion about Alex's proposition, and I valued his opinion more than anyone's. He had more experience than all of us combined, and I had faith that he'd never steer me wrong.

Whether he'd give me enough space to negotiate the deal on my own was another question.

"Sure," I said hesitantly. "Just text me where you want to meet up."

"Okay, will do."

★ ★ ★

We had just ordered enough sushi to fill a sizable boat when Alli started in.

"So what happened with Alex?"

Her eyes were focused on me expectantly. Blake and Heath followed suit.

I swallowed over the knot in my throat. *Here goes nothing.* "He wants to buy Clozpin."

Alli almost choked on her mai tai, her eyes impossibly wide. "What?"

"He wants to take the site to the next level, but he doesn't want to make that investment without ownership."

"What did you tell him?" Heath asked.

I looked to Blake, whose expression held no indication of surprise or disapproval. "I told him I'd think about it. He said he could make an offer if I sent him some financials."

"But we're finally starting to get ahead," Alli said, her lower lip pouting a little. The rush of emotions that I'd experienced earlier playing out in her features. Shock, excitement, sadness, and worry. "Don't you want to see how far we can take it first?"

"We've made some great headway lately, but mostly because of this partnership with Alex," I explained. "The referral commissions we're getting are substantial. Think of how that might translate into a sale for us."

"Alex already knows the profit potential. I doubt he'd bring you an insulting offer," Blake said, breaking his thoughtful silence. "But the bigger question is whether it's something you want to do."

"I honestly don't know. He said he wanted all of us to stay on board. For me, it could mean more flexibility to work on other projects."

He cocked an eyebrow. "Geoff's?"

"Maybe. Or others. It's occurred to me that I could be spreading myself a little thin trying to do everything I want to do. Eventually something's got to give."

"What if he changes who we are though… I mean, the essence of the company."

Alli raised a valid point. I could tell she was playing devil's advocate, and for good reason. She'd uprooted her life in New York to come back and work for me in Boston. For her, Sid, and me, the business was a huge part of our lives. Changing any part of that could have an impact on all of us.

"I would hope that he doesn't. He seems to really value what we've done already. But I suppose that's a risk we take."

"So what are you going to do?" Heath asked, pushing me further toward a decision I was in no position to make tonight.

I shrugged. "I've been thinking about it all day, and I can't say I'm any closer to really knowing what I should do. I have to admit it's a promising idea, though. I sent him the financials this afternoon to get things started. If the offer is fair, I think we should strongly consider it."

Alli blew out a breath. "Wow."

"Well, I think it's a great opportunity. For both of you. You've both worked really hard, and if the time is right, go for it."

When Heath smiled, Alli's worry seemed to melt away, her eyes warming as she gazed into Heath's. I looked to Blake beside me. His arm draped over the back of my chair and he rubbed my back gently. The gesture was a small reassurance of his support and approval. I had a feeling he had more thoughts on the topic that he wasn't willing to share in front of Alli and Heath, but at least for now, I didn't feel so off track considering Alex's offer.

The waiter brought an enormous boat of sushi and placed it in the center of the table. We proceeded to stuff ourselves and down another mai tai each. After another hour of talking wedding details and business, Blake and I said our goodbyes to Heath and Alli.

We walked back to the apartment, which was only a few blocks away.

"Sounds like you had a big day," Blake said, threading his fingers with mine as we walked.

I laughed. "No kidding."

"I can talk to Alex tomorrow and feel him out for offers," he said.

I stared down at my strides over the sidewalk. "About that." I hesitated, bracing myself for the blowback. "I'd like to negotiate this myself."

We slowed in front of the awning of our building.

"We've gone over this, Erica."

His voice was quiet, but tension rippled off of him. I drew in a deep breath and prepared to hold as much ground as I could.

"I know. And I know it makes sense for you to work this out with Alex. Obviously you're both sort of evenly matched when it comes to business. I'm still learning a lot, and I value your advice. I always do. But I've built this business from the ground up. With Alli and Sid, yes. With your investment to help us grow, yes. But if this is really the end of me being an owner, I want to be able to say that I wrote the final chapter."

I looked up at him, pleading silently with him to give me the control I craved to take this next step on my own.

"You must want this chapter to be a good one, more than anything, right?"

I sighed. "Yes, of course. But I can do this," I said quickly, not wanting to show any inkling of doubt. "And if I start to feel like I'm getting in over my head, I'll be more than happy to send Alex your way. After our meeting in California, he probably already thinks I need your permission to order office supplies."

He shoved a hand through his hair. "You know that's not true."

I shrugged. "I don't take for granted that anyone respects me in this business. I've had to fight and prove myself every step of the way. Having you hovering, waiting to jump in when I falter, probably doesn't help much. I appreciate it. I do."

"This is what I do, Erica," he pressed.

My shoulders fell. "I know, but Blake...this is my baby."

He cursed under his breath before meeting my imploring gaze.

"Fine. Negotiate the deal with Alex, but promise me you won't commit to anything without running it by me first?"

"I'm fine with that. I wouldn't anyway."

"And if you decide you want to sell, we'll have my

lawyers draw up the agreement."

I rolled my eyes at his persistence. "Blake, I have my own lawyers. They'll do fine."

He took a step forward, determination clear in his eyes. I stepped back, only to find myself pressed against the front door.

"You're enough to drive a man insane, do you realize that?"

I trapped my lower lip between my teeth, trying to suppress a smile. I curved my hands over his shoulders, kneading them gently. "Yes," I admitted.

He looked away, as if he were trying to hold on to his frustration. I kissed his jaw, the stubble from the day's growth rough against my lips.

"I love you," I whispered.

"My lawyers," he said firmly, his eyes serious. "And I want you upstairs naked, on your knees, waiting for me. I'll be up in a few minutes."

I frowned. "Where are you going?"

"I have to make a call."

"Who are you calling?" I tried to push him away, but he kept me firmly trapped between the door and his tightly wound body, catching my wrists, pressing them above my head.

"Ask me again, and I can promise you'll regret it." His hips shifted, pinning me firmly against him, punctuating the husky promise.

I stilled, weighing the ratio of anger to lust in his words, and how much room I had to push him. I bit my lip for a second but couldn't help myself.

"Are you calling Alex?"

His eyes darkened. The corners of his lips lifted in quiet mischief. "Oh, I'm going to have some fun with you tonight. Get your ass upstairs before I decide to punish you in a more public fashion."

My skin warmed and my nipples pebbled against my shirt, my body's traitorous reaction when he threatened the kind of punishments I was likely to sign up for any day of the week, whether or not they were inspired by any actual infractions. Damn him. Gradually he stepped back, allowing me to escape his clutches.

I turned to go, but didn't move quickly enough when his hand made hard contact with my ass. I felt the sting through my jeans and fought a smile. I pushed through the door and hurried upstairs.

CHAPTER EIGHT

I fidgeted in my chair. My ass still stung a little from the solid spanking Blake had doled out the night before. That was after I'd spent a great deal of time on my knees. God, did the man love to see me on my knees.

But there had been more at play last night than Blake's kinks. Frustration rolled off his tongue with every sharp demand, every fierce drive that took us over the edge again and again. My willing submission had come with a price. I was fighting back for the control I'd once promised him.

And I would keep fighting for the right to call the shots until Alex took over the business. Holding onto that level of control, now that everything was changing so dramatically, was worth it. Sore knees and all.

Plus, I'd left my own marks and had my own fun. Blake never tormented me to any degree without matching it with a heavy dose of sexual satisfaction. The slight discomfort of my ass was a casual reminder of yet another sleep-deprived night in Blake's arms, at his mercy. I crossed my legs, hoping to dull the pulsing ache there.

I pushed sordid thoughts from my mind and read a message from Geoff reminding me about our meeting this week. I was looking forward to chatting with him and learning the details of what he had planned, but now I considered putting it off. I had no idea what my own future looked like. How could I make him any promises of being able to help him?

Finances weren't the issue. If I didn't invest my own money, Blake would invest "ours." But with a sale of the business, I could pay Blake back the loan he'd made toward Clozpin and possibly fund Geoff's business too. Quiet satisfaction took root when I imagined making a tiny seed grow again on my own, without the overwhelming wealth and security of Blake's bank account and business prowess. I could do it, and I couldn't deny the part of me that craved this new opportunity. In the boardroom, Blake had encouraged me to grab what I wanted and go for it. If it made financial sense, that was what I was going to do, but I had to break that news to Sid first.

I sent him a message, and a minute later he was sitting across from my desk. His tall frame overwhelmed the chair as he leaned back with tired eyes and a tall energy drink in his hand.

"What's up?"

I drew in a deep breath. "I wanted to talk to you about a new direction for the business that I'm considering."

His eyebrows went up, a new alertness brightening his eyes.

"Alex Hutchinson wants to acquire Clozpin."

He paused. "What would happen to the team?"

"Alex assures me that everyone's jobs would be safe. He'd add language to any sales agreement to that effect. Obviously you and Alli would be cashing out along with me, but we could all keep running Clozpin as long as we wanted to be involved. He said he really wants me to stay and keep doing what I'm doing here."

A slight frown wrinkled his forehead. I found myself mimicking his expression, waiting to hear his reaction. I'd never been one to make blanket decisions for the team. Alli and Sid always brought something valuable, and Alli's words last night still lingered in my mind. They echoed my own fears. The big, scary what–ifs that I had to consider if everything went wrong. "Interesting," he finally said.

"Interesting, good?"

"Maybe. The financial security on a personal level would be good. I've been able to stash some money away since Blake still won't cash the rent checks for the apartment, but I have my own ideas that I wouldn't mind working on."

My heart fell a little. "You don't think you'd stay?"

He shrugged. "Shouldn't shock you that I'm not that much into fashion. I'll stay as long as you want me to though. I'd never abandon the project. We've put way too much into it. Whether we sell or not, I want to see it successful."

"Are you worried about selling it too soon? Alli thinks we might be leaving money on the table."

He twisted up his lips again. "I guess that all depends on what he's offering and what we want to walk away with. Ultimately, it's your call, Erica. We put you at the head of the project, and so far you've done a good job steering us in the right direction. If you think this is what we should do, I'm behind it."

I released a relieved sigh. "Thanks, Sid. For everything. I can't imagine coming this far without you and Alli. No matter what happens, I want you to know that."

His cheeks darkened and his gaze dropped to the floor. "Thanks. I feel the same way. We've made a good team." The way he said the words sounded oddly like a goodbye.

With each passing moment I felt more and more committed to the prospect of selling, even as I waited for Alex's offer.

Alli popped in, interrupting us. "Hey, um, Alex is on the phone."

"What?"

Sid rose. "I'll leave you to it. Keep me posted."

"Of course. Thanks, Sid."

He and Alli left me alone. My stomach flipped. Had he reviewed the financials so quickly?

I picked up the office line. "Alex, hi."

"Hi, how are you?"

"I'm doing well. You?"

"Good." He sighed, and for a moment, I wasn't sure I believed him. "I looked at the financials last night."

I clicked my pen anxiously. "Okay. Did you have any questions?"

"No, not really. I assume the fact that Blake reached out to me means you are open to offers though, correct?"

My heart stilled. I hoped my shock wasn't obvious to him.

"Y–Yes. I mean, if it makes sense financially." I winced at my stammering.

"Of course. In that case, I'm sending you over our initial offer this morning. There's one issue."

"What's that?"

"I don't typically like to rush things, but time is of the essence on this. I'll need an answer from you tomorrow."

My mind spun. *Shit.* "Okay, is there a particular reason why?" I hesitated to ask, but I wanted to know what was spurring this sense of urgency.

"Nature of the beast, I suppose," he said quickly. "I think you'll be happy with the offer though. We don't have a lot of time for negotiating specifics, so I'll be sending it over with a draft of the agreement. If everything looks good on your end, we can move forward pretty quickly on this."

"Okay." I couldn't hide the uncertainty in my voice. I had boarded a deceivingly tame-looking theme park ride and now I couldn't get off.

Alex ran a few more details of the proposal by me before we hung up, but I couldn't get his comment about Blake out of my head. I didn't bother asking Alex what they had discussed and risk sounding ridiculous for not knowing. Despite my plea to handle the negotiation myself, Blake had reached out to him anyway. I knew it. I fucking knew it. I slammed my hand down on my desk, suppressing the urge to scream out in my frustration. I was marrying the most maddening, controlling man on earth.

Head in my hands, I took a few steeling breaths. I'd deal with Blake later. More importantly, I had a prospective sale to weed through, and Blake was insane if he thought I was going to let his lawyers have any piece of it. I refreshed my email repeatedly until Alex's offer came through. I stared at the message, not sure I was ready to read it, but I was unable to do anything else until I knew what it held. I skimmed through the message.

The offer was seven million dollars, an enormous sum.

I bit my lip, trying to stem my excitement. *Oh my God, this is really happening.*

I hadn't burned through Blake's entire initial investment. In fact, I'd stashed a good part of it away into a business savings account in the event of an emergency. After paying him back and cashing Alli and Sid out from their stock in the company, I'd have enough for Geoff's project and plenty leftover.

I printed out the deal terms and called a meeting with Alli and Sid. We met downstairs at Mocha, which was convenient for privacy and a much needed caffeine boost.

We each read the terms and discussed the concerns until we felt all the bases were covered. We stared at each other. I was desperately searching for signs that this was the right thing to do. A Magic 8 Ball could have done the trick, but I settled for the tentative agreement of the two people who had gone on this crazy journey with me from day one.

"Are we sure?" I asked, looking between Alli and Sid.

"Let's do it." Sid's big brown eyes seemed sure.

More than Alli's, but enough to give me the push I was looking for.

"Okay, here goes nothing, I guess."

I stayed late going back and forth with Alex's legal department. Over email, we'd set the closing for Friday of that week. Days away. It was all so surreal.

Alli joined me when the office had cleared out for the day. "Do you need help with anything?"

"No, I'm just looking over the terms." I hesitated,

compelled to seek her approval once more. "Are we sure about this?"

She smiled weakly and sat in front of my desk. "It's progress, I guess. Nothing can stay the same forever."

"This isn't an easy call for me, Alli," I admitted.

"I know. There's a ton riding on this, but whether it works out the way we want it to or not, we took a risk. Nothing can take away the experiences we've had. Honestly, I'm scared this could push us in a direction we're not ready for, but I'm also scared about turning down an opportunity that we would be foolish to ignore."

"I feel the same way. Change is never easy, I guess," I said.

As much as Alex assured me that he wanted me to keep doing what I was doing, I knew change was on the horizon in one form or another. One didn't make an acquisition of this size, no matter how well off he was, without wanting to get the most out of the opportunity. I had to brace myself for those unknowns and have faith that Alex had our best interests in mind, even if they were secondary to his desire to take profit from the venture.

"Well, the decision has been made, right? I'm going to send this off to the lawyer, and maybe we'll have this executed soon."

She blew out a breath and shrugged. "Another reason to celebrate, I guess."

"Sure, we should celebrate. Drinks or something."

Alli's smile grew wider. "I was going to surprise you, but the bachelorette party is this weekend."

I lifted my eyebrows. "Oh."

"So celebration will definitely be in order. We'll have to feed you some extra shots."

I laughed. "Okay, we'll see how it goes."

She rose and came to me. I stood up and hugged her.

"I'm so proud of us." Her voice was muffled in my shoulder. Suddenly tears threatened, and the emotional cliff of following through with this was fully in sight. This was shaping up to be one hell of a week.

She left, and I sent off my last message to Alex. I sat in the office a little while longer, contemplating the heavy choice I'd made. For so long, my life had been framed by Clozpin, by the experiences that had taken me from dabbling hopeful, to near failure, to veritable success. Alex wanted the business and he wanted me. He'd seen value and taken a chance on both. A ripple of satisfaction went through me. I smiled inwardly. I was proud of us too.

★ ★ ★

Clay dropped me at home. The night had turned dark, and I tried not to think about everything Blake and I needed to hash out tonight. I walked toward the door.

"Erica?" A man's voice approached me, his frame appearing from the shadows. My heart leapt and I stepped back.

"Who are you?"

"I'm with Channel 5 News. I was hoping I could ask you a few questions about your connections with the governor's race and Daniel Fitzgerald."

"I'm sorry, this isn't a good time." I fumbled with my

keys and tried to circle him to get to the door.

"I'll only take a moment of your time."

Before I could tell him to leave, Clay appeared, squaring off with the man.

"The lady doesn't want to speak with you. You need to leave now."

The young reporter scoffed at him. "Who are you? I'm not breaking any laws by being here."

"I'm security for Miss Hathaway and for this building. If you don't leave, I'll call the police." Clay was unruffled, his voice and broad frame intimidating without trying to be. He stood imposing between the reporter and me, staring the man down.

Unfortunately for the man, Clay could probably bench press him. He didn't have a prayer.

"Fine. Sorry. Is it okay to follow up with you by phone?" He glanced around Clay to me.

I shook my head with a sigh. Jesus, these people were persistent. I turned my key in the door and thanked Clay before rushing up the stairs.

I walked into the apartment, dropped my purse on the counter, and silently wished I could unload the suitcase of emotions I'd brought home. Blake rose from the couch while I made a plate of leftovers.

"Is everything okay?"

"Reporter accosted me outside."

His brows knit tightly. "Who was it?"

"Clay dealt with him. It's okay."

The tension in his body seemed to relax a little. "Okay."

He circled the island to where I stood and leaned in for a kiss, but I turned from it.

"What's wrong?"

"What do you think?" I muttered. He was going to make me spell it out. I couldn't wait to hear his excuses for getting to Alex before I could.

He lifted his eyebrows. "Why don't you just tell me?"

I stared up at him. "I took punishment from you last night with the promise that you'd stay away from this deal. This is *my* deal."

"You didn't say stay away. You told me you wanted to negotiate it," he said tonelessly.

I let out a shocked laugh. "So you proceeded to call the person I need to negotiate with directly?"

"I wanted to get a feel for the deal. That's all."

"Really?"

I moved to the dining area with my warmed food. After a moment, Blake took a seat at the other end of the table. Maybe we did need a bigger place. I needed at least two rooms between us right now.

"I don't know why you're so upset. You're the one he's sending the offer to, right? All I did was ask some questions. I didn't pretend to represent your opinions, or mine, in any other way." He paused. "You wanted my advice, right?"

"Yes," I said sharply between bites.

"Okay, well, I can't advise you on something I don't know all the details about. This is your first deal. There are a lot of questions to ask right off the bat to see what the basic structure is going to be. I knew Alex would have something fairly specific in mind. I wanted those details so I could point you in the right direction when the time came."

I shook my head. I wanted to call bullshit on all of it. "I hate you sometimes, you know that?"

His devilish smile weakened my resolve. "I don't believe you."

I looked down, pretending to be unaffected. He wasn't getting away with this by being gorgeous. I was mad, and I was staying mad until he apologized.

"Baby…"

"Don't *baby* me. I'm not going to reward you for meddling in my business yet again."

"Seriously, you're going to nail me on a technicality?"

"It's not a technicality. It's the principle of the matter. You know that. I may be short and blond and seven years younger than you, but I'm not an idiot and I don't appreciate being treated like one."

He flinched as if I'd slapped him.

"What did he say?" he asked after a few minutes.

"Why don't you call him and see for yourself?" I muttered, sarcasm dripping from every word.

He hinted at a smile. "Do you want me to? Because you know I will."

"Fuck you," I shot back dryly.

He relaxed back in his seat, waiting for me to speak.

"He offered us seven million dollars. It's more than enough to pay you back and leave Sid, Alli, and me with plenty to make our next move."

He pursed his lips and nodded slowly. "That's healthy.

Are you happy with that?"

"We all talked about it, and we are."

"That was quick."

"The offer is only good until tomorrow," I explained.

"Why?"

I shrugged. "He didn't say. He seemed kind of stressed. Not like him typically, but maybe that's just how he negotiates. I don't know. He seems to shift from friendly to all business pretty quickly."

"Seems unusual."

"He needs to fast-track things maybe."

"Not really ideal. We don't have time to review everything properly. You should push back and ask for more time."

"But what if he rescinds the offer?"

"He wants the business. He's made that position clear. Don't second guess his interest now."

"Maybe something is keeping him from being able to buy it if we don't move on this quickly. This is a huge amount of money."

"You're getting emotional about this," he said matter-of-factly.

I bristled at his tone. "Of course I am! This is my whole life we're talking about here."

"Is that right?" Blake laughed weakly, but I could see the hurt in his eyes.

I closed my eyes, cursing my poor choice of words. "You know what I mean."

Our eyes met, two stony gazes weakening under our emotions.

"Doesn't matter anyway," I said finally. "We all agreed to move forward. Our legal teams finalized everything today."

He shook his head, a resentful smile pulling his lips tight. He pushed away from the table. "Do what you think is right, Erica," he said flatly.

He disappeared into the bedroom, and I stewed. My jaw locked tight as the minutes ticked by. I wanted to throw things. I wanted to know how his employees handled his compulsively controlling nature day after day. I wanted to know how the hell I was going to be able to live with it.

Unable to get my brain to shut up hours later, I finally gave up and joined him in the bedroom. Moonlight spilled into the room, offering just enough illumination to undress and find the bed. I crawled onto my side, careful to keep enough distance to communicate that I was still very pissed off. But Blake's chest was moving with a slow rhythm indicative of sleep. I willed my own body to unwind. I needed to let go of today.

I curled up beside him tentatively. He was incredibly warm when my lips glided across his shoulder. He smelled like soap. Sometimes loving him was easier when he wasn't talking, or conscious. I wasn't sure he could help himself. I hated when we fought, and even now, I questioned whether any of this was worth fighting over.

This never-ending battle between us. Over what? Power. What did it even matter in the context of two people who loved each other as helplessly as we did?

I'd given him power in our relationship, and he'd

collected on that by reaching out to Alex without my permission. He could have taken it further, but he hadn't. *A small concession*, a little voice reminded me. A concession nonetheless.

The long day was taking its toll on me. Exhausted, warm, and content by his side, I let sleep overtake me. But the black of the night gave way to troubled dreams.

Alex's edgy voice rang out in the background. He was rattling off the details of the deal. Over and over, like a record playing on repeat. Darkness lifted, and he faded away.

We were at my office, but it was empty. Sunlight spilled in through the big front window. The room felt bare and cold without all the people who belonged there. Where was everyone?

I walked to my desk and Blake was there, his feet propped up, a sexy smile on his face.

I forgot I was angry with him for a minute. "What are you doing here?"

"I work here, remember?"

Did he? He seemed so sure. I walked toward him, and he pulled me down onto his lap.

"I don't understand." I curled my arms around his neck.

"I'm here for you, Erica."

"Okay." That seemed right, but I wasn't sure why. I wanted him here. He filled the empty space, and I didn't want to be alone.

I leaned up to kiss him. The room became warm. Energy flowed between us. My body was waking up, all my thoughts turning toward the places where we touched. I skimmed my palms down his chest and forgot about where we were. His hand went between my legs, rubbing me, massaging me through my jeans. I moaned, closing my eyes.

When I opened them, a blanket of darkness had fallen around us.

He'd moved us so I was on my back. I didn't know where we were, but it didn't matter. We were alone, and he was stripping us down, slowly and patiently.

He crawled over me, lifting my arms above me, pinning them. He stared into my eyes. The hunger there stole my breath.

"I need this."

I nodded. Somehow I understood. I wanted this too.

He kept my arms pinned while he moved over me, taunting my body in every way. Skin against skin. The dusting of hair on his chest teasing against my nipples. The slow drag of his scorching cock against my thigh.

I trembled.

He was in control. We'd been here before, and I'd learned not to fight it.

I fell into the sensations, trusting Blake's lead. But no matter what I did, how I moved, he wouldn't move any faster. We were lost in an endless circle of unsatisfied lust.

I whimpered his name. I begged. But nothing I could do could make him satisfy me.

He caught my nipple in his mouth and sucked gently. Unhurried caresses swept across my skin, while a fiery ball of desire grew and grew inside me.

"Please!" I begged, in the hazy confines of my mind, and I screamed it.

Could he hear me?

My eyes flew open. I blinked several times, reacquainting myself with the darkness of our bedroom. Beside me, Blake slept, his breathing markedly slower than mine. I licked my dry lips and lowered my arms. They'd been in the same position in the dream. My clit throbbed, pulsing with the rapid beating of my heart.

What the hell?

Eyes closed, I wanted the dream again but I wanted to be free of it too. I wanted relief.

Blake was on his back, slumbering. I ached for him. I was awake, but lust from the dream lingered on my skin, making it all seem real. We were real, and Blake could ease this agony.

I leaned over him, wanting to kiss him, to wake him. My earlier anger went to war with my lust. I hesitated, a glimmer of an idea sparking in my mind.

I slid off the bed and walked around to the end. I went to my knees, opening the wide drawer at the base. Inside were Blake's toys. *Our* toys. Most of the things were still in packages. *Thank God.* We hadn't used a fraction of them, and I didn't care. All I cared about was one thing. I found what I was looking for and closed the drawer. Returning to bed, I crawled naked over Blake, my bottom against his thighs.

He stirred, humming when I settled over him. I bent over so we were chest to chest. I spread tiny kisses over his face, down his jawline, and to his neck. After a moment, his pelvis arched up and he groaned. I smiled and returned my attentions to his lips. I licked them, nibbled gently at their fullness.

Then his arms encircled me, hugging me to him as he kissed me deeper. I reveled in it a moment, and then wriggled free to carry out my plan. Sitting up, I caught his wrists and moved them so they were above his head, pressed into the pillow.

"What are you doing?" Blake's hoarse voice broke the silence.

I hushed him and fumbled for the leather cuffs I'd retrieved from the drawer. I snapped one onto his wrist, looped it around the post in the headboard and quickly snapped the other.

"Erica." Eyes wide and voice void of sleepiness, he seemed fully awake now.

"I'm playing. Just relax."

His muscles let go a little, and I kissed him again, wanting to soothe him. I didn't want to fight. I wanted to play.

I was shaking loose from my dream too. I was wound up and eager for satisfaction, but my frustration with him seemed to grow with my desire. I moved down his body, loving him and wanting him to feel what I was feeling too. I sucked his skin, teasing my tongue over the soft disks of his nipples until they turned hard. I traced my teeth over the tips as he'd done to me so many times, driving me wild.

The sound of his breathing filled the air. "Fuck. What are you doing to me?"

"You're mine tonight," I murmured, sucking the skin at his neck. The salt of his skin flavored the rough kiss as I breathed him in deep.

I drew lines down his side with my nails. He groaned, flinching. From pleasure or pain, I couldn't be sure, but something in me wanted to mark him. To make him mine. Heat spread through me at the sight of them.

"Take these things off. Now, Erica. I'm serious."

I ignored his demands. Instead, I spread hard sucking kisses over his torso. "Me too. How does it feel to have all your power taken away?" The power of my position now might have been going to my head. I felt light, intoxicated on it. I worked my way south, licking a lusty trail down his abdomen. I nipped at the soft skin of his belly.

The bed jolted when he tested his bonds. I dipped my tongue into his navel and finally made my way to his cock, rock hard and bobbing erect on his belly. I hummed and teased the head with my fingertips. I fluttered a tiny lick at the tip, collecting the small bead of his arousal. I closed my eyes, fighting the urge to take all of him.

I wanted to tease him more than I wanted to please him tonight. He deserved that much.

"Erica." My name left him with a strange sound somewhere between a reprimand and an appeal for mercy.

"Yes?" My voice was light and playful.

The tone that followed was decidedly not. He sucked in several breaths.

"You have to the count of three to get me out of these things."

Big words for a man tied to my bed. He'd pissed me off, and I wanted him to feel it. I wanted to feel his body struggling to contain his desire the way I had countless times. Under his command, his control, his damnable talent.

I laughed softly. "Or what?" I whispered tentatively against the blazing skin of his erection. "Maybe I don't feel like taking orders."

He clenched his teeth, his eyes closing. "One." The single word came out strong, like a quietly rendered threat.

My desire kicked up. My breasts heavy as they brushed against his thighs. I wanted his hands on me, but no...

He hissed when I took him in my mouth. I moaned, loving his musky taste and the way his body strained toward me. He stiffened further between my lips. A few strokes of my tongue and I let him slip from my mouth. I delayed his pleasure, pressing hot, wet kisses over his pelvis. I wanted him as needy as I was. I was wet and aching, walking an almost painful edge from it.

"Two." His voice wavered slightly, as my breasts brushed over his erection.

I smiled a second before I took him into my mouth again. I let the length of him sink in, gliding over my tongue, all the way to the back.

"Fuck, Erica."

I focused all my attentions on pleasuring him, teasing him with light flicks of my tongue before taking him as far as I could, swallowing and undulating over the lush head of his cock.

"I need to touch you," he begged.

Desire coiled tight in my belly. I wanted him to touch me too. He had no idea how much. I hummed, the sound vibrating against him as I took him deep again and again.

His hips snapped up and I released him, blowing a small puff of air over his wet, throbbing flesh. "Say please."

He squeezed his eyes closed. "I can't do this." His breathing became labored, every muscle tensed. I froze, transfixed by the reactions of his body. I was barely touching him now, and he looked like...like he was ready to explode. I grasped his erection and began stroking him steadily.

He opened his eyes, leveling me. Even in the moonlit room I recognized the dark look that told me he was passing the limits of his control. But he had no control now. My breath left me in a rush. Thighs spread over him, I harnessed all my willpower not to slam my cunt down onto him and drive us both over the edge.

"Three... now," he growled.

"Relax," I chided him softly. I feathered my free hand over his chest, pumping him with my other.

He swallowed with a grimace.

"Limit."

He held me in his pained stare as I processed the meaning behind what he'd said.

Limit.

Oh, shit. The word rolled around in my head before I realized I needed to act. I clambered up his body and reached for his arms. Before I could reach him, his biceps flexed into tight balls and then I heard a snap. In a flash his hands were on me, his fingers digging into my hips.

I sucked in a sharp breath as he sat up, bringing us chest to chest. He grabbed a fistful of my hair and used the advantage to arch me back. I cried out. Maybe from the pain of his grip. Maybe from the rapture of having his hands on me finally. Maybe from the rapid twist of having complete control to relinquishing it so suddenly.

He moved me, unapologetically positioning me over his cock. A second later he was inside me, plunging deeply, once and then again, deeper still. I was slick around him, my pussy spasming instantly.

"Blake!" I sobbed with pleasure, clawing at him, wanting to hold him to me, but he couldn't be contained. I clenched around his penetration, the friction and fervency of his thrusts hurdling me straight into an unstoppable orgasm. My thighs trembled, and I grasped at his shoulders as the climax crashed over me.

I could barely come down from the violent rush before I was on my back. Blake's strong hand pinned both of mine above my head. Spreading me around his thighs, he pounded into me, moving us both up the bed in a series of powerful thrusts. I was breathless, grasping but unable to free myself from the onslaught of his passion.

"What do you want, Erica? Do you want me to fuck you this way, or do you want me to lie down so you can play Dom?"

He was taunting me with the very thing I'd tried to strip him of, and hell if I'd never wanted anything more. I was melting around him. I wanted everything he could give me. He was everywhere. Holding me down, pressing against me, restraining me, devastating me from the inside out.

And right now I only wanted him to take what was his—my body, my heart, and God, my submission. If that's what this was, I wanted to serve it up to him on a silver platter because I'd never felt so dominated and so completely aroused by his determination.

"I want you to fuck me," I admitted, no shred of doubt or hesitation coming out with my words. "Just like this."

He slammed into me, his jaw tight. "This is me. This is us," he ground out.

I cried out every time he hit the deepest part of me, all my senses launching into overload. "I want this. I want you," I said between my jagged breaths. My heart twisted, adding weight to the force of the orgasm that hit me. My head fell back, my neck arching off the edge of the bed where his violent fucking had pushed us. He caught my nape, bringing me back. He released my hands to hoist my hips up, fucking me at an angle that sent me into orbit.

The edges of my vision went black. My breath caught. When I found it again, I screamed, tearing my nails down his shoulder while his cock punished the sensitive spot inside of me.

A painful cry tore from his throat and he collapsed over me. I struggled for breath under his weight, but whatever had happened between us had me wanting him close. I wrapped my arms around him, pushing my fingers through his damp hair. Lazily, I caressed the places where I'd marked him harshly until slowly he crawled off and disappeared into the bathroom. By the time he returned, I'd fallen asleep, wrecked.

CHAPTER NINE

The bed was empty when I awoke. I showered, dressed, and met Blake in the kitchen. A small plate of fruit was set at my place at the island. He looked away, grabbed a mug, and poured my coffee, setting it down beside my breakfast.

"Thank you." I stared down at my fruit, moving it around the plate. For last night's exertions, I should have been able to eat a hungry man's breakfast, but my nerves were destroying my appetite.

"What was last night about?"

I felt a flush creep up to my cheeks. Why was I embarrassed? Blake had done far worse to me, but somehow my doing it to him seemed entirely different. The look in his eyes told me so.

"I had a dream," I said quietly, not knowing what else to say.

"About dominating me?"

"No, the opposite actually."

"Really." His voice was so calm, his face the only indicator that anything was amiss.

"I'm still upset with you."

"So you decided to tie me up while I was sleeping?" The question almost sounded innocent.

I winced. "You were half awake, Blake. Not to mention you're twice my size and you snapped the cuffs like a piece of twine. You're acting like I handcuffed you and tortured you."

"Is that what I should expect next time?"

I rolled my eyes and stabbed a piece of my fruit. I chewed in silence a moment. "It didn't occur to me that you had...limits."

His jaw ticked. "It didn't occur to me, either."

"I don't know the rules of this game, Blake. You refuse to talk to me about it."

He laughed roughly. "Is this about the club?"

I answered with my eyes, hoping he'd open up to me about it. "Why won't you talk about it?"

His lips went thin. "Enough about the club! I don't need a label between us to know I want to control your pleasure. And I don't need a fucking safeword."

His anger shot off the walls of the room until there was only silence again. He walked toward me, his palms curling over the edge of the counter near where I sat. I'd rattled him. My playing, which had been innocent enough, had shaken him deeper than I ever imagined. I was playing a game I knew nothing about.

He leaned in and kissed my cheek. I sighed, relieved to sense him softening toward me.

"But you do," he whispered, setting off a new ripple of anticipation. "Because I'm going to push you past every boundary. I'm going to fuck you every way a woman can be fucked."

I closed my eyes at his dark promise. "I'm sorry. I didn't realize—"

"You didn't realize that someone like me doesn't want to be tied up."

"You do it to me all the time," I shot, tears stinging my eyes.

"Did it feel better to pretend that I'm someone I'm not?" His voice was gentler.

I shook my head, regretting all of it. My little foray into dominance was backfiring in a big way. I wasn't satisfied at all. We were both hurt and off balance.

"No." I shoved off from the counter and left for work without him before I broke down.

I was tired and confused, and for once, I longed for the stability of work, the familiarity of the office and the people who filled it.

Clay played defense when another reporter was waiting for me outside the office.

Great. That was all I needed.

Now that the reporters were showing up at work, the thought occurred to me that negative press probably wasn't what Alex wanted either. Maybe fast-tracking was good, because once Alex knew I was potentially linked with the investigation surrounding Daniel, maybe he'd want to distance himself from us. I pushed the thought away and went through my morning routine at the office.

About an hour later, I heard the office door open and Alli speaking with someone. A few seconds later she was at my desk with a small red box that rested in her hands.

"What's this?"

"I don't know. A courier just dropped it off." She set it in front of me on the center of my desk. The box was covered with velvet and tied with a black satin bow. If it was from Blake, I could only imagine its contents.

"No sender?" I asked.

"I didn't ask, but I'd be willing to bet it's from Blake." She shot me a mischievous smile.

I returned a weak one. Was he sorry? The way I'd left this morning had not been good. He hadn't cooled off from the night before, so I couldn't imagine he'd experienced a dramatic change of heart in the few hours since I'd left him standing there in the kitchen.

"Okay, thanks."

I slowly untied the bow. I lifted the lid, revealing bunches of thick black tissue paper. I pushed through it until my fingers met a texture I recognized. Leather. And then something cool. Metal studs. I stared into the box, my heart thundering. It was a ball gag. A flash of red beneath the leather straps caught my eye. I pushed the gag to the side and retrieved a tiny card.

Erica,

I regret that I'll be missing your nuptials, but I would be remiss if I didn't send a gift to mark this joyous occasion in your lives. Here's a little memento from our adventures at the club. Maybe you two can carry on the tradition.

All the best,
Sophia

The handwriting was feminine but jagged, the S looping over the other letters. My hands trembled and I dropped the note. The gag sat inside the box and my stomach rolled. The mere sight of it sent my adrenaline rocketing out of control. Knowing that Blake had used the thing on Sophia was making me physically ill. I wanted to throw it into the trash, but instead I sat frozen, studying the box quietly. The device didn't look old, but it wasn't new. The leather was worn slightly where the hook met the belt hole. My imagination flooded with terrible unwelcome images of them together. Her bound, him seeking his pleasure from her submission the way he had with me so many times.

My eyes burned, and my lips quivered beyond my control. I grabbed the card and crushed it in my palm. Doing so did nothing to relieve the pressure that built inside my chest. I closed my eyes, and in my mind, I screamed every vile name I could think of.

Sophia had hit her mark, and what perfect timing too, after the night we'd had. I was reeling. Releasing the card, I noticed more writing on the back. I straightened the thick crumpled paper and blinked, clearing my vision to read the small text printed on the back.

La Perle, 990 North Hampton Street, Boston, MA

Everything went still. Reading the words seemed to open a valve in my chest. I could breathe again, but it still hurt. Sophia was taunting me, in more ways than one. If the contents of this box were the problem, maybe this hint, however unwelcome, was the answer.

For the rest of the morning, my mind was a war zone. If Sophia had wanted to send me over the edge with imagined memories of Blake fucking her, she'd done a great job. My appetite non-existent, I worked through lunch in a near manic state. I forced my thoughts away from the package that had finally found a home in the trash receptacle beside my desk, but I was consumed by only one thing. I searched the name and address of the club online, finding nothing of interest or anything to indicate what kind of place it was. It was as if the place didn't even exist, save the little red pin that showed its location on the map.

The clock hit three, and I Skyped Alli, nervous energy pulsing through my veins as I did. What the hell was I doing?

Erica Hathaway: I need to borrow your closet. Do you want to cut out early?

Alli Malloy: Sure. Let me ask the boss.

I wanted to smile, but I was too far from levity right now. I shut down my computer, grabbed my purse, and met Alli in the hallway where we quickly descended to the street. We stepped into the Escalade and directed Clay where to take us.

Alli's eyes were wide. "What's the occasion? It's only Wednesday."

"I'm surprising Blake. And I need something…um, really sexy." This shouldn't have surprised her, considering she still believed the mysterious red box had come from him.

She hummed. "Okay, I definitely can help with that.

What are we talking, Vegas-sexy or you're not leaving the house sexy?"

I swallowed hard, the reality of what I was about to do dropping like a rock in my stomach. I wished I could share a fraction of the excitement Alli seemed to have about what tonight would bring. Unfortunately, sex wasn't the only thing I had to look forward to. "Vegas sexy should be fine," I said quickly, shifting my focus out the window.

Clay dropped us at Alli and Heath's apartment a few minutes later. Alli riffled through her ample closet and tossed out a handful of tiny dresses. A few I recognized from our trip to Vegas months ago. At the time, I couldn't imagine walking around in public in these outfits. The normal discomfort I'd feel from being seen in a barely-there mini dress paled in comparison to the unknown of how I'd be received at the club, if they even let me in. This could all turn into one humiliating mess, but Blake still wasn't talking and I needed answers. Tonight, one way or the other, I'd get them.

"This one is fine." I smoothed my hand over a black mini dress made of stretchy cotton sateen that would fit tightly over my curves. I brought it up to my front, gauging that it would hit mid-thigh. The neckline was a revealing scoop, which would accentuate my cleavage. I had no idea what I'd be walking into tonight, but I was determined to at least try to look the part.

The truth of the matter was I had no fucking idea what I was doing.

★ ★ ★

I fiddled with the buttons of the long jacket that concealed the outfit that was hardly appropriate for any old Wednesday night date. Clay turned down a few more streets, and I knew we were getting close. My stomach rolled with my anxiety. I fought the urge to throw up and instead shot off a text to Blake and turned my phone to silent. Thank God Clay had no idea where he was taking me, which gave me some small measure of comfort. He hadn't taken Blake here since he'd hired him to keep tabs on me. Already I had a million questions, and the one that kept pushing its way to the forefront of my brain was when he'd been here last.

Clay turned onto North Hampton, and a thousand scenarios spun through my head. Maybe they'd be closed. I could go home and surprise Blake with this outfit and pretend like Sophia hadn't sent me a relic from their D/s sex life. Maybe they'd take one look at me and tell me to get lost or find the nearest street corner. Heaven knew the outfit I was wearing would warrant such a reaction.

He slowed in front of a row of brownstones. The building was simply marked with a plaque reading 990, with no indication that we were anywhere important. Clay squinted and glanced back at me with a wary look. "This it?"

"Yeah, um, I think so." I scolded myself for sounding so nervous.

"Want me to wait for you?"

I hesitated. Maybe he should. God, Blake was going to skin me alive for this one. Fear shot through me all over again when my phone vibrated for the third time.

"Sure, if you want to until I'm inside." I tried to sound innocent.

"Does Blake know you're here?"

"Yeah, of course. He's meeting me here," I reached for the door handle before I needed to lie again. I liked Clay, and I already felt guilty. He'd no doubt get a verbal lashing from Blake that might rival my own.

"All right," he said after a moment.

Confident he almost believed me, I stepped out and climbed the steps to the broad wooden door. I was running out of time to follow through. I located the buzzer to the right, pressed it, and waited impatiently. I rotated my weight between my feet, careful not to offset my balance and tumble. A minute later the door opened. A girl with long bleached blond hair stood before me. She was dressed entirely in black, a small halter and leather pants. Her makeup was heavy, and I began to feel a little better about my attire.

Our eyes met and she stared blankly. "Can I help you?"

I licked my lips, feeling uneasy. They weren't going to just let me waltz in here, skank dress or not. "I'm meeting someone here," I said, my voice wavering more than I wanted it to.

She toyed with the shiny metal that looped through the side of her lower lip. "Who?"

Oh hell, here we go. I shoved my nerves to the side. "Blake Landon."

Her pierced eyebrow lifted before she shifted her

bored stare past me. She stepped back and lifted her chin a fraction, motioning for me to come forward.

I stepped far enough inside for her to close the heavy door behind me. I moved to follow her, but she raised her hand. "Wait here."

I nodded quickly, as if I knew that was protocol. I knew nothing. I was officially in well over my head. Time stretched on. Every second felt like an eternity as I waited for her to return or for Blake to come barging in after me.

Then I heard someone coming down the hall. My breath caught when, instead of the girl, a man nearly twice her age greeted me. He was dressed well in a black suit and a white shirt unbuttoned casually at the collar. Even in the poor light of the foyer, I could see his skin was dark, not tanned but naturally olive. He regarded me coolly. I knew instantly that I was in the right place, and without question, that this man knew Blake.

"Tessa tells me you know Mr. Landon. Is this true?" His voice was smooth, cultured, and tinted with an accent that I couldn't place among my scattered thoughts.

"Yes. I'm actually meeting him here." I battled the urge to break away from the intensity of his stare. The quiet humor in his eyes made me feel small and vulnerable in his presence, as if he held a wealth of knowledge above me. I had little doubt he did. Still, I sensed that he wanted to believe me, which made it easier to lie somehow. "He should be here soon," I added, just in case this dark and dangerous stranger was having any thoughts about locking me up in his cage in the interim.

He held out his hand. I hesitated for a moment that

seemed too long, and then accepted the gesture. I tightened my grip, expecting him to shake my hand. Instead he turned my palm down and lowered his lips to the top of my hand. The kiss was sweet, but if a kiss could have layers, this one did. Something about the firm but gentle grasp on my hand, the slow purposeful way he grazed my skin, and the dark look in his eyes when he lifted them to mine had my heart racing with fear. And something else, something darker that I couldn't name. This man was a Dom. I was willing to put money on it.

He straightened slowly, paralyzing me with that knowing look. "My name is Remy. Welcome to *La Perle.*"

"I'm...Erica," I replied with a shaky breath. Fuck, twenty seconds with this man and my facade was crumbling. I wouldn't last long in this place. I sent up a silent prayer for Blake to speed here, yet somehow I knew he was.

"Erica." Remy paused on my name and pursed his lips, as if he were letting the sound of it settle over his tongue like a fine wine. "Lovely. It's always a pleasure meeting Blake's friends."

He smiled faintly, as if he knew immediately how those words would rattle me. The muscles in my face tensed, but I tried like hell to calm my features. How could I hide my displeasure at the reminder that Blake had *friends*, and more than one, who ran in these circles?

Too busy trying to lock down my physical reactions, I barely noticed Remy still held me in his clutches, our connection now prolonged but strangely not awkward.

"Join us." He nodded toward a long hallway beyond.

By lowering our hands together to his side, he coaxed me a step closer.

The small moment set me into motion behind him. On shaky legs, I started down the hallway. The old floors creaked below the clicking of my heels, making the journey to this secret place uncomfortably loud. At the end of the hall, a turn brought us to a landing. A thick ornate railing led downstairs where the muffled sounds of the club first hit my ears.

After another gentle tug, I followed Remy down the stairs, clinging to the railing and, oddly, his hand like a lifeline. I strained to hear what was going on behind the door we approached. Music and the uneven tones of voices. Different voices. Quiet and loud, even some laughter. Then a loud cry that sounded like a woman's. I tightened my grip.

He smiled. "Don't be afraid, *cherie*. But stay close to me, just in case."

CHAPTER TEN

Alarms rang out in my brain, shooting fear down my limbs, making me sweat despite the sparse clothing under my jacket. I longed for the reassurance of safety. While Remy's seemingly possessive presence didn't exactly promise innocent protection, I wanted to believe it might. If only while I waited for the only man whose arms could take me away from the terrors of the world.

And I was nothing short of terrified now. My eyes were wide, my heartbeat skipping out of control. Remy turned the old-fashioned knob with a squeak and gave us passage into an enormous oblong room that went on farther than I could see. The place was dim, not completely dark, but before I could bring everything into focus before me, Remy had me walking away from the entrance. We approached an old wooden bar situated against the wall. Afraid to look around, I followed him, a routine that was almost becoming instinct in the few moments I'd known him.

"Let me take your coat."

I hesitated. I quickly sized up the nearly naked people in the room mingling with people in various states of dress. People like me, people in suits, people in street clothes, and many others clad as Tessa had been. Fitting in wasn't a concern anymore, but I wanted to crawl into the shadows now, not put myself on display.

Against my better judgment, I shrugged off the coat, which Remy quickly took. With a barely noticeable flick of his hand, he summoned a tall brunette with luminescent blue eyes to where we stood. She took my coat and disappeared just as quickly.

"Have a seat. Can I get you a drink while you wait?"

I sat on the smooth wooden stool, pulling down the hem of my dress as I did. I took in every small detail of my surroundings as quickly as I could. The walls were a deep red, made darker by the sparse lighting.

"Erica."

I turned to Remy, my heart stilling at the familiar tone. Blake had that tone memorized when he wanted to get his way.

"What will you have?"

A modest but decidedly expensive collection of liquors was displayed along the wall. "Lagavulin," I said. "On the rocks."

He regarded me silently.

"Please," I added softly, as if his look compelled me to.

Remy's face registered only slight amusement at the last part of my request. He relayed the order to the female bartender. She slid my drink toward Remy, her eyes cast down. He murmured a thank you and pushed it into my hand. His fingers lingered over mine only a second. I resisted the urge to pull my hand away.

My nerves were tearing me apart. I wasn't as brave as I thought I was. I lifted the drink to my lips and took the first burning swallow. I breathed in deeply through my nose, the sharp scent of the smoky liquor filling my lungs. I took another sip before setting the glass back down.

The low, unrecognizable beat of the music was broken with the cry of a woman. I turned in my seat and froze at the visual that lit up before me. On a small but brightly lit platform in the center of the room stood a woman. The strangled cries had come from her. She was bent at the waist, hands gripping her ankles tightly, and clad only in a black corset that covered neither her breasts nor her bottom half. The shiny leather decoration clung to her torso as she jolted under the whip of a long black flogger against her backside.

Another cry tore from her as the figure of a man unleashed a torrent of lashes. A look of tormented lust pinched her lovely features. She flushed red, from her cheeks all the way to her small breasts that bounced from her body with every new assault.

I gripped my drink, letting the cut glass of the lowball mark indentations into my cold fingers. Heat flooded my face as I recognized the woman's sweet agony. Remy's voice broke the spell the woman's sexual torture had put me under.

"You are new here, and I like to know about my patrons. Tell me more about you, lovely Erica."

"Not much to tell," I lied, my voice too light, almost comical in the context of where we were and what we were watching.

"How long have you been with our Mr. Landon?" His dark eyes glittered as they fixed on me.

I licked my lips anxiously under his penetrating stare.

His eyes lowered, fixing on the motion.

"Since May." *Since I graduated from college and my whole life changed.*

"So…you are *his*?"

The fleeting sweep of his index finger over the well of my throat disturbed me more than I let on. His touch was feather light, but an unspoken challenge lay there. From the moment we'd been introduced, he touched me like he had the right to. The boldness reminded me of the man who did. Every touch seemed like a silent proclamation.

"I'm his." I found my voice, determined to leave no doubt as to the truth of those words. I wanted to recoil away from him, but determined to play the part, I sat frozen in place while his gaze swept over me.

"And he has you here without a collar?"

My chest tightened with panic. A collar? What the hell had I gotten myself into? My hand went to my throat. I felt suddenly naked without the symbol that would prove I was Blake's, truly. I looked down, the glimmer of my ring bright in the low light.

"We're engaged." I wasn't sure if I should have revealed the detail, but it was all I had now.

"Ah." Remy smirked, looking away a moment. "The ultimate collar. You must be very special indeed, to be his wife and his slave."

When he returned his attention to me, I glared, loathing the way the word flowed off his tongue so easily.

"I'm no one's slave."

The dark wing of his eyebrow lifted, an unspoken challenge lighting his eyes. "You don't serve to please him?"

"Y-Yes, of course I do."

What kind of question was that? I wanted to please Blake. In every way. With sex, of course, but in life, I wanted his happiness. I craved it almost as much as my own. But I hated the way Remy painted what we shared. For all the progress I'd made with embracing submission, I bristled at this man's easy assumption that I was less—a slave, a submissive.

He hummed softly. "I'm very curious now what brings you here. Tell me, did you come to play? Or to learn?" He looked into the main area, a new activity beginning to take shape where the other had ended. The room was lined with small booths, shrouded in darkness. The shadows. I wanted to hide there until Blake came for me, but I feared whatever already lurked there.

I followed his gaze, spying with shame on the various debaucheries that played out before us. Still, I couldn't tear away from the scene at the far end of the room. A young man had become the focal point of the evening's current entertainment. Bound by his wrists and ankles to the brick wall by heavy metal holds, he appeared distressed. Tessa was pacing back and forth in front of him. She came up close. I couldn't hear their exchange from this distance, and I could barely see what happened next. He grunted, as if someone had punched him in the gut.

Tessa moved to the side, revealing the man's now exposed penis jutting forward from his pants. Without warning, she slapped his rigid member, eliciting more painful grunts. His bare abdomen tightened with every unwarranted slap, and then released when she rotated her assaults with gentler strokes. He sucked in a sharp breath with a hissing sound when the weapon of play made contact again.

Then she was very close to him, her mouth against his ear. I tried to imagine what she was saying to him, scolding him for some imagined wrongdoing no doubt, reminding him of the rewards of his obedience. As if watching a movie, I caught myself empathizing with his struggle, with his experience. Once again, that look of pleasure mingling with evident pain released an unwanted sensation through my body. Watching Tessa tease and taunt him woke unexpected stirrings too.

"Or perhaps you came to watch."

Remy's words interrupted my blatant gawking at the scene in front of me. Heat suffused my cheeks. He'd caught me being one of those people. His lips lifted with a satisfied smile, as if he were watching a child experience a new wonder for the first time.

"It's all right, *cherie*. People here love to watch. There is no shame in that."

Shakily, I brought my drink to my lips and tried to forget what dominance might feel like. Real dominance. Not just being on top. Heat prickled my skin when I remembered the brief moment of power I'd enjoyed the night before and the incredible intensity from Blake I'd inspired. I'd crossed a line, and I still wasn't sure what to make of what had happened between us then.

I twisted uncomfortably in my dress, the layered fabric suddenly too hot against me even with all it revealed to

Remy and others. We weren't alone at the bar, and despite the many distractions before me, I could feel his eyes on me every time. His and other men nearby. The number of Doms per capita was high in this building.

Would I always recognize that kind of man when one crossed my path, because of the way Blake made me feel? Maybe, but something was different with Blake—everything was different.

I began to panic that he'd misunderstood my earlier text. I'd only told him to meet me at the club. Maybe I should have been more clear, sent an address. Jesus, what if I was stuck here in this godforsaken place at Remy's mercy? My previous thought of him having a cage reared up in my mind.

I inhaled a steadying breath and tossed back the rest of my drink. I turned my wrist only to realize I'd left my watch at Alli's apartment. Time ticked on, and I was no closer to my goal.

"Are you certain he's coming?"

"Yes," I replied quickly. "Is this your place?" I hoped to distract him from Blake's absence.

"Yes, I own *La Perle*. I have for many years."

"Has it always been…like this?" I tried to sound casual, but I was certain Remy wasn't mistaking my novice curiosity with anything akin to confidence.

"Always." He motioned for the bartender and pushed my empty drink toward her. Turning back to me, he asked, "Do you know what it means?"

"What?"

"*La Perle*."

"It's French for 'pearl' isn't it?"

"Of course, but do you know why?"

I shook my head and he leaned in as if to tell me a secret. He was still standing, but his body was close, too close. Suddenly tense, I swiveled toward the bar as the bartender placed another drink on the dark wooden surface. Remy's hand went to the back of the stool. His whisper was hot, an unwelcome sensation against my skin. I tried to mask a shiver.

"You are wise to be afraid. If I didn't know Landon, I would show far less restraint with you."

I exhaled a panicked breath and stared down at the bar, unwilling to look into the man's eyes and give anything else away.

"Because this is not a place for restraint," he continued in a slightly less predatory tone. "At least not for men like me. Perhaps for you…but only to reveal *la perle*, the succulent treasure at the center of you, *cherie*."

I frowned. I didn't know what he meant, and I didn't want to.

"The pearl, like your submission, Erica, is an object of great beauty. The most precious pearls are found in the wild…in unexpected places."

He tucked the hair that had fallen between us, obscuring my face, behind my ear. His touch fell to my shoulder, trailing down to my elbow with heavy intent.

"Unearthing them can be, at times, somewhat…violent." He trailed the tip of his nail down my forearm, with enough pressure to put me on edge but not enough to cause pain.

I shivered again, straining away from his touch. Squeezing my eyes closed, I forced myself to stay calm. But I was struggling for air, scrambling for any semblance of comfort in this dark place. I needed to get out of here…soon. I needed to get away from this man. Where on God's earth was Blake?

Remy seemed to read my thoughts and faced the bar, shifting his focus from my body to the snifter that had been set in front of him.

"*Merde*, where is your man?"

I had no idea, but I now cursed myself for texting him too late. Remy's patience was waning with mine, and he didn't seem like a man who deprived himself of many pleasures.

"Tell me about the other women." Blake would be here soon. God, I hoped he would be. But in the meantime, I wanted to know as much as this dangerous and magnetic man would share.

Remy sipped his drink and sighed. "Blake and I are…well, we are not friends per se, but he is a paying member. I would hardly betray his trust. His proclivities are his to tell. I'm sure he will tell you what you truly need to know." His attention diverted from me, a regretful smile set on his refined features. "Or perhaps he will show you. Here he comes. Finally."

I swiveled in my chair, eyes wide, heart flying. Blake was walking toward us in determined strides. His gaze was steady on me, his jaw set tight, as tight as his fists at his sides.

Remy leaned in, his breath again at my ear. "If you

came here to learn, I'd say punishment might be your first lesson tonight."

My whole body tensed at Remy's proximity and the vision of Blake closing in on us. "I've learned that lesson already," I replied weakly.

Remy laughed. "Have you?"

Before I could explain myself, Blake caught my hand and pulled me off the stool. I struggled to my feet, holding onto him for balance. He positioned his body in front of mine a fraction. Instinctively, I turned toward him, my chest against his arm. I knew he was angry with me, but I also knew he wanted to protect me. And right now, I felt an overwhelming and very present need to be protected.

"Landon." Remy straightened as if to shake Blake's hand.

"Stay away from her."

Remy lifted his hands in supposed surrender, leaning casually back against the bar. "No need to be protective."

"No?" Blake shot back. "Since when does that ever happen around here?"

"I was simply keeping the vultures at bay. It was very brave of you to let such a beautiful creature out of your sight. She wandered in here like a lost kitten." He smiled affectionately, his gaze sliding over me as shamelessly as it had before.

Blake tightened his grip, and I sighed, my entire being relieved to have him near, no matter how angry he was. The way I clung to him now left no doubt that I was his and only his. I chanced a look into his eyes. He cast me an emotionless look. I weakened against him, apologizing without words.

"She escaped," he said in a low tone.

"Ah. I see." Remy smiled again. "Seems unlike you to tolerate such disobedience. She's new to all this, no?"

I suppressed the urge to roll my eyes. Perhaps Remy did keep his women in cages, and between the two of them this all made sense. First I was a slave, and now I was a runaway.

"She's none of your concern, Remy." He turned to me. "Let's go. Now."

"No." I tightened my grip on his hand and pulled him back.

His eyes were wild with frustration now, the calm mask gone. "No?"

"I want to stay."

"Let her stay, Landon," Remy chimed in. "Perhaps she will learn something. You know as well as I do, sometimes they need to learn the lessons the hard way. This kitten has sharp claws. She needs training."

Blake shoved a hand through his hair, his gaze passing over the rest of the club. He murmured a string of curses under his breath.

"There's a little booth there waiting for you. Have a drink. Enjoy the show. And each other, of course." Drink in hand, Remy stepped away. Crossing the room, he settled into an unoccupied plush red chair guarded by a petite, half-naked girl kneeling at its base.

"This is where you want to be?"

I opened my mouth to speak, searching for the words. The truth. All I wanted was the truth.

"Do you have any idea how fucking stupid it was for you to come here alone?"

"I'm fine," I insisted, though my body was still riddled with anxiety over the past several minutes here without him.

"This isn't a martini bar, Erica. You walked through these doors and into a world you know nothing about."

"I want to know about it," I said quietly, suddenly embarrassed.

"You don't."

I pulled my hand from his grasp, only to have him band a protective arm around my waist.

"If it's kink you're after, we can go home right now, and I'd be more than happy to get creative. Needless to say, punishment is in order." He paused, his anger seeming to fade somewhat. "This is not the place for you."

My palm found his chest, and I let my forehead fall to his shoulder. His heart beat rapidly beneath his shirt. I breathed in his scent. A familiar scent, bringing me back to what I knew, back to us. "Tell me what this place means to you," I pleaded softly.

He sighed, clutching me tighter. "Beyond wanting to get you the hell out of here, it means nothing."

I looked up, determined to hear the truth from him. "That's not true. If it were, why would Sophia want to send me here?"

He gritted his teeth, his arm flexing around my waist. "Goddamnit."

"You came here together." I wasn't asking, but I decided to start with getting him to admit to the obvious.

"Yes, we came here together. Is that what you wanted to know, or is there more? Maybe we can continue the interrogation at home, without all the prying eyes." The words lashed out at me.

He was furious. I knew he had a right to be, but I couldn't stop.

"I want to know you." I fought the urge to cry. I hated Sophia and every vision my imagination had created of Blake loving her. I despised the fact that she'd had a part of him that I might never know. I pressed my body along his, my cheek against his chest. "I want to know what and who drew you here for so long. I'm one of two relationships you've had in a decade, and this place filled up too many of the nights in between." I took his silence as consideration and it gave me hope. "Don't I have the right to know? All I want is the truth," I whispered.

"Have I ever lied to you?"

I looked up. "No, but you've never told me anything unless you had to. You want more from me...you *demand* everything. And I'll give it to you, but..."

He caught my face in his hand, his thumb restless against my cheek. I leaned into his touch, oblivious of the people staring at us with lust and envy and passing interest.

"This is the past," he said slowly, but firmly.

"This is now." I touched his cheek, a silent call for the darkness that always simmered below the surface of the man I loved. "Indulge me."

CHAPTER ELEVEN

Blake's jaw bulged, displeasure written across his features. I had pushed him, yet again. I'd likely pay for it, but if he opened up to me, it would be worth it.

He began to walk, pulling me toward him as Remy had before.

"I'm not leaving," I hissed, refusing to go any farther.

"We're not leaving, for fuck's sake. You want to see what goes on in here? Like it or not I'm going to show you. It'll be punishment and education all in one filthy fucking package."

I couldn't speak. I couldn't move until he tugged me toward him once more. This time I went willingly and without argument. Shuffling unsteadily on my heels, I followed him until we slowed in front of the dark, empty booth Remy had offered to us.

Only steps away, the corseted woman from before was now being forced into another compromising position at the hands of the man who I presumed to be her master, at least for the night. He was a thickly built man, his shirtless body on display. He gripped her hair and she gasped, her eyes hazy with lust and whatever intoxicant flooded one's body in these helpless erotic moments.

Blake was behind me now, his hands resting possessively on my hips. "You wanted to come here and taste this life. Maybe I should take Remy's advice, break

160

my own rules, and give you a very public lesson."

I stood stark still at the husky threat. For all the fear that being in Remy's presence had elicited, I could barely breathe anticipating what Blake would actually do to me now.

The muscles in the man's arms flexed as he made fast work of his leather trousers. Seconds later he was in the woman's mouth. Hands bound, she took his thrusts, letting him make lusty use of her mouth as a means to come.

"Would you like that, Erica? Would you like for me to make an example of you that way?"

I shook my head. No. I didn't want that. I couldn't fathom it, being bound or bent over for anyone's public pleasure. It was horrifying, yet I couldn't tear my eyes away.

"Are you sure? That could be you," Blake whispered, skimming his hands down my dress. "I think they'll finish soon. He won't last long that deep in her mouth. Then I can show the people here what a bad fucking sub you are."

I drew in a breath through my nose, trying to ignore the unwelcome pulse between my legs, but all I could smell was sex. The woman was gagging herself with every attempt to draw the man to the back of her throat. He'd kicked her legs farther apart with the thick toe of his black boot. Her body quivered, need seeming to ripple through her as she pleased him. Then a jolt when the same man whipped her ass from above. She gasped for air, whimpering loud enough for us to hear when he peppered her with a series of hard lashes.

"You wouldn't do that to me." My voice was laced

with challenge, but suddenly I was uncertain of how much I could trust Blake in the confines of this establishment.

"Why not? Don't you deserve it?"

I shivered at the fresh edge in his voice. Maybe I did. I couldn't answer, but I sure as hell wasn't going to admit it.

"Do you think he loves her, Erica?"

My heart hurt when he said the words. I turned my head. I couldn't watch anymore. Then I heard the man's groaning pleasure. I couldn't see it, but I was certain he'd come.

"Your turn, boss." Blake circled my body, catching my wrists when I went to move away.

My eyes flew open. "No. I can't."

He hauled me against him, securing me again by the waist. The part of me that wasn't in a full-blown panic reveled in the full contact of his hard body against me. I was frightened, aroused, and completely confused. The only bright spot was the certainty that no one here gave a shit.

"I think you can. You're brave. Look how brave you've been tonight already. Not to mention last night. Thinking about that makes me want to punish you all the more."

"No," I whimpered, hating the cold, teasing tone of his voice.

"No doesn't hold much weight here, Erica. Did you know that when you walked in here?" His voice was softer, almost sympathetic.

I wanted him to take pity on me now. *Save me from*

this chaos, and I'll never do it again, I swear.

"Go ahead," he urged.

"I can't do that in front of everyone," I cried softly. "Please don't ask me to. Please..."

I couldn't breathe. The furious beating of my heart was the only sound in my ears. I was trembling in his arms, the safeword on the tip of my tongue. Fucking on the conference table unbeknownst to Greta a few feet away was one thing. Having sex and taking punishment in public, no matter how much my twisted mind might have fantasized about it, wasn't something I was capable of. Not tonight, and very likely, not ever.

Oh God. What if this is what he wants, what he craves?

"Come here," he said quietly.

"No, please," I begged, but his intense embrace had softened and he was leading us to the booth.

Relief crashed over me that he wasn't forcing me to go through with it. Would he really have? I didn't want to believe that he could have, but how could I know? I didn't know what kind of man he could be here. That's why I had come.

I huddled against him, my enemy and my savior, waiting for my nerves to calm. He hushed me, running his hands over my arms and sides, the way he always did when he needed to take me away from my thoughts and back to the moment, back to him. I opened my eyes finally, peering around the dark club. Through my lashes I caught a glimpse of Remy across the room. He sat in his throne-of-sorts. We were shrouded in darkness but somehow I could feel Remy's eyes on me, his unwelcome touch a memory on my skin.

Blake rested his hand on my thigh. I was still pressed close to him, not sure who or what to be terrified of.

The poor young man from earlier was now being led around the room on all fours, his tortured penis bobbing as he followed Tessa around. She ignored him mostly, engaging in conversation with other patrons. This was a place for fantasies of the darkest variety. If I'd learned anything, I'd learned that.

I swallowed hard, almost too afraid to speak after that close call. "You did…these things?"

"No," Blake answered swiftly.

I looked up, silently questioning him.

"I've always preferred the privacy of a room." He gestured upward with his index finger. "Upstairs."

I looked back to my lap, violently cursing myself for asking. I bit my lip, wanting to puncture the skin with my teeth. Jealousy would make me ugly indeed.

"How does that make you feel?" Blake thumbed my lower lip, freeing it from the tense vise of my teeth.

"Terrible," I admitted bitterly.

"This is the past. You…only *you* are my future."

I wanted to believe him. But… "Don't you ever think of this place?"

He relaxed his embrace, putting a small distance between us. I allowed it, but I didn't like it.

"Sometimes. Mostly when I'm thinking about you, the things I want to do with you. I won't lie. Places like this can be…inspiring. I was driving over here in a blind rage, and I couldn't help but imagine the things I could do with you here." He tipped my chin up. "What really scared me was the thought that someone else wanted the same thing."

I wanted to look away, shameful and embarrassed, but he didn't let me.

"You're strong and willful. I respect that, and God help me, I love you for it, but do not ever...*ever* fucking do anything like this again."

I nodded as much as his grip would allow. I'd never set foot in this place again. Certainly not without Blake, and apparently a collar, just to make damn sure men like Remy stayed hands off.

"I won't," I said weakly.

"I don't believe you." His eyes were hard and emotionless.

"I promise—"

"You've made me this promise before. Remember, the one where you agree not to throw yourself in harm's way for the sake of saving me, or in this case, simple curiosity? Is punishment or the threat of it the only way to get your attention, Erica?"

The sense that we were falling into place filled me. He'd been shaken, seeing me here. Despite everything, he seemed almost at ease now. In control. Calm and commanding in his world.

"Answer."

"I'm sorry. I was stupid to come here without you. I just—"

"You just do whatever you goddamn want anyway. Isn't that right?"

Squeezing my eyes shut, I fought his words along with the string of regrets rattling through my brain.

Then he kissed me.

My fractured thoughts vanished the instant our lips touched. Rough and pent up, the kiss was all consuming. I lost myself in it. His tongue breached my lips, tangling with mine. Never had I wanted Blake to be the man touching me more than now.

We struggled for air, breaking the kiss only long enough to catch a breath before coming back to each other. His hands were everywhere, stilling me by the hair. Then down my chest, the heel of his hand lingered over the hard point of my nipples pressing through the dress. My eyelids became heavy, my nipples tender and needy to the point of pain. Desire was a living thing, blazing under every touch, demanding more. I needed his skin on me. I needed relief from all of this.

I gasped against his lips when his hand found its way between my legs and he coaxed his way up the center of my thighs. I clenched them together, wanting his touch, but not here…

"Do you want to be punished? Is that why we keep finding ourselves in these situations?"

I shook my head, suddenly uncertain of my answer. He slid his hand to the hot apex between my legs and nudged them apart. I squirmed, but he was firm. Bypassing my panties, he dove into the place where I was soaked with arousal. A soft cry left my lips. I pressed my chest against him, wanting him closer, wanting his body to somehow shield the world from the way he was turning mine upside down.

"Fuck." He parted his lips slightly, his eyes going dark.

He retreated and lifted me over so I was astride him. My dress slid up and I struggled to push it back down. I was completely open for him. Lust and shame battled for real estate in my brain. What was he doing to me, and why did a little part of me undeniably want him to?

"They'll see," I whispered in a panicked hush.

"No one can see us."

His kissed me again, and I forgot my vulnerability. His tongue drew a decadent path from my ear down my neck where he sucked hard at my collarbone. He was marking me. I wanted him to.

I moaned. My hands stopped fighting his advances and went to his shirt. Fisting the fabric, I held onto him, as if somehow he could anchor me through this storm that he'd created inside of me. He stroked my wet flesh, thumbing my clit and plunging his fingers deeper into my pussy. I fought the impulse to arch my hips into his movements as I would have had we been anywhere else.

"Blake, we shouldn't." My voice seemed far away, lost in the riotous emotions that outweighed any words.

He was silent, using his mouth instead to kiss me breathless. All my reservations were in vain. The need to come overwhelmed the voices in my head shouting at me to stop this madness.

He nipped at my lip. I shrieked at the flash of pain. His eyes were dark, lust and fire burning in their depths.

"You're right, we shouldn't do this. I should be punishing you, not fucking you. You make me break all the rules, Erica. I just want to see your face when you come. I want to hold you when you fall apart."

His fingers curled up, grazing the sensitive spot inside of me that made me see stars. I sucked in a sharp breath, my entire body seizing.

"Blake, oh God. What are you doing to me?"

I was going to come. A flick of his fingertips would send me over, and I was helpless against it now. I surrendered to the chase for more of Blake's touch, my hips moving in time with every little shove. This was crazy, but all I could do was feel.

Fuck it. I wanted the world to know he was mine and I was his. I didn't care who was getting flogged or sucked, and I didn't care who was watching them or us. Remy or Tessa or any of the other nameless faces. The only person in my world was Blake.

"Blake. Oh no, I'm coming."

"That's right. Come so I can take you home and fuck you until you scream."

His thumb worked a tiny magical circle over my clit and I was lost. I bit down on his shoulder, determined not to cry out. I couldn't be one of these people.

Using his hips for leverage, he went deeper. A helpless, shuddery cry left my lips as the orgasm tore through me, stripping me of everything that didn't matter.

I was one of these people.

★ ★ ★

Rational thought began to return, very slowly. Blake held me, caressed me. When he licked my arousal from his fingers, my body immediately responded. A sharp ache inside me demanded more. I wanted to please him, and I desperately wanted him to follow that mind-bending orgasm with several more.

Reaching down between us, I found his cock hard and bulging in his jeans. I moaned, brushing my breasts against his chest. I kissed him feverishly, tasting myself on his lips. I was so out of my mind with desire, I might have done anything. Limits seemed like a far away concept.

He closed his eyes, his jaw going tight as I massaged him and kissed him.

"I want you," I whispered, nibbling along his jaw.

"Not here."

"Please."

He caught my wrist, stilling my torments. "Let's get out of here."

I drew in a deep breath, sobering myself. I eased myself from him and after a slight adjustment, Blake stood, bringing me with him. We went for the door, traveling the same path I'd taken going in. I was nearly running after him to keep up.

"Wait!"

A woman's voice rang out down the hall. The girl who'd taken my coat earlier ran toward us with the garment.

"Thank you," Blake said, taking it from her.

"You're welcome, Mr. Landon."

She flashed a look to Blake and ducked her head

demurely, hiding those stunning blue eyes. My nostrils flared. I didn't like what I saw there. Something too familiar, like adoration.

The girl disappeared down the hall, and Blake held out my coat for me to put on. "Let's go."

We walked across the street where Blake's Tesla was parked. I slid into the passenger seat, my thoughts suddenly an epic jumble. What had we just done? Who was the girl? What the hell was wrong with us?

Blake pulled out of the spot and began driving home. I stared out the window, unable to keep my curiosity in check.

"Do you know her?"

"Who?"

"That girl."

He shrugged. "I don't know. Maybe."

Maybe? A new surge of jealousy sent a wave of adrenaline through me. How many of these women had been with him? Blake reached for my hand.

I moved away, avoiding his touch. "Don't touch me."

His laugh was acid in my veins. "Really? Don't touch you? You almost begged me to fuck you in the booth a few minutes ago. Now you don't want me to touch you?"

I stared silently out the window. *Go to hell.*

"Erica." His voice was softer. "You came to a sex club I used to frequent and you expected me to be anonymous? You opened the door. Honestly, what did you expect would be on the other side of it?"

"I guess I wouldn't know, since you never told me."

Emotion was thick in my throat. He was right, and I

was a fool.

"How many of those women have you had?" My voice cracked. I kept asking questions I didn't really want answers to.

He stared toward the road. "I couldn't tell you. I didn't go there to remember. I went there to forget."

My heart fell. "To forget Sophia?"

He paused. "Maybe at first."

I was silent. I had tortured myself enough. I wasn't going to coax out anything else that could hurt me tonight.

"Her needs appealed to a compulsion for control that I was still trying to get a handle on. When our relationship ended, the club was all that was left. A game. Going through the motions toward a foregone conclusion."

"Is that what I was too? A foregone conclusion?"

He was quiet for a long time and my misery only grew. We parked in front of the apartment and ascended the stairs in continued silence. Tossing the keys down inside, he put his hands on the counter, seemingly lost in thought. After a moment, he straightened and faced me.

I lingered by the door, waiting for him to make the next move. This night had been twelve shades of messed up.

"This is going to hurt, but it seems like you're on a quest for answers tonight, so I'm going to give them to you." He drew in breath. "You're not the first woman I've seduced, and you're not the first woman I've fucked. I'm sure you already know this."

I winced. I wanted to believe that we'd had nothing but love from the start, but I knew it wasn't true. Not even for me. Lust, preoccupation, obsession. Somewhere in the tornado of all those things we'd found love. Still, I wasn't sure I wanted the truth anymore. I was already hurting too much.

I walked past him into the bedroom. His footsteps followed behind me. I slowed in front of the bed and tore off the tight dress Alli had lent me.

"Are you going to listen to me?"

"No," I answered brusquely. I went into the bathroom and turned on the shower. "I was a conquest, I get it. I don't want to hear anymore about your sexual exploits, Blake. I think I've had enough eye-opening for one night. Clearly I'm way out of my depth."

I was trembling again. My stomach knotted and tears threatened.

"Baby…" His fervency was fading. "Whatever you're trying to find out about me is right here, wishing like hell you would just let us be us. Together, now. Fuck the past, and fuck the people we used to be and the people who made us that way."

Tears stung behind my eyes. "Just leave me alone." I stepped into the shower, shut the door, and let the too hot water scald my skin. When I opened my eyes under the stream, Blake had left.

CHAPTER TWELVE

Tension released in muscles I didn't realize were holding any. I lathered up, eager to wash away the club. Remy's touch. The air in the place, thick with sex and strangers. Christ, all I wanted was Blake and the comfort of his arms, and now I was pushing him away. All I'd wanted was the truth, and now I couldn't stand to hear it. But Blake was my truth, even when it hurt. He was my home, the one person in my life who gave me a reason to stay still and keep faith that together we could be more than our pasts.

I hid in the shower for a few more minutes, determined to pull myself together when I emerged. I toweled dry and found the bedroom empty. I wandered into the living room. Blake sat on the couch, a tired and bleak expression on his face. I sat beside him, tucking the towel in place at my chest. He didn't move to look at me.

"I'm sorry. For what it's worth, it's been a crazy day, and an even crazier night. Sophia sent me something."

He looked toward me then.

"A...gag. She said it used to be yours and hers. Sent it with her best wishes." I grimaced at the snide tone of her note and how deeply it had hurt me. "She gave me the address of the *Perle*. It was a complete mindfuck. This whole thing has been. Ever since I overheard your conversation with her that day, I haven't been able to stop thinking about the club and what it means to you."

"I know," he said quietly.

I sighed, relieved that he'd at least sensed my struggle if I hadn't always verbalized it. "I love you, Blake. I want to know everything about you. Even the things you think I don't want to hear…"

A few empty minutes passed. "Sophia's a bitch," he stated matter-of-factly.

I smiled. "That I think we can both agree on."

He closed his eyes, pinching the bridge of his nose. When no words followed, I inched closer. I feathered a touch over his hand. He turned it up and I laced our fingers together. I leaned my head against the back of the couch. "Talk to me."

He exhaled unsteadily. "I honestly couldn't tell you what I wanted to happen between us at first. I know I was incredibly attracted you, and yes, I wanted you in my bed. Nothing's changed there, except now I love you, deeply and beyond all reason. And the person I was back then, at the club, wasn't capable of loving anyone."

I tightened my hand in his.

"I love you, more than you'll ever know, Erica. But under that, I want to make you mine in every way. I'm hard every time I think of you and we're not together. I think I could live the rest of my life making love to you. I don't know what it is… Call it chemistry. Call it you being the most frustrating female I've ever met. You defy me like it's your fucking job. It drives me crazy." He ran a hand through his hair, leaning his head back against the couch. "The twisted thing is I think it turns me on…and getting you to submit to me afterward is turns me on even more."

I closed my eyes, trying to ignore the way it turned me on too. "Why?"

He lifted his head and looked at me. "I have no idea. It's a fucking kink. Why do you get impossibly wet when I spank you? Why does your body go soft when I dominate you? We could psychoanalyze it all damn day."

"But she's the reason why."

"She turned me onto it, yes. I won't deny it. But she took it too far. She wanted me to choke her, mark her. Then the drugs. She was a self-destructive mess, and the way she needed me made me question everything. I need control, Erica. I thrive on it. It's so deeply embedded in how I live my life now. It puts the world in order for me. And for a long time, after Sophia, I couldn't imagine bringing someone else into that kind of relationship and have it be a healthy one. Even now, I question everything it's doing to us."

He shook his head. "Even knowing your past with Mark, I couldn't stay away. I tried to be someone different, someone better for you. Then you kept coaxing me back to the person I knew how to be. I've been walking this line, trying to be the man you deserve and give you everything you want."

"You are, Blake, and you do."

"Yeah, but sometimes things go too far. For all my wanting control, I lose it. Sometimes I can't turn it off. I wish I could always pick and choose our moments. I know your body and I know what you want. But sometimes I can't turn off what I used to want, and it scares the hell out of both of us."

My throat worked on a swallow, thick with emotion. "Blake…"

"I don't want to hurt you, Erica, but I know I have. You worry that you're not good enough. You say it sometimes, and I can see it in your eyes. It kills me, because you have no idea how many times those words have echoed inside of me. Because you don't deserve me dragging you into all this darkness. I don't have to worry about not being good enough for you, because I already know I'm not."

"No." I stopped him, pressing a finger to his lips. I crawled over him, resting back on his strong thighs. "Don't say that."

"It's true."

"Stop it. Blake, what happened back there…wasn't easy for me."

His eyes dimmed. "I know I pushed you, and I shouldn't have."

"I took a risk going there. I know that. But seeing what goes on there, knowing that was a place that brought you solace…" I licked my lips, nervous about what I was about to ask, because I wanted to be what he needed. "I don't know if I'll ever be like those girls."

"You'll never be like them."

"But are you going to resent me because I haven't done those things or maybe never will be able to?"

He winced. "No. Of course not. Baby, of all of my kinks, wanting to do them in front of a bunch of perverts isn't one of them."

I laughed, relief filling the place where all my worry

had taken up residence this past week.

"I guess I worry about not being as experienced as you want me to be. Maybe that's why I couldn't let this go."

He brushed his knuckle across my cheek. "I want to do everything with you. Seeing your face when I give you a new kind of pleasure is more than half the fun. I'm in no rush to use up my bag of tricks on you and transform you into a connoisseur of kink."

My hand found the edge of his shirt. I pushed it up, lazily stroking the soft skin of his abdomen.

"You're the pro."

He smiled. "I don't think of it like that. But if I am, think of the results as practice for giving you a lifetime of mind-bending sex."

"Can't argue with that."

"I'm glad. We've had enough of that for one night."

I closed my eyes and leaned into his gentle touches. "I shouldn't have gone there without you."

"And I should have told you about the club when you asked. I didn't want to think about that part of my life or the person I used to be."

"I know how that feels too, but I've shown you my past. It hasn't always been easy or pretty, but I've never trusted anyone else with it the way I have with you. No one's ever been strong enough to handle it without judging me or making everything hurt all over again. You're strong enough. And so am I. Trust me with it."

He feathered a touch along my jaw, pushing a damp strand of hair back from my face. "I do trust you," he murmured.

"Then don't hide from me. We're sharing a life, Blake. You're my home. You're everything to me."

Lips parted, he held me close against him. His eyes were bright green, staring deeply into me. "You're in my soul, Erica. I couldn't hide from you if I tried. Just…"

I knit my brows together. "What?"

"Just be careful while you're in there, okay? You have more control than you think."

My heart seized, love pulsing out from the center of me through every limb, making me warm and soft in his arms. My lips trembled. Heaviness lifted. I traced the lines of his face in wonder, so in love with this man.

"Thank you," I whispered, seconds before he captured my lips in a kiss. Deep and passionate. I drank in his addictive scent, the essence of his tongue sweeping over mine. One kiss melted into the next. Soft licks went deeper, devouring.

"I need you now."

I nodded, the flash of desire hot on my exposed skin. The terry of the towel itched over the places where I wanted his touch. As if reading my mind, he reached for the large knot and loosened it from between my breasts. Baring me before him, he let out a breath. His gaze followed his touch, down my arms, kneading my breasts.

"Love your tits. Perfection." He thumbed over the sensitive peaks before sucking each one into his mouth. Gently, and then harder, grazing his teeth until I jolted under the pressure. The sharp edge arrowed to my core, making me hungry for him all over again. He kept on, teasing and torturing until they were both tender, swollen, and pink from his kisses and soft bites.

Leaning in, he kissed and licked the valley between my breasts. "I could lick every inch of you. One day, I just might. But tonight I can't be that patient."

I sifted my fingers through his hair, tugging gently, letting him know without words that I was burning for him too. He thrust his hips up with a rumbling growl, but otherwise he didn't act on his urgency. Mouth moving over my skin, hands restless over my curves, he kept us climbing, slowly. My breathing had changed into soft pants. I was ready to explode. I'd been so built up over the course of the night, I wasn't sure how much more I could take.

I stilled his movements, forcing his gaze to mine. There, lust and dark craving mingled. "Tell me what you want, Blake."

He licked his lower lip. A stab of need shot through my core. I undulated over him, brushing against his still clothed body, wishing he were inside me already.

With a firm hand, he stilled me. "You're all I want. Just this, just us."

"Then take me," I whispered against his lips.

I reached for the edge of his shirt and tugged it off. I went for his zipper, and he lifted his hips, shoving his jeans and boxers down just enough to free his engorged cock.

I reached for him eagerly. His velvet skin slid warm against my fingertips. I circled him, loving the way his eyes went dark when I touched him this way. He sucked in a sharp breath, lifting his pelvis into my grasp. I gazed up at him through the veil of my lashes.

"I want you inside me, Blake. I don't want to wait anymore."

My chest rose and fell in time with his. With my legs wrapped around him, he lifted us and stumbled forward, bringing us to the floor. The rug was soft and forgiving over the hard wood. He moved over me like an animal seizing his prey, making my pussy clench, hungry to be filled. He found his place between my thighs and took what was his.

I groaned in satisfaction and toed his pants down to his calves. I tried to touch him everywhere. The muscles of his back bunched under my hands as I lifted into his thrusts.

He gasped, increasing his pace. He cupped my ass, lifting me higher so his cock dragged over the sensitive bundles of nerves inside. I closed my eyes against the overwhelming sensation. My thighs gripped him, and light and color flashed behind my eyes.

"Look at me." His voice was full of gravel and need.

I opened my eyes. A look of love softened the lines around his eyes. I reached up, my hands restless over the muscles that flinched with his efforts.

I wanted to touch him, to soothe him and tell him without words how much he meant to me. His heart beat against me, his body white hot around me, inside me. When I couldn't find the words, my body spoke the truth.

Love wasn't enough. This—our bodies together—was more.

His hips hit mine with a strong thrust. I cried out his name, struggling to maintain eye contact.

"Blake…I love you," I sobbed with pleasure.

Vulnerability swam behind his glittering eyes, a silent answer to my proclamation. Wrapping his arms tightly around me, he silenced me with a deep kiss. He swallowed my cries, every breath. He was everywhere. We were as close as two people could be. I clawed at his sides, bowing off the floor and into his strong embrace.

Hips moving like pistons, he took us over the edge.

"I love you, Erica. God, I love you so much."

I came apart, tears burning behind my eyes.

★ ★ ★

My swollen eyes opened and I groaned at the sight of morning spilling into the room. My body hurt, fatigue and a general achiness that I couldn't quite pinpoint. I felt Blake's touch on my back. I flinched when he grazed over a particular spot on my shoulder blade.

"Ouch."

He pressed his lips to it. "Rug burn."

I groaned again and turned my face into the pillow as memories from last night flooded my brain. Jesus. What a night.

"See, this is why we need a bigger place," he said.

I turned to face him. His dark hair was a mess, spiking in every direction from sleep and...other things. But he looked more rested than I felt. He looked content, and that warmed me through.

"Why do you say that?"

"I need more rooms to fuck you in. Or at least more surfaces."

I giggled. "You're crazy."

A content smile spread across his lips. "Yeah, well, that's your fault."

I rolled to my back and stretched. The sheet slipped, baring my chest to him.

He moaned, his gaze roving over me hungrily. "What are you doing today?" he asked suggestively.

I closed my eyes, my ever-full daily calendar appearing behind them. "I have a million things."

His lips came over my nipple. "I guess that means I can't hold you hostage here."

I moaned and arched into his mouth. "I don't think Alli would allow that. I have a dress fitting. I have a meeting with Geoff too, to go over some of my questions."

He lifted up on his elbow, staring down at me with affection.

"What are you going to tell him?"

I pulled the sheet up over me and shifted to my side. I drew tiny circles over Blake's chest, tracing the beautiful curves of his body. I couldn't imagine him in any pose that would diminish my complete and utter awe of his body.

"Erica?"

"Hmm?"

His eyes were still lazy and low-lidded from sleep. "What are you going to tell Geoff?"

I hummed with a smile. "Sorry, I was just cataloguing your most gorgeous qualities."

He laughed. "After last night, I wasn't sure you'd ever talk to me again."

"I can't say I'd do it all over again." I fell back against

the pillow. "Well, maybe some of it."

"Don't do crazy shit like that anymore, okay? I mean it."

I met his serious gaze with a tentative one of my own. Going to the club alone had been a stupid move. I could have let him come around with it, but there was something about knowing I was going to marry the man that made it impossible for me to handle secrets between us. No matter how far into the past they were lodged, no matter how far away we'd come from them. I'd shown him everything. Every scar, every insecurity. Finally, we were on our way to turning the tables and Blake trusting me with the shadows from his past too.

"I won't as long as you make me a promise."

He was silent for a moment. "We're not back to ultimatums, are we?"

"I'm not a fan of ultimatums, but you wanted me to give you my trust. It's a two-way street. I don't want any secrets between us. If you don't trust me not to do things like I did last night, don't ever give me a reason to consider it."

I looked down, running my finger along the edge of the sheet. The memory of Sophia's words rattled through me. She'd sent me on this journey, and she'd threatened the validity of what Blake and I had. I hated her for it because she didn't believe we'd survive if I knew Blake's past. I wanted to prove her wrong in every way.

"I don't know what was worse, listening to the terrible things she said to me or feeling like I was in the dark about your past."

He toyed with a strand of my hair. "No more secrets."

I looked up, hopeful. "Promise me."

"I promise."

CHAPTER THIRTEEN

The next couple days were filled with preparations for the sale. We broke the news to James and Chris, whose shock was soon followed with support. The decision had been made swiftly, and the execution of it was right on my heels. Everything was happening so quickly, a circumstance that made it easier to quell the anxiety we all seemed to have around the impending transition.

I was days away from signing a piece of paper that, to the rest of the world, meant that the business as we knew it no longer belonged to us, but to Alex Hutchinson. A seasoned businessperson, a mogul, a man with vision we could only hope aligned with ours.

When Alex walked into the office on Friday morning, the air was heavy with anticipation. An edgy energy rippled off him as he sifted through the papers we had to sign. The past couple times we'd met in person, I couldn't get a read on him. Then again, I didn't know him that well. He was Blake's colleague more than mine, until recently.

Focused on the logistics of making the sale transition, I skimmed over the documents I'd already reviewed numerous times. Dozens of papers passed between us. I signed them all with trembling hands, trying to ignore the emotion tingling in my throat.

Maybe I was allowed to be emotional this one time, but I couldn't bring myself to lose it. I still had to work with Alex, and I wanted him to believe I was stronger than I sometimes appeared. I'd made this decision on my own. I'd written this chapter, and I wasn't going to end it in tears, at least not in front of him.

Then it was done.

The whole process took less than five minutes. I dropped my well-used pen and sat back. Alex held out his hand, the tension around him seeming to ease, the colleague I'd been used to shining through again.

"Congrats, Erica."

I shook his hand firmly. "Thank you."

"The funds were wired this morning, so they should hit your account sometime this afternoon."

"Thanks. I'll keep an eye out. Um, do you want to grab lunch or anything?"

He checked his watch. "I'd love to, but I have another meeting to catch this afternoon. Let's touch base on Tuesday though. I'll give you a ring. I have a few ideas I want to run by you." He collected his copies of everything and stood to leave.

"Okay," I said, feigning excitement, but I was already anxious about any impending changes that would be beyond my control from here on. I stood and showed him out.

The door shut behind him, and I gazed at the Clozpin logo etched into the glass. A rush of emotions hit me at all once. Relief, excitement, terror. I struggled to process the magnitude of what had happened in such a short span of time. My whole world shifting. Placing my trust in the hands of a man I hardly knew. I reached for faith and hope, believing along with Alli and Sid that this was the right decision for us, as hard as it may have been to make. I closed my eyes. Somewhere in the swirling of my mind and heart, I might have registered regret, but I pushed it down.

★ ★ ★

I'd come home early to catch a nap before the big night out with the girls. I was eager to celebrate. Too much on my mind might make the champagne flow more freely, but I'd earned a little reprieve from the epic week I'd had. Navigating Blake's intensity, selling my business, and dodging reporters thanks to Richard. I needed my girls. Some laughs, some drinks, and some memories to remind me I was twenty-two.

I took a shower and dressed for comfort. Sifting through outfits, I tossed a few options into my bag. We'd agreed to meet at Simone's, so I would have to consult with Alli and dress there. Plus I didn't want Blake to see me all decked out yet. I wanted to surprise him. I also didn't want him going all over-protective on me before I could get out the door.

I heard the door open and close. I shuffled out to the kitchen to find Blake. "What are you doing home so early?"

"I had some shopping to do." He set a plain brown paper bag down on the counter, a deceptively innocent look on his face. "I wanted to catch you before you left."

I lifted my chin, trying to peer into the bag. "What's in the bag?"

"We'll get to that in a minute." He moved it out of my view. "How did things go with Alex?"

I sat down on one of the stools. "Good, I think."

He cocked an eyebrow. "You think? What does that mean?"

I shrugged. "It's done. I guess I thought it was going to be more climactic. It was over in a matter of minutes. Just like that." I snapped my fingers.

"That's usually how it goes."

"Good to know I didn't miss anything, then." I still couldn't believe it was done. The extra zeros on my bank balance had made it a little more real, but the whole week still seemed like a dream. Maybe tomorrow I'd know what to think of it all.

Blake raked a hungry look over me, distracting my thoughts. "Is that what you're wearing?"

I glanced down at my outfit and pursed my lips, feigning offense. "You don't like it?"

He hooked a finger over the band of my pants, snapping them back. "Yoga pants and a little T-shirt? You look hot, but I doubt this will pass Alli's bachelorette party dress code. I should be so lucky. What are you really wearing?"

I clucked my tongue. "Did you really think I was going to let you have final approval on my outfit?"

"I could always demand it." He pulled his bottom lip between his teeth.

I shook my finger at him. "Uh-uh. You'll have to wait and see."

He glanced over the bag. "I was hoping to make one small addition to it, actually."

I lifted an eyebrow. Intrigue fluttered through me. I liked Blake's surprises. "Oh?"

"You could even call it a gift."

"Is it sparkly?" I teased.

He smiled broadly, revealing his teeth. "Funny you should mention that." He reached into the bag and retrieved a plastic package.

I came closer to get a better look. He opened it and revealed a clear plastic toy, with a faux diamond shimmering at the end.

I wrinkled my nose. "You bought me an anal plug. How romantic."

He laughed loudly at that. "I thought so. You can wear it tonight. Then no matter how much fun you end up having without me, you'll still be thinking of me."

"A pain in my ass. How appropriate."

His eyes narrowed. Curving a hand around my nape, he pulled me against his chest. His lips melded over mine. I moaned until, sucking my lip into his mouth, he bit down.

I yelped, flinching back. He brushed his thumb over the sore spot.

"Watch your mouth."

I glared at him, but he only smirked.

"Come here." He led me back to the bedroom, sat on the edge of the bed, and patted his lap.

No way was lodged somewhere in my throat, not able to emerge from my slightly swollen lips. Instead my legs moved me forward. I stopped in front of him and stood between his legs.

"You're serious about this."

He rubbed up the outsides of my thighs, massaging his path. "You're going to be out in the city without me. Very likely drunk and dressed to kill. I don't want you forgetting all about me."

"How can I ever forget about you? You're all I ever think about." The sting of his earlier wound was forgotten, overwhelmed by the indisputable truth.

Satisfaction swirled in his eyes. "Now this will guarantee it." He patted his knee, a reminder to comply.

I stiffened in place. "I don't think I can't do this, Blake."

"Yes, you can. It's easy. It could be easier if I tied you up though. Would you like me to?"

Maybe.

Instead of testing his resolve, I lay over his lap. A slow moving hand slid up my thigh and traced the band of my pants. Swiftly he moved them down with my panties, baring my ass and upper thighs. I tried to breathe normally. I didn't want to give him the satisfaction of my embarrassment, but it was almost impossible to control myself. I heard the unromantic squirt of lube. I braced myself, flinching when his hand came down on my ass with a light slap.

"You have a pretty little ass. I'm so enamored with your tits, I might be neglecting it a bit."

I closed my eyes. "I have a feeling that's not going to be a problem soon."

"I have a feeling you're right," he said without humor as he spread my cheeks.

My teeth came down onto my sore lip when one well-lubricated finger breached me. I couldn't believe I was letting him do this. I took a deep breath and tried to think of something else.

A merry-go-round. *The Wizard of Oz.*

Anything but the pressure of the cool plug slowly making its way into my body. I tensed, squirming away when it probed deeper.

"Stay still."

I gripped the comforter. When Blake had shown me the toy, it looked small enough. Sparkly and innocent. Cute almost, much like the fashion accessory he pretended it was. Now it felt enormous in the narrow passage trying to accommodate it.

I sucked in sharp breath. "It's too much, I can't."

"Almost there, baby."

My face heated, and I almost cried out when the widest part cleared and relief swept over me. I relaxed, tension leaving my body. Thank God that was over.

"How does that feel?"

I tensed around it, noting the pressure in my pussy. "I feel full."

"Perfect."

He patted my ass again and slid my pants back up. I

stood up awkwardly, coming to terms with my new accessory.

I sighed, resigned to my fate. "Do you have any more presents for me before I go?" My words were a mix of sarcasm and distant hope. Maybe I could get an orgasm for the road.

He seemed to read the dark thought. A growl hummed from his chest and he pulled us down to the bed. I rested over his chest and kissed him softly. He pushed my hair away from my eyes.

"Be careful tonight. Don't do anything crazy."

"I know you think I'm unpredictable, but I'm not the crazy one in this crew."

"I know. Don't get too drunk, because I need you conscious for what I have planned tonight." His eyes glimmered with unspoken thoughts.

I bit my lip and swiveled my hips, trying to connect my clit with his thigh. He was already hard beneath me. "Can I get an advance?"

"I want nothing more than to have you stay and play, but Alli has her plans. She'll come barging over here if I don't give you up."

On cue, my phone dinged with a text. It was Alli, requesting the shoes I'd borrowed for the club the other night. I got up and searched for them in the closet, acutely aware of the plug with every casual movement.

"I can't believe you're making me wear this all night." Desire was already pooling in my belly. I wasn't anywhere near drunk or debauched, and my skin was prickling with awareness.

"Don't you dare think of taking it out."

I tossed the black heels into my bag. "Wouldn't dream of it. Anyway, I should head out."

Blake stood and reached for my bag. "I'll drive you."

"You don't have to."

"I want to. Plus, I want to make sure my care package is there."

"Care package?"

He grinned. "You'll see."

Blake and his surprises. I rolled my eyes and followed him downstairs to the Tesla.

A few minutes later we were pulling up to Simone's apartment. Simone was wearing a backless dress that hugged every ample curve. Fiona, who was always the picture of class, wore tight black jeans and a strapless top that revealed her delicate frame.

"Erica!" Alli's initial reaction was a mix of disgust and reproach. "You are *not* wearing that."

I laughed, tossing my bag down. "No shit. You think I was going for a night out on the town and not making you dress me?"

She shook her head and poured a glass of champagne for me. "Here. You drink. I'll primp you."

As she disappeared into the bedroom with my bag, James walked out wearing only a towel around his waist. Simone whistled and plastered a lusty kiss on his lips.

I turned away, stealing a look to Blake. He didn't look concerned. In fact, a smug smile tugged at his lips. "What?"

He nodded to James. "Looks like the care package is here."

I frowned.

James approached when Simone released him from her clutches. "Sorry. Girls have been hogging the bathroom."

Blake shook his hand. "Keep your dick in your pants and we're good."

James rolled his eyes. "Right. Anything I need to know before we head out?"

"Just don't let her out of your sight, and when they're ready to go home, call me. I'll come pick her up."

"Alli has a limo."

"I don't care. I'll collect her myself."

I waved my hands between them. "Excuse me. When did this all get worked out? This is a bachelorette party. *My* bachelorette party. No boys allowed."

I swiveled to find Simone leaning against the couch, listening to us bicker. She shrugged, tossing back the last of the champagne in her glass. "Talk to Blake. We already tried negotiating."

I returned my glare to Blake.

"There's no way I'm unleashing these girls on you without someone on hand to stay sober and make sure no one gets hurt."

"We're going to drink too much and dance until we pass out. No one is getting hurt. I don't need a freaking bodyguard."

"You are *not* passing out, as previously discussed. And you do need a bodyguard. Do I need to remind you of your propensity for finding yourself in dangerous situations?"

I groaned. "Whatever."

"Here, wait." He caught my hand before I could turn to leave. He pressed a small wad of bills into my palm.

"What's this?"

"Fun money."

I tilted my head and tried to pull away but he didn't let go. "I'm flush with cash now, Blake, remember?"

He smirked, brushing his thumb over my wrist. "I insist."

"Whatever," I huffed.

"No strippers," he said firmly.

I laughed. "You really need to stop making rules and get out of here."

"I'm serious, Erica."

He released me and I turned with a wave. "Me too. Goodbye."

I disappeared into the bedroom to find Alli. I heard James and Blake talking for a few minutes longer before the door shut.

I let out a sigh of relief. I wanted to let loose tonight. I wanted to be free and have fun. I was pretty confident James wasn't interested in ruining our fun, but Blake's meddling never failed to grate on my nerves. Fiona and Simone joined us, and we talked over which club to hit first.

By my second glass of champagne, I'd nearly forgotten about James and Blake entirely. Alli twisted my hair up into a sexy, messy up-do and applied heavy makeup to my eyes and cheeks, leaving my lips nude and glossy. I slipped on a simple number, a strapless hot pink sheath covered in black lace. The tiny dress showed off every asset, and I was grateful all over again that Blake wouldn't see me leave in this.

I was definitely looking forward to coming home in it though. The thought reminded me of the plug. I fought the heat creeping into my cheeks.

"You okay?" Fiona asked, her eyes far too innocent for the truth of what was making me blush.

I fanned myself, trying to get hold of my body's rioting. "Yeah, I think it's the champagne. It's warm in here."

Simone opened a window, mercifully closing the subject.

Darkness fell before we finally headed out, but not before Fiona decorated all of us with sashes bearing our titles, as bride-to-be and bridesmaids. She tucked a tiara that could not have been made of more than two dollars worth of plastic into my hair.

"Perfect. Oh wait." She fussed with it a minute more until it began lighting up, red and white lights. "Now you're perfect."

We laughed and James took our pictures. Then the five of us piled into the limo. A bubble of happiness grew in my belly being surrounded by my friends. Even James, who had become a loyal friend despite our ups and down. Simone cranked up some music, and before long we were laughing and shouting over each other.

"James, you're going to have so much fun babysitting us," I teased, nudging him with my elbow.

He smiled and looked out the tinted window. "I have little doubt."

We drove until the limo dropped us at the club. Alli led us to a booth reserved for our party. We ordered a round of drinks and watched the club fill up.

Out of the masses, a cute blond bartender approached again, balancing a tray of shots, enough for each of us. His gaze lingered on Fiona. She reddened and toyed with her diamond hoop earrings.

"What's this?" Simone reached for one of the shots.

"The lady up there ordered these for you." He gestured to the upper level. The club was smoky and I couldn't place who he was referring to.

Alli leaned over the tray, her nose wrinkled. "What are they?"

Simone tossed hers back and dropped it back on the tray with flare. "They're yummy."

He cleared his throat. "Um, they're called 'shit on the grass'."

Simone grimaced.

"What?" Alli studied the shots, their green liquid settled aptly over the brown. "Who sent them?"

I looked past the man, squinting until, through the lighting and crowds of people, I settled on a familiar face. Fucking Sophia. She sat at a high-top bar table on a platform overlooking our VIP sofa. Our eyes met and she offered a small wave, a conceited expression set on her face. I glared at the bartender, momentarily hating anyone remotely connected with her.

"Sophia," I said.

"What a bitch." Alli spat.

Simone wrinkled her lip. "Are you telling me I just

drank shit on the grass?"

Fiona started laughing. The bartender flashed her a smile and returned his attention back to me. "She wanted me to tell you congratulations," he said, his mouth tensed into an awkward line.

"Send them back." I waved my hand for him to go away.

"They're paid for." He attempted one last effort to offload the drinks and extricate from this evident long-distance catfight.

"I don't care. I don't take drinks from people I don't trust."

He hesitated. "What do you want me to do with them?"

I chewed the inside of my lip, an idea forming. "Take them back to her and give her a message. Tell her the ball gag she sent over this week fit perfectly. Blake and I both send our thanks."

His eyes went wide, and I knew that would be a hard order to fill. I reached into my purse and fished out a handful of bills. I dropped some of the hundreds Blake had given to me onto the tray. "For your trouble. Make sure she gets the message."

Barely obscuring his smirk, he turned to leave. I sat back on the couch, feeling as smug as Sophia's face. I glanced over at Alli who was staring at me wide-eyed.

"Ball gag?"

Whoops.

I grabbed my drink and sucked up some more liver-damaging liquid through the straw. "Doesn't matter. I'll tell you about it later."

Or not!

Simone shook her head, her eyes a drunken haze. "I knew you guys were freaks."

Alli's wild laughter set off my own, and before I knew it we were doubled over, tears threatening our mascara. Alli's was still perfect, but I had a feeling mine was probably traveling all over my face at this point in the evening. We finally caught our breath.

"Want to dance? I feel like I'm hitting a wall," Fiona said.

"Sure." We jumped up and pushed in the crowd. James followed obediently behind, emerging from somewhere in the shadows where he was giving us our privacy. Whatever orders Blake had given him, he seemed bound to following through. I hoped it had more to do with caring about our well being than accommodating Blake's overbearing tendencies.

We danced through several songs. With our matching party sashes and my obnoxious blinking tiara, we attracted stares from everywhere. The attention only motivated our dance moves, as the four of us went from tipsy, cute partiers to sweaty, drunk disasters. Simone shimmied her ass against James, who, while on duty, didn't seem to mind the small distraction from the evening's task of keeping me "safe." Alli and I clung to each other, laughing and yelling and reveling in our general awesomeness.

As one song rolled into the next, the persistent pressure in my ass combined with watching Simone grind up on James reminded me of some other fun I could be having.

The night had been a blast, but I was now all sorts of horny. I needed my man and I needed to stay upright for the wild night he had promised me. I leaned against Alli.

"I want to go home and see Blake."

She laughed. "I'm picking up what you're puttin' down, babe. Let's get out of here before I pass out."

CHAPTER FOURTEEN

I sucked in a deep breath when we emerged from the club. The night air was cool, refreshing on my damp skin. Fiona and I had our arms linked as I scanned for our ride home.

"This way, ladies. Your chariot awaits." James led us toward the shiny black limo parked along the curb.

"Erica."

I stopped abruptly, nearly tripping Fiona. James caught her and helped her into the limo. Simone and Alli were taking selfies a few feet away, loudly critiquing each one as not quite right.

A warm arm wrapped around my waist, lifting me to my toes. Blake had me pressed tightly to this chest.

"Blake!" I pressed a sloppy, slightly inappropriate kiss to his lips. I felt him smile under me.

I heard Alli whoop loudly behind us. "Oh my God, I love you two together. Aren't they the cutest?" She nudged Simone, whose focus was locked onto her phone. "Blake, I love you. Have I told you that? I really do."

He laughed. "Thanks, Alli. I love you too."

Her eyes brightened. "You do? Aww, let's all just get married and have babies. I want babies. Don't tell Heath, but I want his babies."

"Maybe you can tell him yourself."

He nodded toward the limo where Heath emerged. The uncomfortable smile on his face told me he'd heard her. She'd been almost shouting every word for the past three hours, so I wasn't surprised.

"Heath!" She squealed and bounded into his arms. He lifted her up, letting her wrap her legs around his waist. She caught him between her hands, kissing him as passionately as I'd just kissed Blake.

"Wow, they are going to have some fun tonight."

Blake slid his hand down my spine and grabbed my ass. "I'm more interested in the fun we're going to have. You still up for it?"

I rubbed my body against him with a helpless moan. I was ready to take him right on the street. I slid my hands around his nape and went for his mouth again.

He chuckled softly, breaking our kiss. "Okay, I'll take that as a yes. Let's get you home." He led me by the hand toward the car.

Despite my efforts to crawl across the console to assault him all the way home, he kept his cool until we got upstairs to the apartment.

But as soon as the door closed behind us, he had me pinned to it. I whimpered, every touch lighting fire over me. I arched into him, lifting my leg to wrap around his thigh, shifting the plug inside. "Fuck, I need you. Like right now."

He thumbed the thundering pulse at my neck, pressing a kiss there. "Slow down, baby."

"I can't slow down. Not tonight."

"Slow down, or I'll have to tie you up."

"I don't care. Tie me up. Do whatever you want." *Just fuck me, for heaven's sake.*

"I just might. I have plans for you. And your ass." His hand slid under my dress and nudged the sparkly tip of the plug, reminding me again of what I'd been feeling all night. Friction. Fullness.

"I'm ready now." I wanted this plug out. I wanted relief. I tugged off Blake's shirt and threw it hastily to the floor.

He laughed. "Trust me, I know. I want to play a little first though."

I splayed my hands over the gorgeous planes of his chest, all the way down to the band of his low-slung jeans. I wanted those off. "What are we playing?" I asked, only vaguely interested.

"You'll find out soon enough. First, I want you to undress for me."

I shot him a playful smile and reached down for my heels.

"No, no." He caught my hand, helping me regain my balance. "Keep those. Everything else goes."

"Kinky Blake," I murmured as I shimmied out of my tight dress. I unhooked my bra and stepped out of my panties. I stood before him naked and blissfully tipsy.

"Where would you like me, Master?" I toed the tip of my shoe on the floor, letting a little bashfulness seep into my intoxicated boldness.

He nodded toward the living room. "Over the back of the couch. Ass in the air."

I obeyed, sashaying to the other room. I bent over the cream fabric, balancing on the tiptoes of my high heels. I waited for his approach, but I'd heard him leave the room and return a couple minutes later. The delay only added to my vulnerability. I closed my eyes, listening as his footsteps stopped behind me.

"Did you misbehave tonight?" The timbre of voice was low, warm, and a little threatening. A shiver slivered up my spine.

"Yeah," I breathed. Already the night had become a blur, but if he wanted me to be bad, I'd gladly play the part.

"Oh? That's not good."

A cool flat implement rubbed across my backside, over the curves of my ass and down my thighs. I was breathless, but in the most wonderful way. I wanted to moan and arch back into it—whatever it was he wanted to give me.

"You drank too much, huh?"

"Mm-huh." I fidgeted anxiously, wiggling my ass impatiently. Warmth radiated in my belly, causing my pussy to twitch in anticipation. I wanted to know how far he would take this, yet a part of me didn't want to know. It was the not knowing that drove me wild every time.

"Did you let anyone touch you?"

I quickened, not quite sober enough to resist the temptation to stir his jealousy. "Maybe."

"Is that so?"

His hand left my ass and was swiftly replaced by the hard smack of what could only be a paddle.

"Shit!" *Yeah, that still hurt.* He'd joked about the paddle, but I never expected him to actually use it. I'd had plenty of fun under the palm of his hand. Thankfully the alcohol was working its magic. The sting of the blow numbed quickly.

"It was crowded. I didn't mean to," I said, suddenly eager to soothe his jealousy.

He paddled me again and the pain melted a little faster.

"I'm sorry, Blake."

"I'm glad. But we have a long way to go."

I mewled in my dissent, even as a little voice in the back of my mind begged him to keep going.

He leaned down over me, holding the paddle still against my stinging ass. I tensed, uneasy, not knowing what he had planned.

"Do you think you deserve punishment?"

Yes.

I shook my head *no*.

"No? You have quite the list going. Tying me up and trying to have your wicked way with me. Running off to a sex club unattended. Tell me now, do you think you deserve punishment?"

"Yes," I breathed softly, an admission that only the couch could hear.

"I can't hear you," he said sharply.

"Yes, I deserve it."

He swirled the paddle over my ass, causing my stomach to clench anew with anticipation. The fog of the alcohol was lifting with every passing moment.

"That's what I thought. You're going to get to know the paddle tonight, and no matter what, Erica, I don't want you to come. Take everything I give you, and you'll get your reward after."

I loved a solid spanking as much as the next girl, but the paddle was unforgiving. The threat of climaxing against his wishes was weightless. I'd get my reward, no doubt, but not before he made me feel the sting of regret.

I bit my lip and braced myself for the lesson.

The paddle came down, a solid slap against my skin. I groaned, trying hard not to squirm away. He delivered blow after blow, spacing them out, spreading them over my ass and thighs. Hard stinging licks that fell just shy of my sex. Fear mingled with desire, as I prayed he wouldn't make a mistake and hit me there and hurt me. Yet I fantasized about any kind of contact there. His fingers, his mouth, his cock. Anything. The intensity of the blows went straight to my head. Unbearably needy, I grew wet, a fact that couldn't be hidden with my ass on display, my legs as far apart as he'd wanted them.

He delivered another blow, harder than the others, and I yelled loudly, the sound echoing off our walls.

My entire body tensed, the defensive instinct resonating most noticeably where the plug nestled inside of me. The pressure there was so concentrated. The nagging desire that its presence had inspired all night had morphed into a powerful reminder of what Blake wanted from me tonight.

I rubbed my chest against the rough linen of the couch cover. Every cell stood on edge. I wanted more. I wanted everything tonight.

He paused long enough to twist the plug. The reminder of the pressure, the friction was too much. I could feel it in my pussy, acute enough that I could almost...come.

My hands fisted into balls. No, I wasn't supposed to.

When I thought I couldn't take another second of his punishments, he stopped. I flinched when he soothed my hot, prickly flesh with his palms. I let out a breath I didn't realize I was holding. He felt like heaven, like a wonderful, tender gift. Water in the fucking desert. Blood thundered in my veins, pulsing arousal through me. Desire surged, and I hurdled to the edge of orgasm. I trembled with the effort not to come.

"Blake!" I pleaded. If I had to bear one more sensation, I was going to lose it.

He hushed me, stroking my back and the burning skin of my ass. Leaning over my backside, he kissed me on the shoulder. "You did well. I'm going to fuck you now, baby. You ready?"

Slowly, he pulled out the plug, but I registered anything but relief.

I struggled for breath, the pressure of my own body suddenly too much against my chest. I nodded, trying not to think of how I could withstand more pain. I was already weak and barely able to stand.

He tugged me upright. "Let's sit down, and then I want you to straddle me."

I stood still, processing his directions, but not sure how this was going to work. He dropped his jeans to the floor. His thick cock stood ready, shamelessly erect from his body. Was he still planning to…?

"I thought we were…"

The corner of his mouth lifted with a wicked grin. "I'm having your ass tonight. But I want you to be as comfortable as possible this time."

We circled the couch. Careful to keep my balance, I settled comfortably over his splayed legs. The hunger in his eyes was enough to take my breath away. I knew what he wanted tonight, but my body wanted him other places. Places I knew would bring me unspeakable pleasure.

He'd promised me pleasure, but I still wasn't convinced it was possible for me this way. "This is going to hurt," I said, my expression bordering on a pout.

He reached for the bottle of lube on the table that I hadn't noticed earlier. He applied a generous portion to his palm and spread it up and down his length. He was big. He got even bigger when he was about to come in me. His generous endowment was a feature that never failed to please me during sex. Making all of him fit comfortably inside of my ass was another matter altogether.

My jaw fell slightly, my heartbeat kicking up as he stroked more lube over the head of his cock.

He lifted an eyebrow, seeming to notice my reactions. "See something you like?"

I swallowed hard.

His expression softened. "Have I ever hurt you? In a way that you weren't begging for more by the end?"

I turned my gaze to his slick erection. The noises of his strokes were impossibly distracting.

"No," I admitted. Tonight was evidence of that. I'd been paddled like a precocious child, and I would have withstood twice the punishment if he'd wanted it. He never steered us wrong. Yet doubt crept over me.

"This will be no exception. It'll be intense, but you'll enjoy it. We'll go slow, and I'll talk you through it."

I couldn't argue with that. I was primed, thoroughly ready for release, and his promised dirty talk could be the icing on the cake—if I could handle it. My hands were hot against my thighs. I rubbed them up and down anxiously, suddenly not knowing what to do with them.

"Come closer." He scooted farther down the couch, while I shimmied up so his cock lined up at a better angle. "This will give you more control."

I snorted. "Not your style."

"Try not to remind me." His eyes darkened.

I bit my lip, not wanting to fuel his vengeance when I really needed him to be gentle and patient with me.

"We'll go slow. We can even stop. But by the end of the night, I'll be in your ass. So wrap your head around that. The best thing you can do is try to relax."

I nodded and held onto the small comfort that I did officially have a safeword now, even if I'd never had to use it.

He hushed my silent worries with a soft kiss. "When we're done, you'll be asking me why we never did it sooner, I promise."

I sighed. "You sure know how to give a girl cold feet."

He explored with his fingers, lining us up.

"Don't worry. Your feet are going to be toasty warm in a few minutes." Rubbing over the tight bud between my cheeks, he pressed firmly, seeking entry. "Open up for me," he ordered gently.

Against every instinct, I released my muscles, easing his passage into me. One slick finger and then two stretched me, with the same decadent sting as they had before. I closed my eyes, remembering how hard I'd come before when he was inside me this way. Could it be like that? Before I could wonder, he pushed the blunt head of his cock into me a bare inch.

"Now come down onto my cock, nice and slow."

My thighs trembled. I struggled to stay steady as I took a little more of him. I felt like we were moving one millimeter at a time. I was petrified, but there was no urgency in Blake's eyes or body language that forced me to hurry my movements. After a few minutes of careful progress, somehow I felt more ready for him. After all, the plug had been marking his place inside of me for the past several hours.

My liquefied thoughts pieced that together, making me bolder. I dropped down more, but my eyes shot wide open at the first dart of pain that halted everything. I whimpered at the discomfort and withdrew from the progress we'd made.

"Breathe, Erica. Give your body a chance to accept me."

He held me still, his hands firmly at my hips. We were still connected. The pain had subsided, and he coaxed me back, regaining the lost ground. I sucked in a tentative breath, surprised when the pain wasn't as intense as it had been. The relief was quickly replaced with the intensity of being filled, breathtakingly stretched. The pain came and went and we slowed around it until it passed, until I could catch my breath and my courage.

Blake's eyes closed a moment, restraint tightening the muscles in his face. He opened them, his hooded expression sweeping over me. "I can't wait to be all the way inside you, Erica. Can't wait to make you come this way."

Air filled my lungs, and my body went lax at his dirty promises. With gentle ease and determination, he had me clenching around him, the way I had around the plug when he'd paddled me. Except this was more intense and way more intimate.

He caught my chin, focusing my gaze to him. "Look at me. Feel me." Lust and strain washed over his countenance. He stared deeply into me. "Little by little, you're giving a piece of yourself to me. I'm inside you, the same way you're inside me."

He worked me down over him until I couldn't believe he could fill me any farther. I licked my dry lips, unable to still their quivering. Heat spread out from my heart, covering my skin with an unbearable sizzling need. My hands trembled over his chest, rising and falling over his labored breaths.

My heart swelled, and any last resistance gave way as I relaxed around him. I thought I'd taken him to the hilt when he thrust up, taking us the rest of the way. *Oh fuck.*

"There." He released a shuddery sigh. Leaning forward, he kissed me. A slow, hard, penetrating kiss. "You're always inside me, Erica."

Another wave of heat washed over me, making me slick with sweat where our bodies met, which was nearly everywhere. I wanted to move. I wanted him to deliver on this promise of pleasure already budding inside of me.

Blake's hands roamed restlessly, pulling me against him

tightly. His teeth grazed my neck under hot, hard kisses. I quivered over him.

"Fuck," he growled. His breathing grew rapid, but he wasn't moving.

"Is everything okay?" My voice was a whisper. "What do you want me to do?"

"You don't have to do anything. I'm just trying like hell not to come right now. Feels fucking amazing."

He held me close for a moment. I tried to relax, but I was too wound up. Too edgy. Too desperate for him to take me. I closed my eyes, acutely aware of this new possession.

He stilled and drew in breath.

"I'm going to move now, but I'm not going to last long this way. Now that I'm inside you, it's going to be fast and a little rough."

I nodded, drunk now only on lust and the intoxicating love and trust I felt with Blake. He could take me anywhere, do anything. I didn't know what a limit was anymore, because everything became a step to being closer to him.

Fingering my folds, he brought the moisture that had pooled between my legs up over my clit. He started slow strokes over the firm nub. His touch was gentle but the sensation was sharp. My body clenched tightly around him, heightening the intensity of everything. I clutched the couch behind him, needing to dig my nails into something.

Blake cursed, and then he pulled out enough to thrust. He sank into me with careful thrusts that grew in strength and speed as the seconds passed. The sensation entirely new and overwhelming in the way intimacy with Blake always was.

I bit my lip, trying to focus on the pleasure over the sting.

"You okay, baby?" His cheeks were flushed, his voice breathy.

"Yeah," I whispered.

He looked into my eyes, seeming to hear the hesitation in my voice. He slowed and lifted me enough to glide his fingers from my throbbing clit, lower to the entrance of my pussy until he was pressed deep into my tissues.

I sucked in a sharp breath. Suddenly exquisitely filled, I exhaled a small cry. My hips snapped forward, seeking more. Liquid fire burned its way through me, sliding into my veins, growing and demanding oxygen.

I felt so…taken.

"Better?" The low rumble of his voice vibrated through me.

I moaned, quivering—impossibly wet, impossibly tight around him. He was right. Neither of us would last long this way.

Our once painstaking pace ticked up to a rugged tempo as he fucked me faster and harder. I threw my head back with a wail. The friction was intense, the burn of his initial entry lingering, bringing an edge to the unexpected pleasure. I was losing my mind this way. My brain scattered, every thought disappearing in a sea of cries and prayers and "oh fucks" as he buried his cock inside of me over and over. He slid his fingers into me deeper, the heel of his hand working over my clit until I saw stars.

There was no blissful climb to the top of the cliff. The orgasm rose from a source I couldn't place and shattered through me. Possessed and filled and stimulated in more ways than my tired mind could comprehend, I screamed. I came hard, electric pleasure shooting through every limb, down to my toes and the fingertips that ripped into the fabric behind Blake's head.

"Oh God, baby. Just like that," he groaned.

I faltered, my legs weak and my senses overwhelmed. His fingers left me, and he took command of my hips, driving me down onto his slick cock the way he wanted. He used both hands and the force of his hips to impale me. Tension lined his face.

"Nothing's ever been this tight. So fucking tight." His voice was raw, unrestrained.

His hardened abdominal muscles came together, revealing their impressive definition. He was beautiful. He was mine. I was his, unmistakably his, in every way.

Hauling me tight against him, he unleashed a series of powerful thrusts, exploding in me with a hoarse cry.

We stayed like that, molded tightly together, quivering from the potent release. Hours could have passed before my brain started functioning again in any reasonable way.

"Oh my God," I breathed. I opened my eyes to the world as if I'd just woken from a coma. A sex-induced, thought-obliterating coma.

He laughed, his breath cool on my damp skin.

"Good?"

"Mmm." I hummed a lazy affirmation, gazing at him through sleepy eyes. "We should have done that sooner."

He kissed me, a satisfied smile curving against my lips. "I told you."

★ ★ ★

I lingered in bed the next morning while Blake caught up on work in the living room so I could rest. I was ready to slip back to sleep when my phone rang. It was Daniel. We hadn't spoken in weeks, but I'd been waiting for him to reach out to me again.

"Hello," I answered.

"Erica."

"How are things?" I tried to sound cheerful, but my voice was still raw from a long night of partying and orgasms.

He was silent and my stomach tightened with anxiety.

"I need to know who's leaking this information. The press is up my ass. They're starting to ask about Patricia." Frustration and determination weighted his words, which worried me even more.

I swallowed over the dryness in my throat. "They've been hounding me too. But I told you before, I don't know."

"What does Blake say?"

I tensed, not liking my fiancé's name anywhere in my conversations with Daniel. "He doesn't know either."

He was silent again.

"It's out now, Daniel. Don't you have enough on

your plate without vengeance? What's the point of trying to hunt someone down?"

"Because I'd like to know who's costing me this campaign. I'd like a chance to look them in the eye."

He wanted the chance to put a bullet in them, more likely. I started to feel sick knowing that might very well be what he was after.

"Tell me."

"I told you, I don't know." I struggled to keep my voice steady. I desperately wanted him to believe me.

"I can only assume it's Blake then." The finality in his voice sobered me on an entirely new level. I sat up straight from the bed, my heart racing with fear.

"No!" I nearly shouted. "Blake has nothing to do with this." God, anything but having Blake back in his crosshairs.

"Then who?" he shouted back. I jumped, tensing the phone in my grasp.

"I don't know," I insisted. I couldn't tell him. How could I? I couldn't trust Daniel not to do something drastic. I hated what Richard had done to Marie and to me, but what if it cost him his life?

"I'm losing my patience, Erica. I have ways of getting information. The easiest option is for you to tell me."

Silence stretched between us, and I couldn't ignore the foreboding feeling that he was not going to let this go, possibly ever. I rubbed my forehead, willing away the headache that had resurfaced suddenly.

"I'm afraid," I admitted. "I'm afraid you'll do something terrible again, and I'll get caught in the middle of it. I don't want to lie to protect you anymore." The truth, finally. Words I'd wanted to say for a long time.

"Did the police talk to you again?" His voice was quieter now and tainted with a different kind of concern.

"No, but it's only a matter of time."

He paused again. "What if I assured you no one's life would be in danger?"

I wouldn't believe you.

"I don't know." They seemed to be the only words I knew. If I kept saying them, I wouldn't have to give him a real answer.

"You'll never be rid of me until you give a fucking name. It's Blake or it's someone else. You decide."

No, no, no. Tears formed in my eyes. Why was he doing this to me? Why was he so set on revenge?

"Erica!"

I stifled a whimper. "Richard Craven."

"Who?"

"His name is Richard Craven. He's a reporter for *The Globe.*"

He exhaled audibly. "You told a fucking *reporter?*"

"No," I said, irritated that he would think that about me.

"Then how the fuck did he find out?"

"Stop yelling at me!" I shouted, unable to take this aggressive line of questioning with him any further.

I heard him breathing on the other end of the phone. "Explain to me, please, how the reporter Richard Craven knows that I am your biological father," he said more calmly, but with evident strain.

I brushed a tear away angrily and took a steeling breath of my own. I had no idea how to explain this without throwing Marie into harm's way too. That I wouldn't do. I wanted to believe he'd never hurt someone close to me, but I could never know for certain with him. His moral compass had proven to be calibrated quite differently from my own. Still, I knew he wouldn't let this go without some answers, and I didn't want him believing I'd leaked the information myself. As much as I didn't trust Daniel, I knew he didn't exactly trust me either.

"He's been dating an old friend of Mom's. She…" I closed my eyes, praying that I was doing the right thing. "She's been like a mother to me since Mom passed. She knows who you are. She didn't mean to hurt either of us. He's been manipulating her to get information about me to hurt you."

"Who is she?"

"I gave you what you asked for, and I expect you to keep your promise. I don't agree with what Richard's done any more than you do, but I don't want any more blood on my hands. Daniel, promise me. Promise me that no one's going to get hurt."

A second later, the line went dead. I stared at the phone, stunned by what had just happened. I replayed the conversation over in my head, second guessing everything I'd said. In the end, he'd left me with no reassurances.

Somewhere in the flurry of emotions, I felt relief that I'd spared Blake from Daniel's wrath. The relief quickly dissipated when I realized I could have put another man's life in grave danger.

CHAPTER FIFTEEN

Even after Daniel's disturbing call, I managed to sleep away most of the weekend. Monday morning came quickly, and I tried to ignore the niggling worry that I'd put Richard in danger. I toyed with the idea of meeting with him. I had plenty I wanted to say, but maybe I could somehow convince him to give up this interest in Daniel's world. Somehow…

I ducked into Mocha to dodge a reporter and grab my morning fuel. Simone let me sneak to the back and get to my side of the building undetected. Opening the door to the office, I stood frozen.

My heart pounded frantically, my palms damp at the sight before me.

At our conference table sat Sophia, and beside her, the man who'd been trying to nose his way into my business for months, Isaac Perry. Alli sat across from them, tensely silent.

"What's going on here?"

Relief washed over Alli's countenance when our eyes met, quickly followed by concern. She got up and walked to me.

"They've been here since I opened up this morning. They wouldn't tell me why. Said they had business to discuss and you needed to be here."

I stepped around her, glaring at them. "What are you

doing here? Get out."

Isaac rose, looking far more tentative than Sophia. "Erica, have a seat so we can talk."

I stood by the table, ignoring his request. "Out." I pointed toward the door, glaring at Sophia.

She sat back casually in the chair she occupied next to Isaac. She wore a tight black paneled dress, her long legs crossed over each other. A pen pressed to her curved lips. "Have a seat," she said flatly.

Fine. I dropped down at the head of the table. "Talk. Quickly."

Isaac drew in a breath. "First of all, congratulations on the sale of the business."

I stilled. "How did you know about that?" I asked quietly.

"Alex Hutchinson and I have been working on our own deal for quite some time. We came into town last week to finalize everything."

He averted his eyes but I continued to stare, trying to penetrate him with a look designed to kill.

"What deal?"

Sophia leaned in, spreading her manicured fingers over the table. "The deal where Perry Media Group acquired Clozpin, along with several other entities under Alex's domain."

My stomach fell to the floor. Sickness tore through me.

Alli let out a sound of pure shock. "Why would you do that?"

Isaac cleared his throat. "I know this comes as a shock,

but this deal has been in the works for a long time with Alex. Acquiring Clozpin was a new development, but one that made sense for us."

"Who's us?" I asked.

"My company, and Sophia. She holds an interest in Clozpin and will be taking an active role in the business. Remotely, of course, but we're here often so we can meet as frequently as you need."

I let out a caustic laugh. Isaac was talking like Alex. Like this was all business as usual. Except I had no business relationship with Isaac. Blake had wanted it that way, and ultimately I had supported his position. And I sure as hell wasn't doing business with Sophia.

"We'll be making some changes over the next few weeks." Sophia's smug look met Alli's still stunned expression. "Alli, regretfully, we won't be able to keep you on through this transition. Under normal circumstances we would give you two weeks, but due to the nature of this acquisition, we feel it's best if you leave the company, effective today."

Alli's eyes grew wider, her jaw dropping farther. "What?"

"Isaac already has a full marketing team. Your services are no longer needed."

I stood up, my hands flat on the table. "You can't do that. We had an agreement. The staff stays."

Sophia's gaze darted up to mine. "Sorry," she quipped, without a trace of regret. "That clause doesn't hold in the case of a third-party acquisition. Perry Media Group, in this case, is the third party. Did you read the agreement closely,

Erica?"

Her words punched the breath from me. I went to war with the tremors of anger coursing through me.

She'd fucked me. She, and Alex, and Isaac. They had all royally fucked me. I tried to collect myself, tried to pick my dignity and my jaw off the floor, though I was certain she noticed my reaction.

If Alli was out, I was probably going to be right behind her. No one hated me more than Sophia, and it was obvious that Sophia—not Isaac—was running this show.

"So I guess that means I'm next," I said, hoping to beat her to the punch.

A smile twisted up the side of her face. She tapped her nails on the table. "Oh, no. We want you to stay. We have plans, and you're just the one we want to see them through."

I sat back down. Not out of defeat, but because in that moment I couldn't have held myself up for the world.

"You've got to be kidding me."

Tension hung in the air between us. I didn't want to show weakness, but I silently pleaded with Isaac. The look he returned was almost pained, as if Sophia were literally twisting his arm up behind his back, forcing him into a situation that was only pleasurable for her. I wasn't entirely convinced in that moment that Sophia wasn't a sadist in her own right. For all her wanting to be Blake's submissive, she really seemed to get off on hurting others.

"We'll be bringing on new staff, of course. People from my agency and Isaac's team. You'll work directly under them to carry out the new vision for the site," Sophia said, smug authority dripping from her voice.

Under them. Under *her*.

I leveled a glare at her, but I was growing numb. The air was thick, and the silence in the room was deafening. Blood hummed in my ears. I vaguely noticed James and Chris hovering on the sidelines of our conversation, waiting. They were all looking to me, waiting on me to make the next move.

"You can't do this." My voice was thin, not my own.

They couldn't make me do this.

"You have no ownership stake, Erica. You're now an employee of the company, and what we say goes."

Something had snapped. It wasn't a punch in the gut or even a slap in the face. I sat there, stripped. Gutted. The pain and the shock of what she was saying gave way to something else. Reality, the choices I'd made, and the choice I was now facing.

Sophia wanted to run me into the ground. She couldn't have Blake, so instead she was aiming for the singular pleasure of ruining the thing I'd worked so hard for, and forcing my hand to help her do it.

"You're not going to top me, Sophia."

Recognition shadowed her eyes. "Well, someone needs to. Unfortunately, Blake left me in a somewhat precarious position when he pulled out from the agency. I was forced to diversify. Isaac and I were both surprised when Alex told us how receptive you were to selling. But don't worry, the business is in good hands now. You'll get to see firsthand."

No fucking way.

I shoved out the chair and stood. "I won't be a part of this. I'm not going to watch you ruin what I spent years building."

For the first time since she'd entered the office, Sophia showed an inkling of displeasure, her eyes narrowing slightly. "You'll lose everything if you leave now."

"Maybe I will. Maybe this is the best hand you can play, Sophia, but you should know that I'm not playing this game with you. Not like this."

She let out a curt laugh. "You'd give everything up, just like that?"

"Just like that," I said quietly before turning toward my office.

I struggled to fill my lungs with air, but all I could manage were shallow dizzying breaths. I couldn't believe this was happening, but it was. In a matter of minutes, days, everything had irrevocably changed. Of all my worst-case-scenario worries, this one topped them all.

I went to my small partitioned space and stood in silence a moment, surveying the contents of my desk top. None of this was mine. Not anymore. For the first time for as long as I could remember, none of it mattered. The paperwork, the lists, the schedule I'd written out for my day. Hell, the pop-up sticky notes on my desk that I couldn't normally live without. None of it mattered if Clozpin wasn't mine. I wasn't being fired from my nine-to-five job. I was leaving behind an era of my life that I would never, *ever* get back.

But what other choice did I have?

I closed my laptop and shoved it into my bag along

with the framed photo I had of Blake and me.

"Erica, don't do this. We want you to stay."

I flashed an angry look up at Isaac who had joined me. "Of course you do. So you can force me to watch Sophia ruin everything."

"We aren't going to ruin everything. I didn't spend all this money to flush it."

I squeezed my eyes tight, willing the emotions away. "How could you do this to me? What did I ever do to you to deserve this? Was it that night…with Blake?"

I shook my head, in disbelief that Blake defending me against Isaac's terrible behavior could plant such a seed of vengeance in him.

"I was talking to Alex before I even met you. I was interested in the market, and that's one of the reasons I wanted to meet with you. When I realized he was working with you as a partner, we discussed adding you to the acquisition. I knew you'd never sell to me directly, and based on our last meeting, I wasn't even sure you'd continue the partnership knowing I was involved."

"You're right. I wouldn't have."

His shoulders sagged. "It's done now. Let's make the most of it and figure out how to work together."

For a second, I believed that could be possible, until Sophia's terrible face entered my mind. I shoved the last of my personal things—meaningless trinkets—into my bag.

I was being rash, maybe even irrational. I had no metric for normal or logical or even sane. My entire world had tilted on its axis. The business that had kept me grounded for so long had been torn out from under me. As much as I wanted it back, I couldn't imagine letting this play out through Sophia's meddling plans. I couldn't imagine Blake would want me to either. His silent voice in my head offered the smallest measure of reassurance that what I was about to do was the right thing.

"It's not possible, Isaac. I told you I didn't want to work with you weeks ago, and I meant it. Just because you've coerced me out of a position of control doesn't change that. I didn't trust you then, and I sure as hell don't trust you now."

"I can talk to Sophia about bringing Alli back. Just go home and unwind, and let's start fresh tomorrow. This has been a lot to take in."

I stepped out from around the desk, hating the tears brimming my eyes. Like it or not, I was exposed. She'd wounded me where it could hurt me the most, and she'd done it in plain view.

"I don't know what she's got on you, Isaac, but it's enough that she's here. She's lodged herself into your business, and now mine. You screwed me on this deal. You and Alex, and she's next in line. Except I'm not going to give her the chance."

He stared at me a moment. "You're really leaving? I knew you'd be upset, but you can't just walk out on us like this. Alex wanted you to stay, and so do I. We need you."

For a second, I wanted to give in to the plea. To be needed by the business was what had driven me for so long. It was like a child, a baby I'd nursed from the very beginning when neither of us were anything at all. I wasn't just walking away from Isaac, Sophia, and this whole fucked up situation. I was walking away from something precious that I'd created.

I swallowed over the emotions threatening to spill out from my eyes. "Good luck, Isaac. You'll need it."

I brushed an errant tear away before emerging into the main area. I left quickly, Alli on my heels, without giving Sophia another look.

I had to get away. I couldn't leave fast enough. I had to go before I changed my mind, before I gave Sophia the satisfaction of knowing she had won.

I wouldn't play this game with her.

I stepped out onto the street. The air felt different. The sound of the cars driving by was foreign. I resented the aroma of coffee tainting the air as a patron left Mocha. None of it was mine anymore. I had no place here, and I'd never belong to this part of my life again.

"What do we do now?" Alli's sad voice broke through my numbness.

The Escalade was parked across the street with Clay waiting in the driver's seat checking his phone. Glancing up and down the sidewalk, I had no idea where to go, which direction to move in.

I needed to walk. I needed air. A stiff drink. A hug. All of the above.

"I don't know," I finally said.

"Did you have any idea that Sophia was involved with the deal?"

How the hell could I have seen it coming? I ran every moment through my mind, looking for some clue that could have triggered this knowledge.

"Alex gave me no indication. It was all roses and rainbows. A deal that would work out for both of us. Worked out for everyone but me, I guess."

"And me, don't forget. Not that I would want to stay without you, Erica, but what did I do to deserve this? I know she hates you, but our paths have crossed before and I've never seen that kind of venom from her. I'm completely blindsided."

I gave her a vacant stare. "Heath."

She shook her head. "But Heath and she are friends."

"He broke the news to her about pulling his and Blake's investment from her agency."

"She fired me because Heath was the bearer of bad news?"

"No." I worked my jaw, not wanting to tell her more. She and Heath had enough issues to work through without me throwing a skeleton from his past into the spotlight.

She stepped closer, squaring her small body with mine. "Tell me."

"Ask Heath about her. I'm sure he can probably tell you more than I can."

"Erica, I am standing out here on the street, jobless from a company I've put my heart and soul into right alongside you. Don't tell me I should go talk to Heath about it. If you know something about her that I should know, tell me."

Fuck. I didn't want to get into this right now. I had a thousand things running through my head, and outing Heath's supposed interlude with Sophia years ago was not something I wanted to share with my best friend.

"Erica, please." Alli's eyes were wide, and the wavering in how she said my name told me she was moments from tears. We both were.

"They have history, Alli."

She made a small sound of shock. "W–What?"

"Blake has been taking care of Heath for a while, through some rough times. You knew this. Sophia was into the drug scene too. They partied together, and Blake doesn't know for sure because neither of them would admit it, but he thinks they might have hooked up before Blake sent them both off to rehab. And when Sophia got out, Blake left her. Maybe because of that, but he had a lot of reasons. She stayed close to Heath, and obviously they both invested in her company to help her get off the ground. Consolation prize for Blake breaking her heart, I guess. But I'm beginning to wonder if she stayed close to Heath just to have an in with Blake. He'll do anything for Heath, and she plays the victim so well when she wants to."

Alli's eyes narrowed, tears threatening at the corners. "If they were together at any point, why wouldn't he tell me? He introduced me to her back in New York like they were old friends."

"They were. I honestly don't know what happened between them. Only they do. And if it was anything more than friendship, I'm sure Heath didn't want to hurt you by telling you."

I closed my eyes. Blake had done the same for me. Spared me the details of the past to save my feelings. Like a fool, I sought them out anyway. Had I learned all that much from unearthing his past? Maybe not. Maybe there was some greater good for having the dirty details out in the air.

"Looks like I'm hurt anyway. Sophia couldn't get me out of here fast enough." Alli wrapped her arms around herself.

I wanted to do the same thing. I wanted to curl up and disappear into the concrete. I wanted to feel nothing—not an inkling of what that vindictive woman was putting us through.

"I can't believe you left," she said quietly, bringing me back to the moment when I'd given up.

I shrugged, surrendering to what had unfolded over the past hour. "I had no other choice." I stared down at my feet.

Alli came up to me and squeezed me tight.

"We'll get through this. Right now it doesn't feel like we will. But I have to believe that tomorrow will feel a little less horrible."

I hugged her tighter and fought the tears, not wanting to break down where Sophia might still be able to see us. We'd get through this. Right?

Alli pulled back and brushed away the tears crawling down her cheeks. "Okay. God, I need to get it together. Let's talk tomorrow, but call me if you need anything tonight, okay? I need to go home and try to figure this all out."

"I will. And I'm sorry, for what it's worth, which unfortunately, probably isn't a lot right now." I stared down at the ground, wishing it would swallow me up and take this all away.

"You don't have to be sorry, Erica. Please, don't blame yourself for this. Go home and talk to Blake. Maybe we can find a way out of this."

She shot me a sad smile and turned, walking toward home.

Seemingly paralyzed by the afternoon's events, I felt around my purse until I found my phone. I dialed Alex's number and began walking down the street. His receptionist picked up and I asked for him.

"Mr. Hutchinson isn't available at the moment."

"You tell him this is Erica Hathaway, and I will call you all damn day if I have to. Put him on the phone."

"One moment, please," she mumbled with an agitated tone.

A minute later the line picked up.

"Erica." Alex had the decency to sound a little tentative through his greeting.

"You sold my business to Isaac Perry. Is that right?"

He sighed. "Yes, I met with him after you on Friday."

"Well, he and his pal Sophia Devereaux fired my marketing director on the spot."

He was silent for a moment. "I didn't realize that was in their plans. I was clear that you wanted the team to stay."

"This isn't about what I want. This is about revenge."

"Not for me, it wasn't."

"Then what is it about?" I harnessed all my energy not to shout at him through the phone.

He paused. "This is business, Erica. It's about creating opportunities and taking profit. Companies change hands every day. I realize this has been an emotional process for you—"

"Fuck you, Alex." I couldn't hold it back any longer. His condescending tone. As if the sole reason why I was unraveling right now because I was some over-sensitive woman, floundering in a man's world.

"It's just *business*," he said flatly.

"Business, huh? What about morals, and ethics?"

"I did nothing unethical. I negotiated a fair deal."

"You misled me. You withheld critical information that has my best friend and me unemployed at the moment."

"You left?"

"Yes, I left." What other choice did I have? Sit there and take orders from my fiancé's diabolical ex-girlfriend? Not in this lifetime.

He sighed loudly. "There's nothing I can do now, Erica. I'm sorry things panned out this way for you. It's just the way it is, I guess."

"That's just great, Alex. Pleasure doing business with you."

I hung up, knowing the longer I stayed on the phone with him the more I was going to lose my cool. Already I regretted half the things I'd said. My desperation for a way out of this nightmare had me sounding emotional and vulnerable. The problem was he simply didn't care. Not the way Blake or the people I'd surrounded myself with would care.

I walked a few more blocks, not knowing where I was going, no aim in sight. With shaking hands I dialed Blake's number. He picked up after the first ring.

"Hello?"

My lip trembled as I searched for the words to explain what had just happened. Then the tears began to fall. Everything that pride had cooped up inside of me was letting loose. I was falling and I needed a soft place to land.

"Erica, are you okay? Talk to me."

I suppressed a sob, wanting to crumble at the sound of his voice.

"I need you."

CHAPTER SIXTEEN

After two hours of solid crying and a glass and a half of Blake's most expensive scotch, the rage had dulled to a numb sort of hopelessness. Blake had held me and promised that we would get through it. But the more I tried to believe him, the less convinced of it he seemed. He paced the living room, looking repeatedly at his phone as if he were holding back from launching into action at any moment.

"I'll fucking ruin him," he muttered.

Under any other circumstances I might have pitied the person Blake wanted to ruin, but not today. *Ruin away*. But deep down, I knew there was nothing to be done. Even in the tired haze of my mind, I knew Isaac wouldn't have dropped all that money on a business only to have his lawyers leave a convenient loophole for me to hold any of it back. No, he would have covered all his bases. The way men like Blake always did.

"Why bother? He's wasted enough of our time." I shrugged, the motion nearly imperceptible from my slouching position on the couch.

"Because he deserves it."

"It's just business," I sang softly, mimicking Alex's earlier words, except there was nothing funny or cute about the position he'd left me in. And I hated him for it. I lifted the lowball to my lips, acutely aware of how much less I hated him the more I drank.

Blake leaned down and took my glass. "You've had enough."

I slapped my empty hand down onto the couch. "I have a very long shit list right now. Do not make me add you to it."

"You're going to be on your own shit list tomorrow if you don't slow down. I'll get you a water."

I sank back into the couch, defeated. Utterly defeated. I wanted to drown myself until I couldn't think about today anymore. If I couldn't permanently erase Sophia's face from my mind, I wanted to blur it out thoroughly for the next few hours.

Blake returned with a glass of water. I wrinkled my nose at it, but held it obediently in my lap. He sat on the coffee table across from me, framing my legs with his.

"I can buy it back," he said matter-of-factly.

I stared back at him, confused. "Why?"

"Because the business should be yours."

"But I sold it."

"So we'll buy it back. I'll make Isaac an offer he can't refuse."

My eyes widened. "I don't like the sound of that."

That lightened the grimace that had marked his face for most of the evening. He stroked my knee with this thumb. "Don't worry, I don't use Daniel's methods."

I shook my head, not wanting to think about that on top of everything else that had gone horribly wrong as of late. "It's not worth it, Blake. I sold it. He said he genuinely wanted it. So…now he has it." I sighed, the reality that owning the business was officially in the past settling over me. "At least I cashed out. I can pay you back now. I wanted to give myself some freedom to do new things, so now I just have to figure out what to do with all that freedom. Ironic, huh?"

Blake released a frustrated groan. "For the hundredth time, you do not need to pay me back. It's a moot point. We'll be sharing assets soon enough. This isn't about the money, and you know it."

"The business was always more than the money. But…" I bit my lip, closing my eyes. It was gone, all gone now. "I have to learn how to let it go. I have to figure out how to start over."

I opened my stinging eyes and saw the resentment that we both shared now in his. It cut through me, his emotions validating my own. Nothing felt quite like betrayal, or finding yourself on the floor because you were too blind to see it coming.

I couldn't help feeling that Sophia had won somehow, but I was powerless to change what had happened.

★ ★ ★

The next few days went by without incident. Blake had taken some time off to be with me, to make sure I didn't go catatonic, even though everything in me wanted to. But eventually, work called him back to the office. He had responsibilities. Purpose. Two things I now lacked.

Alli called. So many people had called. Even Marie, but Alli's were the only calls I'd answer. I couldn't handle telling people the story over and over again. Listening to their pitying reactions. Asking me what I was going to do now. Alli was the only one who understood what I was going through.

"Have you heard anything?" I asked.

"I talked to James last night. I guess Sid left."

"Good," I muttered, picking at the rip in my jeans.

"James is staying because he needs the job right now, so he's waiting this out."

I nodded. "I can't blame him. It's a messed up situation."

"No kidding. I really don't think they expected you to leave, Erica."

No one was more surprised than I was.

"Did you talk to Heath?" I asked tentatively.

"Yeah."

I waited for her to tell me more. I didn't want to push if she didn't want to talk about it. It was their business.

"Are you guys okay?"

"We're fine. We talked, a lot. I'll tell you about it later. It doesn't really matter now."

"Okay," I said, content to leave it at that.

"Marie called me. She was worried when you weren't answering your calls and they said you weren't at the office anymore."

I closed my eyes, unable to comprehend facing Marie and adding one more hurtful thing to the pile of ashes my life had become. I didn't want to think about the invisible barrier that had crept up between us. Her knowing I was angry with her, and my unwillingness to let it go. I wasn't sure how we would get past it. As much as I wanted to hold on to my resentment, I wanted her to admit Richard was using her and hurting us both. Maybe she would. Maybe enough time had gone by.

"I'll text her," I finally said.

"You should call her, Erica. She's really worried."

"Did you tell her about the business?"

"Yeah, I didn't figure you'd mind."

"I'd rather someone else tell her. I might even tell one of the reporters who keeps calling so they can broadcast it to the world. I never want to have to tell that story."

"Erica…"

I swallowed down my tears. I didn't hate a lot of people. I didn't have room in my heart for it, but I made a special place for Sophia, Isaac, and Alex. A place untouchable from forgiveness or pity. A place that couldn't be erased with time. I would never forgive them. Never.

"I have to go."

She was quiet. "Okay. Call me if you need to."

"I will. Thank you."

I hung up and promptly cried myself to sleep.

★ ★ ★

By day five, I realized I needed to leave the apartment. I was a wreck, and I needed to get back out into the world, even if it was only in a small way.

I took a walk down the street, parked myself on a bench, and watched people for about an hour. Across the street, people went in and out of the market. Going in empty handed, they left with bags full of groceries and wine.

We'd been living on takeout and Blake's sometimes-successful cooking projects. I was starving for a home-cooked meal. I felt empty in so many ways, and somehow I wondered if a lot of pasta could fill up those places. At least for an hour or two.

A pang of sadness hit me when I thought about my mom. Maybe she was what I was looking for, but I'd have to settle for recreating one of her delicious meals. I walked across the street and threw myself into shopping for every one of my favorite dishes that she'd taught me how to make. I had more bags than I could comfortably carry. When my phone rang, I cursed.

I stepped to the edge of the sidewalk and set the bags down to dig through my purse. The number was local but not one I recognized.

"Hello?"

"Erica?" A man's familiar voice greeted me, but I couldn't place it.

"Who is this?"

"Richard."

My jaw set, my stomach clenching.

"Richard Craven?"

"I know who you are. You're the reason I've been fighting off reporters for the past couple weeks."

"Right. I'm sorry about that."

"Are you?"

He sighed. "Listen, I was hoping we could talk."

"No." My tone was pure acid.

"Hear me out."

"I won't be giving you an exclusive, if that's what you're after. Not to you, and not to anyone else. Find someone else to give you the story you're looking for."

"I have."

The knot in my stomach grew in size, settling like a rock.

"Really." I kept my voice steady, not wanting to reveal my concern.

"I want to talk to you about your father."

"I don't have anything to say to you about Daniel," I said quietly but firmly.

"I have information you might find interesting. You might change your mind."

I shook my head. As if any news about Daniel would shock me.

"Will you meet me?"

If he had a story, I'd read about it in the papers, but I wasn't going to star in it. Maybe I already was destined to though.

"Just ten minutes," he pressed.

I cursed silently. "Fine, ten minutes. That's all you're getting."

"That's all I need. Can it be today?"

"My calendar is wide open." I took small pleasure in the sarcasm only I understood.

"Great. There's a little bistro across from the news office. *Famiglia.*"

"Fine. I'll be there in an hour."

About an hour later I got off at the T-stop nearest the

destination. Blake had given Clay some much-needed time off. I wasn't getting out much anyway, so I didn't care. Now that I was out, I appreciated the moment of freedom. I couldn't be more free it seemed. No one hovered. No one needed me.

No one had told me freedom could feel so empty.

Ignoring the sentiment, I took quick strides toward the restaurant, and my phone rang, lighting up with Blake's face. I answered.

"Hey, do you want me to pick anything up on my way home?"

"No, I bought food."

A car horn blared behind me.

"Where are you?"

"I'm meeting Richard. He called me. Said he wants to talk."

"Are you sure that's a good idea?"

"Not really. I'm sure he just wants to pump me for information, but I have a few choice words for him too."

"Just be careful. He's a reporter. He'll use anything you say and twist it. You're in the spotlight enough as it is."

"I know. I don't plan on saying a lot outside of four-letter words."

"Fair enough. Where are you meeting him?"

The restaurant was just ahead. "At this Italian place across from his office."

"Is it safe?"

I glanced around. People walked the streets the same carefree way they did on our side of town. "It's fine, Blake.

It's a busy area and I'm in broad daylight."

"Okay, I have to wrap up a few things here. I'll swing by when I'm done and pick you up."

My phone beeped. "I have another call coming in. I'll see you after."

"I'll call you when I get there."

I pulled the phone away and saw Daniel's name on my phone.

Shit. What impeccable timing. I considered ignoring the call but worried that he'd simply keep calling.

"Daniel." I swallowed and tried to sound firm.

"Where are you?" he barked.

I tensed, remembering his wrath from the last time we spoke.

"I think I told you to stop yelling at me."

"I don't have time for discussing manners, Erica. Where the fuck are you?"

I started losing my cool. I was pissed, but I was scared too. I glanced up and down the street, suddenly petrified that he could find out where I was.

"This isn't a good time," I said quickly.

"Erica, you're—"

I hung up the phone and silenced the ringer, dropping it back into my purse. No way in hell was I telling him where I was. All I needed was him and his henchman Connor showing up at the restaurant confronting Richard. I closed my eyes and asked myself why I cared, why I still let him be a part of my life in any way. I'd be better off without him. Just like my mother wanted. Why hadn't anyone given me the cliff notes on him before I'd stupidly

241

started seeking him out?

My purse vibrated against me. I knew it was Daniel again. All he cared about was his campaign. All he ever did was hurt me. Physically, and emotionally, he'd put me through hell. Yet here I was, fishing for what Richard might know that could damage him or compromise his freedom.

I reached for the door handle of the restaurant, determined to push thoughts of Daniel out of my mind. I caught Richard's profile ahead of me. He held his cell phone to his ear. I approached, not caring that I was interrupting. Dropping down into the chair across from him, I leveled a contentious look his way. Expressionless, he looked over at the front window, repeating the name of the restaurant to whoever was on the other line.

"See you then."

He hung up and set his phone down between us. "We meet again."

"What do you want?" I snapped, eager to let him know how unimpressed I was with him and how he'd hurt one of my best friends to further his own career.

"I'm not here to fight. I just want to ask you a few questions."

I let out a short laugh. "Right. For the record, I have nothing to say to you."

"I had a feeling you'd say that. So why are you here?"

I leaned in. "I want to know how you sleep at night."

His eyes narrowed. "Listen, I just want the truth."

"So you manipulated someone I love for information? What kind of person does that?"

He sighed and pinched the bridge of his nose. "I care about Marie."

"For someone who wants the truth, you're full of shit. Does she even know what you did?"

He worked his jaw, avoiding my eyes. "We talked."

"And?" I waited. I wanted him to tell me he'd revealed his true self to her. But if he had, he would have destroyed her too. I couldn't forget the hurt look on her face when I'd called Richard out. She loved him.

"Not surprisingly, she didn't understand my reasons or my obligations as a member of the press."

"What about your obligations as a decent person? Marie is a good, kind person, and you probably broke her heart. For what? A story?"

He shook his head and looked past me. "Look, I know there's more to Daniel Fitzgerald than meets the eye. He's skirted past every major controversy that's come close to him over the past decade, and no one digs any deeper with this guy. I want to know why, and I'm going to find out."

I stared at him, my lips sealed into a tight line. He wasn't getting shit out of me.

He leaned in as if he were warming up to convince me of something. "You come into Daniel's life out of the blue, right? Weeks later, his stepson is dead. Apparent suicide. And he's carrying on his campaign as if nothing's happened."

"He's a politician. Do you have any idea how many people they answer to, how much money they sink into these things? This is years in the making."

He shook his head. "No, there's more to this story.

The police know something, and I have a feeling you do too."

My heart sped up at the mention of the police. Richard digging around was one thing, but as much as I respected the law, I was scared to death that I'd lied to cover Daniel's crimes.

"Erica, this is your last chance."

My questioning gaze flew to his. "Last chance for what exactly?"

"To tell the truth. He's going down. You have to ask yourself whether you want to let him take you down with him. I realize he's your father, but how far are you willing to go to protect him?"

I grimaced. "You have nothing on him. Or me. He's my father. So what?"

He smiled, and my stomach fell.

"I have a lot more than that, sweetheart."

"Then why isn't he in jail?" I hope he couldn't hear the growing hysteria in my voice. What else could he possibly know?

"I've been researching his affiliations. Making connections."

"And?" I held my breath, wondering how much Richard would actually divulge to me in an effort to get me to talk.

"I found someone."

I held my breath. "Who?"

"Someone from his network in Southie who wants to talk. In fact, I'm meeting with him as soon as I'm done here. He has information about what happened the night

Mark MacLeod died."

My heart beat loudly in my ears, fading out the quiet murmur of the restaurant.

"So like I said. This might be your last chance."

"This has nothing to do with me." I wished that were true. I wanted nothing to do with what Daniel had done. I didn't regret that Mark was gone, but I didn't want to know anything more about it. I didn't want to walk around with the knowledge that he might have died because of me and that I'd lied to keep Daniel from justice.

"This has everything to do with you. I've been a reporter for half my life, and this has you written all over it. Talk to me, goddamnit."

The sound of my phone vibrating in my purse distracted my rising panic.

"I have to go. Good luck, Richard." I rushed up out of my seat. He called my name, but I wanted nothing more to do with this. I wasn't going to help him. And an insane part of me wanted to warn Daniel.

I stepped out of the cafe and paused in the middle of the sidewalk. I scanned the street for a cab to take me away from here, but my eyes fixed on a man across the street.

He was tall and thickly built, a faded gray scally cap shading his face.

Our eyes locked. I knew him. I knit my eyebrows as I tried to place him.

"Erica, wait."

Richard was beside me, but I couldn't tear my gaze away from the man. He didn't belong here, but his eyes were trained on me. He must know me too, but how…

Before I could piece it together, he raised his arms in front of him, the shiny metallic of a weapon pressed firmly in his hands.

No.

My mouth fell open in a silent scream, but I couldn't move fast enough. The loud blast of shots echoed through the air.

An explosive pain ripped through me. The world stood still.

I had no idea how badly I'd been hurt because all I could see was blood. I was soaked. I dropped to my knees.

Oh God. This isn't happening. This isn't real.

The street was chaos. The blur of frightened faces running from the danger. The noise. Screams and more shots and the screech of a car. More commotion on the street and men's angry voices.

I held my shaking hands against the places on my belly that radiated with pain. Richard lay unmoving beside me. More blood.

My head swam, and I dropped down onto my side on the pavement. With waning strength, I gritted my teeth, trying to hold on for help.

"Erica!"

Like an angel's, Blake's arms came around me. With careful speed, he lifted me and carried me into the restaurant. He lowered me onto the carpeted floor in the back of the restaurant. The tension I'd been holding onto released, and I grabbed his hand as he reached for me. I squeezed it hard, unwilling to let him go.

"I've got you, baby. Everything's going to be okay.

Help is coming."

His voice sounded foreign, like he didn't believe his own words. I looked into his eyes, fixed on that single point, but the pain there was almost as unbearable as the pain pulsing through me. He twisted out of my grasp and lifted my shirt up past my bra.

He exhaled in a rush.

"Fuck."

He pulled off his T-shirt and pressed the cloth hard against my belly. I cried out.

He hushed me, never moving his hands or easing the pressure. "You're okay," he said again.

I wanted to believe him. I closed my eyes, feeling weaker with each passing second. Blake's warm hand cupped my cheek. Warm, he was so warm.

"Look at me, baby. Keep your eyes open."

I opened my eyes halfway. Somehow that was as far as they could go. Everything felt slower, the breath that filled my lungs, the beat of my heart. The chaos around us moved in slow motion, a blur of sounds and activity. But he was all I could see, the only voice I could hear.

The heaviness of the pain had waned, and my body felt lighter in its weakness. Using all my strength, I raised my hand to his face.

"Blake…I love you."

I didn't recognize my own voice, but I felt the words in my heart. I loved this man. With every ounce of my being, faded as the world was becoming. I closed my eyes again, lightness wrapping around me in the dark.

"No," he ground out. "Don't say that. You stay with

me."

I rested my hand over his. The wet blood sopping his shirt was barely warm on my skin now. I couldn't. I couldn't keep my eyes open. I wanted to. I wanted to be home, with Blake, wrapped up in his arms.

I let out a breath, relief and a sudden dizzy rush washing over me when I imagined that's where we were.

"Stay awake, baby. Please try to stay awake for me."

He was hurting. The agony in his voice lanced through me, one last strike through the numbing pain.

Blake... His name was a whisper, or maybe just a whisper in my own mind. I repeated the word like a mantra until he was gone. I couldn't hear him or feel him anymore. His voice, his face, even the dream of us had vanished into nothing.

CHAPTER SEVENTEEN

The persistent beep was like a fly that wouldn't go away. I frowned, searching for the strength to make it stop. I was cold. I didn't know this place. Everything was blurry, but the room was brightly lit, lights buzzing a quiet hum above me.

Slowly and with great effort, I brought more things into focus. The rough texture of the white blanket covering me. The hard tubing invading my nostrils. A soft rustling sound beside me.

Then Blake's face filled the widening frame of my vision. I wanted to reach for him, but a needling pain shot through my hand as I went to move it. I winced. He caught it between his palms, stroking softly and warming it at the same time.

"Blake." My voice cracked when I spoke. My throat was dry, but suddenly grew moist with the tears and emotion. Seeing Blake overwhelmed me. We'd been apart for too long, yet I couldn't explain why. "What happened?"

"You were shot."

I closed my eyes and reached for the memories. Everything was so blurry, but slowly, like the room, the last memories of my conscious mind came into focus.

The restaurant. The shots and the screaming. Blood. God, there'd been so much blood. Richard's too.

Richard was hurt…or worse.

"Is Richard okay?"

Hesitation swam in Blake's eyes. He shook his head. "He didn't make it."

Oh, no. I couldn't believe it. We'd spoken. Contentious as it was, I couldn't believe he was dead. Blake tucked a hair behind my ear, moving a tube that blew cold unwelcome oxygen into my nostrils. I wrinkled my nose and went to pull them out.

Blake stopped me, replacing its position. "No, keep that."

"I don't want them."

"Christ, Erica. You've been shot three times. Can you please leave it? At least until the doctor comes."

I relaxed back into the pillow, giving up the fight and feeling the small surge of energy that had woken me vanish. I was exhausted, but I didn't want to leave Blake yet.

"Sorry," I muttered.

He sighed softly. "Are you in pain? I can call the nurse."

I did a mental scan of my body. The pain in my abdomen was more localized than I remembered, but I still had no idea where I'd been hurt. Heaven help me, that man. He was the one who'd taken the shots. I closed my eyes and tried to remember his face. Dark hair and dark eyes. Shadowed as he was, I couldn't make much of him out. But his presence, his build, and the way he dressed had set him apart in my mind. He wasn't another suit, a young professional on the streets.

"The man who shot me. He…"

"He's dead, baby," Blake said.

My eyes flew open. "The police shot him?"

"No." He rubbed the stubble that covered his jaw. "It was Daniel."

My heart stopped. "Daniel?"

"After you and I hung up, he called me in a panic. He said you were in danger and needed to know where you were. I didn't want to tell him obviously. I wanted to get you myself but he insisted. He was…frantic. Somehow he knew whatever was about to go down. He showed up a few minutes before me. He pulled his bodyguard's firearm and shot the man dead a few seconds after he opened fire on you."

Then suddenly I remembered. The tweed cap. The muscled man who reminded me of Connor when I'd first seen him. I touched my trembling fingertips to my mouth. "I remember him."

I looked to Blake's concerned expression.

"I saw him when I was with Daniel, a long time ago. This seedy bar in Southie called O'Neill's. He was manning the door. He seemed to know Daniel. That was him. I remember."

He shook his head. "Why would he want to hurt you?"

"I have no idea. But Richard…" I frowned, trying to remember our conversation. He'd had something on Daniel. Something that spooked me enough to want to leave suddenly.

"Richard wanted me to talk about Daniel, to reveal what I knew about him. He suspected him of being involved in Mark's death. Richard said it was my last chance to tell the truth. He was going to meet with someone from that neighborhood who was going to tell him everything he didn't know about Mark's death."

"Do you think he knew you were going to be there?"

"Maybe. Richard might have told him."

Blake stood up and began pacing a small path beside the bed. He pinched his lower lip between his fingers. "The press has been quiet other than saying that Daniel shot him. I wonder how much they really know."

A nurse entered the room, and a tall man with short brown hair dressed in a white doctor's coat followed behind.

"Look who's awake." The nurse patted one of my feet through the blanket and checked my chart.

The doctor followed, an optimistic smile on his face despite the fact that I'd clearly had better days.

"I'm Dr. Angus."

He sat in a stool and rolled up beside me. Blake stood back while the nurse bustled around the other side, taking my vitals. She jotted them down while the doctor inspected the bandages under my gown. I focused on the bare white ceiling. I wasn't entirely ready to see what had happened to my body. I was still grateful to be alive, to have Blake with me. I wasn't sure how much more I could handle.

"Everything looks good. The surgery went well, and I think these will heal just fine."

I met his eyes once I was covered again.

"Surgery?"

"One of the bullets passed through, but we had to

remove two of them and try to repair some of the damage."

Damage. The word reverberated in my already foggy brain.

"Damage?"

The optimism in his eyes dimmed a bit and he shifted his gaze to Blake. "You should rest a little more. You've been through the wringer. I'll be doing rounds again tomorrow morning, and we can discuss it more then."

"No, I want to know now." I tried to shift upwards in bed, but a sharp jolt of pain stopped me from going any farther. "Ouch."

The nurse found a beige cord beside me and pressed it a couple times. "Press this for pain, honey."

"Thank you," I mumbled, hating how restricted I was in this bed.

A moment later, the nurse had disappeared, leaving a growing air of tension in her absence.

"Perhaps we could chat a moment alone." He looked questioningly to Blake and then back to me.

"No, you can say anything. Blake is my fiancé," I insisted.

The doctor coughed quietly and stared down at his clasped hands. He drew in a breath and made eye contact again.

"All right then. One of the bullets skimmed your side here, but passed through, as I said." He placed his hand over my left side, and the heat radiated down to the place where I registered a faint pain. "And then two shots entered your abdomen. There was some damage to your reproductive organs."

All the air left my lungs. Silence hung in the air, like we were all standing there frozen in time.

"What does that mean?" A surge of panic flowed through my veins. My breathing became rapid and tears formed in my eyes.

He glanced to Blake again, whose face showed no emotion. "We repaired the damaged tissue of your uterus. That should heal in time, but we were not able to repair the rest. Your ovary was lost." His lips wrinkled into a sympathetic line. "I'm very sorry, Erica."

"What about…" I swallowed hard, trying to form the words. Words we'd never even said as a couple, yet here we were in front of a stranger who was threatening all of it. "Does this mean I can't have children?"

"You will probably want to consult with someone who specializes in these things, but if you had plans to conceive… well, it's not impossible, but it may not be easy. You have one ovary now and the damage to the uterus could affect implantation and carrying a pregnancy to term. Only time will tell."

With the exception of my heavy breathing, silence stretched over what felt like several seconds. I couldn't speak, and Blake's eyes never left the doctor. I wanted him to look at me. But I was terrified that he would and of what I would see there.

The doctor finally spoke. "Do you have questions for me?"

No. I shook my head. The doctor squeezed my hand gently before he left, saying something to Blake that I couldn't focus on. My thoughts were swimming. Tightness formed in my throat. I pressed the button on the beige cord a couple more times. I wanted to feel numb. There was too much pain. Suddenly it had all become unbearable.

Blake caught my hand, caressing his thumb again around the place where the IV connected to my vein. He lowered his lips to my skin, pressing softly. He didn't speak. He simply caressed my hand lightly. His jaw was tight, his full lips drawn up even tighter.

"Blake. I'm sorry." He couldn't know how sorry I was.

When he finally looked up, his eyes were misted. He blinked and cast them down again quickly. A painful sob wanted to burst out of my chest, but I held onto it, afraid to unleash it. Why? All I could ask myself was why, and there was only silence to answer me.

Blake shifted beside me. Reaching into his pocket, he retrieved my ring. Sparkles danced off the band of beautifully cut diamonds. I glanced down at my pale bruised hand. They must have taken it off for the surgeries. For all my wounded nakedness under the gown, I suddenly felt bare without it.

He caught my fingers and slipped the band carefully over my knuckle. I closed my eyes and let the tears roll down my cheeks. Warm lips pressed against the skin above the ring, the same place he'd kissed the same day he asked me to be his wife, reminding me of our promise.

★ ★ ★

Blake doted on me for weeks. We hadn't talked about

the doctor's words, and a part of me wondered if Blake was trying to pretend like he hadn't said them at all. Perhaps he was only trying to help me heal. I played along, pretending my injuries—all of them—would heal and we could go back to our lives. Pick up the pieces of our lives.

I sipped my tea, my thoughts blanked out by the television blaring in front of me. I startled at a knock. Blake looked up from his laptop and went to the door.

"What the hell are you doing here?"

I sat up carefully, peering over the top of the couch. Daniel stood tall in the doorway, seemingly undeterred by Blake's threatening posture. "I came to see Erica," he said calmly.

A tense moment passed between them before I spoke. "It's okay, Blake. Come in." The part of my mind that was used to doing whatever it pleased wanted to stand up and greet him, but I was still couch-bound. At least Blake insisted I was. I wanted to move around, but he restricted me to mandatory movements only.

Daniel came into the living room and sat on the opposite couch. I shut off the noise of the TV. I had a thousand questions. The news had been extremely vague, and I hadn't wanted to reach out to Daniel and raise suspicions. I worried that his visit wasn't a good idea now, but I desperately wanted to know what this all meant. I needed to know why someone would want to kill me, and why Richard had lost his life because of it.

What had really happened that day? I silently implored Daniel as his gaze skirted around the room.

"Do you want something to drink?" I asked weakly,

not sure how to break the ice.

He eyed the wet bar at the other side of the room but shook his head. "No. Thank you."

I had many questions, but one burned in my mind. "Who was he?"

He looked down at his folded hands, but didn't answer.

"I recognized him. He worked at O'Neill's. That day we went there."

"He worked for me."

I nodded slowly, fingering the knot in the blanket over my lap.

"He was trying to blackmail me. He wanted money to stay quiet about Mark's death."

"He knew the truth?"

He nodded.

"Why did he know?"

He lifted his gaze to mine. "Why do you think?"

I swallowed hard. *God.*

Blake came around and sat beside me. He leveled a dead stare at Daniel.

Daniel cleared his throat and began. "He heard about you in the press. When he found out you were my daughter and linked to my campaign, he must have figured you were pretty important to me. He threatened to come after you if I didn't pay him off."

"And you wouldn't."

"I would have. If I'd thought that would be the end of it. I was hoping for a more permanent solution, but by the time I figured out what he was up to, all I could do was try to get to you before he did."

I closed my eyes against the burning behind them. "And Richard. Was that…an accident?"

"Maybe he thought he was Blake, or maybe he was simply too close to you. Someone important to you would presumably be important to me."

"It's all so terrible. I still can't believe it. It's like a dream. One that I'll wake up from and it'll be that day, before everything happened. I just stood there, waiting for him to do it. I couldn't figure out who he was, but I knew his face."

Daniel sat in silence, his lips pressed tightly together.

"Well, we came around to the permanent solution anyway. The police matched a print from Mark's apartment to him. He used the same weapon against you as he used to kill Mark. He wasn't as bright as he was ambitious. Unfortunately for him, fortunately for me. The case is finally closed. They'll be announcing it any day now."

Emotion flooded through me. The relief was unmistakable. Could it really be over? It seemed impossible, but I couldn't imagine going through any more of this.

"I can't believe it."

"It's done. I promise you. My lawyers are taking a much-needed vacation. The police shouldn't bother you anymore. Neither should the reporters."

Thank God.

"How are you feeling otherwise?"

I opened my eyes, and a new kind of pain shot through

me, a pain far deeper than the physical pain that had slowed me down the past couple weeks. Blake's hand tightened around mine. My free hand rested over my belly, that wasteland where I could have held a life. That possibility was now just a number, a slim chance that anything could be normal. I swallowed the tears that would come every time I thought about it.

"You should go." Blake said quietly, but firmly. "She doesn't need any upset right now."

"It's okay," I said, but my voice cracked.

"It's not. This is his fucking fault. Look at what this has done to you."

A tear fell slowly down my cheek. "Stop, please."

Daniel frowned, fresh concern awash on his features. I didn't have the physical or emotional strength to keep them from tearing each other apart if they stayed in the same room. I gave Blake a pleading look.

"Blake, can you give us a minute?"

His eyes narrowed as his gaze slid back over to Daniel. He looked back to me, his expression softening only slightly. He rose and retreated to the kitchen.

"What happened, Erica?"

"I'm fine. It's just. Um, it might be hard… Having kids, I guess, will be a challenge now. There was some damage there."

"Jesus." For the first time I saw genuine fear in Daniel's eyes. He seemed pale as he looked me over. "Erica, my God, I'm sorry. I've made such a mess of this. I wanted…"

His head fell into his hands. He rose abruptly, went to

the wet bar, and poured himself a drink. He drained it quickly and poured another. He stared into the glass. The answers weren't there. I wanted to tell him I'd already checked. I'd thought my way all through the bad news the doctor had given me. I could stack up the regrets and rewrite history, but nothing would change the damage that had been done.

My life was a mess. At least we had that in common.

"What are you going to do about the governor's race?"

He gulped down another mouthful of Blake's expensive scotch and exhaled. "Fuck, I don't know. There're only a couple weeks left. What more can I do? There's more news about the shooting than the campaign at this point."

"I could try to help."

His eyes widened, that glimpse of fear there again. "No."

"I know I haven't been very supportive," I said.

"You've had good reason not to be. And now you have an even better reason. You shouldn't be anywhere near my campaign or me."

I wilted. "I literally don't have anything else to do. The business is gone. I'm stuck here." I didn't want to go down the list of everything that had led to the utter wreckage of my life in its current state.

He came closer, sitting beside me on the couch. "What happened to the business?"

"It sort of got sold out from under me. It's a long story, but suffice to say, I now have lots of spare time on my hands. I could help if you wanted me to."

"You should be resting, and I want you far away from all of this." He caught my hand. "I want you far away from me too." He let me go, sliding his hand away as if the touch burned him.

"Daniel."

"I've done enough damage. Every time I think I'm taking care of a problem, three more crop up. I've brought nothing but terror to your life since you found me, Erica."

He stood, avoiding my eyes.

"This is done now. The investigation is closed. We can sever ties. You don't need to worry about me bothering you anymore. I'll leave you alone. Hopefully the only time you'll see me is in the news, and even then... Fuck, I don't know." He shoved a hand through his graying hair. "Nothing makes sense right now."

Fresh tears formed in my eyes. "Why are you saying that?"

"Because it needs to be said. Because this is why... *This* is why I left your mother." His blue eyes blazed into me, emotion igniting there that I'd never seen before. "You've seen glimpses, but you have no idea what it's like to have this life. You had no way of knowing that finding me would bring you this far down into it, but I warned her too. I told her we couldn't be happy that way. Erica..." He rubbed his forehead, doing nothing to resolve the grimace there. "I wanted to be with Patty. I swear on my life, I loved your mother. I wanted to marry her and be a family, but I had no choice. You can't understand it, but I have no choice. It's all laid out, and for all the years it took to get here... Christ, here we are. Here I am. No better off, really. And you're not safe around me."

He stared into the now empty glass. I didn't know what to say to him. I couldn't argue that my life had turned into a life-threatening shit storm since I'd found him, but the thought of him leaving and never coming back was slowly devastating me.

Before I could argue, he took a step toward me. He leaned down and kissed the top of my head, where my hair met my forehead. He lingered there a moment and began to speak in a whisper.

"You're my daughter. My only child. I love you, but it's time for me to go now."

He stepped back with eyes cast down. He left the apartment as quickly as he'd come, leaving me in stunned silence.

CHAPTER EIGHTEEN

Daniel had left in a rush, and I didn't know what to make of it all. I turned the television back on, wanting to drown out my swirling thoughts. I couldn't talk to Blake about the knife Daniel had lanced through me with his words. Blake didn't want me to care. No one did. What more could the man do to me to earn my hatred? Still, it slipped through my fingers, and only a sad emptiness remained. A shell of what could have been. Lingering regret over what had come to be.

"You look tired. Do you want to lie down?" Blake was seated at his usual perch on the opposite couch, his gaze heavy with the usual concern.

"No, I want to get up."

He gave me a tentative look. "How about a bath? That will relax you."

I sighed. A trip to the bathroom was probably all he'd allow. A bath sounded nice though.

"Fine. But I'm walking there myself. You have to stop babying me, Blake."

He stood quickly and helped me up. "You can walk there, but I will never stop taking care of you until the day I die. So you can give up on that right now." He caressed my cheek. "I almost lost you."

I closed my eyes, leaning into his touch.

I almost lost you too. The thought was too terrible to

comprehend.

I'd spent the past several days feeling sorry for myself in every way. Losing the business seemed far less tragic in the face of nearly dying. And the very real possibility that Blake and I might never have children, as soul-crushing as it was to contemplate—and I'd tried very hard not to— paled to the reality that I could have died in Blake's arms that afternoon. The man who'd killed Mark under Daniel's direct orders had not hesitated to attempt to end my life.

As much as I couldn't grieve for Mark's death, I couldn't believe that someone could have so little value for human life. These were the kinds of people who Daniel kept in his life. Or perhaps they'd always been there. For all of Blake's secrets, Daniel's existence seemed far darker, with shadows I never wanted to shed light on.

Blake was filling the bath when I joined him. "Let me help you," he said, pulling my T-shirt off with too much care.

"Are you coming in too?"

He chewed his lip a moment, eyeing the bathtub topped with an appealing layer of bubbles. "I'm not sure if that's a good idea."

"Please… I miss you." I missed the happiness in his eyes. I even missed his temper. All he had for me now lately was pity.

He sighed. "Fine. But you know we can't—"

"I know."

I cut him short, not wanting to hear the reminder. No sex for weeks. I didn't see how it mattered, but the doctor had ordered it and Blake insisted on following everything down to the letter. Denying ourselves wouldn't bring back what had been lost. It only guaranteed that another long expanse of time ahead of us would be filled with more wait and worry. Frustrated anew, I tugged at his T-shirt, urging him to take it off.

"You're too serious lately. You're playing nursemaid to me all day, and it's wearing on you. I just want to relax and be close to you, okay?"

I feathered my fingers through his dark hair, pushing the messy strands back from his forehead. He seemed tired, and somehow, just as run down on the outside as I felt on the inside. We'd been through so much.

"Okay," he murmured softly.

I turned to the mirror while he undressed. I pulled my hair out of the messy bun that was holding it up. I winced at the small pain in my abdomen caused by lifting my arms. I looked terrible. Even being bound to the couch for weeks, I was thinner. And pale. I'd missed the last warm weeks of summer. I wanted to look and feel like myself again, and less like the fragile broken creature I'd become in the wake of these terrible events.

I dropped the hair tie into my make up drawer. Set amongst cosmetics, my opened pill case stared up at me. I picked it up. I'd been halfway through the month's cycle when it happened.

Blake paused. "What's that?"

"Just my pills." I shrugged, trying to seem casual, but nothing was casual about my fertility now. The topic had become a giant elephant in the room. I dropped the pills on the counter. My thoughts spun, and I laughed to myself.

"What's so funny?" Blake met my gaze in the mirror.

I looked down quickly, not wanting to revisit the pain I'd seen in his face when the doctor had delivered the news. I was alive, but damaged. Then again, what else was new?

"I don't know. I spent years trying not to get pregnant, worrying that I would, and now I couldn't even if I wanted to. But because there's a chance, I'll probably still need to take those damn things."

He took the pills and threw them back into a drawer. "Forget about those. Come on, before the bath gets cold."

Eager to forget, I pushed the thought out of my mind. Blake helped me into the tub and I lowered into the warm water. I relaxed, grateful for the relief. When he joined me, his legs slid to the outsides of mine. His hair was rough against my skin. I exhaled heavily at the simple contact, the reminder that we hadn't touched each other much since all of this happened. Somehow, between the weeks of being poked and prodded with needles and coddled like a helpless victim, I'd forgotten the simple pleasure of having Blake's skin on mine. His touch alone could soothe me, heal me.

I leaned my head back against the lip of the tub. "I feel a little decadent."

"Yeah? How is that?"

"It's a Tuesday afternoon, and we're lounging in the bathtub."

He laughed softly. "Maybe we deserve a little decadence." Beneath the water, he caught my foot and began to massage my muscles. The sensation was almost overwhelming. God, I missed his touch. Even the simple ones, my hand in his, a gentle kiss, made me want more.

"We deserve a lot of things."

He stilled a second. I regretted the words when I said them. I hurried to change the subject.

"Have you heard from Fiona lately? She must be frustrated. All that planning just to put everything off. I'm feeling better now, so maybe we can start planning again."

"You were shot three times, Erica. I don't think rescheduling the wedding until you're well is an inconvenience. We're all happy you're alive. The nuptials can wait."

I ran my fingers through the bubbles. A question, one I was terrified to ask, lingered on my lips. We hadn't talked about what the doctor had said after we left the hospital. We hadn't spoken a word of it.

"You haven't changed your mind?"

Seconds ticked by as I waited for his answer. Avoiding his eyes, I imagined all the things he might say. No matter how many times he reassured me that I was the only one he wanted, doubt managed to creep through time and again.

"Why on earth would I change my mind?" His voice was serious, hoarse with emotion.

I struggled over the next words, forcing myself to meet his eyes. "Things are different now."

His jaw set. "Things are different every day, but what hasn't changed and what will never change is how much I love you. I asked you to be my wife. I want that now more than ever."

I took a breath, my nerves suddenly on edge. "But don't you want a family, Blake? We never really talked about it, but now… What if I can't give that to you?" My heart beat wildly over the painful ache there. Maybe he'd never admit it, but if this changed things for him—for us— I wanted to know now.

The look he gave me was unwavering, void of doubt. "I want *you*."

I exhaled heavily. "This is important. We should talk about what it means for our future. This wasn't something either of us could have predicted. I don't want you to resent me if I can't—"

A flash of irritation broke his determined stare. "Jesus, Erica, come here." He caught my hand and, leaning forward, carefully lifted me from the other side of the tub so that I was straddling him. We were chest to chest. He held my face in his hands. They were warm and slid over my skin slowly.

"We'll figure it out, okay?"

My heart hadn't slowed. I still didn't believe him. "But what if we can't?"

He winced. "Stop talking like it'll never happen."

"There's still a chance, I know." Unlikely, but there was a chance.

"Exactly."

I nodded slowly. Maybe he was right.

"Have you ever known me to not get what I want?"

"No," I admitted.

"Good. If we want a baby, we will have one. One way or the other. First things first. We're going to get you well. Then you're going to toss those pills."

I stared at him in shock.

"We're not going to be able to plan anything anyway. If we try to do that, you'll just worry and I'll worry. Let's just live our lives. Let me make love to you every night, and if it's meant to be, it'll happen."

I opened my mouth to speak, but he stopped me, pressing his finger to my lips.

"No what-ifs. I can be quite determined when I want to be. I'm pretty sure if you want a baby, I'm going to give you one."

His words nearly knocked the wind from my lungs. They rushed in over the daggers of my pain. Soothing and pure. I believed him.

I leaned against him, finding the broad toned muscles of his chest. His heart beat a steady rhythm under my fingertips. Sometimes I had to remember that he was human like me, because to me, he was always more. Larger than life, stronger than anyone I knew, with determination that matched my own. In my heart, I believed we could do anything together.

I lost myself in his eyes, a tornado of hazel and passion that reflected between us. "I love you," I whispered, kissing him sweetly. Starting soft, I reveled in the simple pleasure of his full lips against mine. Then the sweep of my tongue, an invitation for his. Then his taste. I kissed him deeper.

He touched my cheek and pulled back a little.

I shifted over him, all too aware of his growing desire. "All this talk of babies, Blake, for the first time in my life, is actually making me want to make one. I wasn't expecting that."

A ghost of a smile passed over his lips. "We can't. Not today…"

I felt for him under the water and smoothed my palm around his cock. He sucked in a breath, closing his eyes slowly.

"Erica, we can't."

"I know," I said, hushing him with a kiss. "The doctor didn't say I couldn't please you, though, did he?"

"You don't have to—"

I silenced him again, deepening our kiss. I tightened my grip around him and quickened my motions up and down his length. His hands moved restlessly over my shoulders, fisting into my hair as we devoured each other's mouths. His muscles flinched under me where our bodies met, and my core clenched in response. Something awakened. That passion that could never be tamed between us lit up inside of me. I wanted release. But right now I wanted his more. I wanted to show him how much I loved him, thank him for walking through hell with me now and having faith in our future. I couldn't imagine my life without this man, and I prayed he wouldn't resent me if I couldn't give him the family he wanted.

He grasped my hips and then released abruptly. "Erica, I want to, badly, but I can't do this. You're driving me nuts. I want to touch you, but I'm scared to death of hurting you right now."

I slowed my upward stroke and drew back from his body slightly. His face was tight, every muscle coiled and ready for release. I wanted to give him that, but I needed to take the fear in his eyes away somehow too.

"Put your hands on the rim of the tub."

He winced slightly, maybe at the tone. I knew he wouldn't hurt me, but if I made it sound like an order, maybe he'd feel safer that he wouldn't. He lifted his hands out of the water and rested them on the edge of the tub the way I'd asked him to.

"Now keep them there. Don't move them until I tell you, okay?"

His bottom lip disappeared from view as he sucked it into his mouth, his white teeth biting into the plump flesh.

I cocked an eyebrow. "Okay?"

He nodded, and I circled both hands around his cock. I stacked my hands, sliding up his length, so that I was touching every inch of him. He flinched beneath my touch when I thumbed over the soft sensitive head.

"God, I miss you, Erica." He exhaled, his head rolling back onto the rim of the tub.

I leaned against him, my nipples grazing his chest above the water. "I love you, Blake." I sucked at his skin, licked the salty flavor from it. "And I love watching you come."

With white knuckles, he held tightly to the edge of the tub. He lifted his head and gazed at me with intense eyes. He was close. I kissed him hard, until he gasped for air.

"Come," I said, mimicking the order he'd given me so many times.

Hips thrusting upward into my rapid effort, he climaxed with a violent shudder and a strangled moan.

★ ★ ★

After numerous attempts, Blake finally lured me out of the apartment to come to work with him. I was trying to grasp onto the positive, but memories of what I'd been through would inevitably drag me back down. I didn't want to leave the house. I didn't want to come face-to-face with the world that had maimed me. Also, I couldn't stomach anything remotely close to an office knowing that a few blocks away, Sophia and Isaac's new business was carrying on without me day after day.

Sometimes I wondered if they knew about the shooting. Of course they would have heard about it. The question was—did they care? Did it matter at all that I'd almost died?

It's just business, I muttered to myself in my best mocking Alex voice. I needed to move on and find hope with new things. Everything had changed, like it or not. I had to accept that.

My thoughts kept returning to Geoff's project. Even as I mourned Clozpin, I found myself thinking through the logistics of his venture. I had too much free time not to. But I'd ignored Geoff's last emails from before the shooting, and he hadn't reached out to me since. I wasn't sure he even wanted my help anymore. If he did, what could I offer? Money, but no guidance. Investment alone would be an empty kind of support. I didn't want to just fund things. I wanted to be a part of them, but I didn't know what I was really capable of after all this.

I could barely manage to get farther than the grocery

store these days.

Instead of venturing out and trying to start over, I turned my attentions to the apartment. I cooked every night. I ordered decor online, determined to bring a piece of myself into the space that previously had been dominated by Blake's simple minimalist world. Blake didn't argue. He seemed content that I was getting up and around, even if I refused to leave the house for more than short trips. Even with Clay in toe, I felt uneasy.

I tried to start painting rooms, but Blake wouldn't let me, afraid the physical effort would upset the healing I'd already done. But despite his fussing, I was better. I still felt the pain, but I was better. The garish red wounds had faded slightly. Not enough to blend in, but the doctor promised me in time that they would. My skin tone would be forgiving. I had to take solace in the small things.

I tensed as we walked toward Blake's office. His hand touched the small of my back, a reminder of his constant support. I slowed in front of the door, but Blake stopped short.

"I want to show you something first. Let's go up." He motioned toward the elevator.

"What's up there?"

He grinned. "You'll see."

I followed him in and waited for our ascent to begin. As the elevator doors opened, he covered my eyes with his hands. "What are you doing to me?" I laughed, trying to hide my nervousness.

"It's a surprise. We'll be there in a few seconds. Walk with me."

Carefully I followed his guiding motions until we slowed to a stop. I heard voices, and they seemed familiar. Blake moved his hands, and I winced at the sudden brightness. I faced a door much like the one leading into his office below. On the frosted glass read, *E. Landon, Inc.*

My heart beat heavily in my chest. "Blake…"

Through the clear glass of the lettering, I saw faces I knew. Opening the door, Alli greeted me from inside. She smiled broadly. "Surprise!"

I laughed, not entirely sure yet what the surprise consisted of. "What is all this?"

Work stations filled the long room. Sid and Cady were standing by one where they'd been talking, their focus on me now. Geoff stood up from one of the desks, his blue eyes bright with the excitement that everyone else seemed to share.

I felt like Dorothy, reunited with all of her best friends after an adventure of the most strange kind. But what the hell? I looked to Blake.

"Do you want to tell me what this is all about?"

Alli beat him to the punch "When you were on the mend, Sid and I got to talking. With the payout from the sale, we didn't have to jump into anything else just yet. Then Blake introduced us to Geoff. He told us how interested you were in the project. And we decided to get together and see if we could help make it happen."

My hands trembled as they reached my lips. The news was overload. "This is too much. I can't tell you how happy it makes me to see you all here."

Sid gave me a shy smile. "We feel the same way.

We've missed you."

I swallowed over the emotion tight in my throat. "I thought we'd lost everything. Honestly, after everything that's happened lately, I started to realize this is what I missed the most. Working with everyone again. I never thought we'd get another chance."

Alli's lip trembled, threatening to set off tears of my own. She pulled me into a hug, full of meaning and understanding. I couldn't have gotten through this without her. She pulled back and wiped a tear away with her hand. "Well, go look at your office. It's so awesome."

Blake caught my hand, excitement glimmering in his eyes.

I brightened with a smile. "Sure."

He led me to the far end of the room and into an expansive private office. The door clicked behind us.

He'd spared no expense furnishing the space. A large executive desk filled the room, along with a small couch and an enormous write-board. Small items that I'd stashed in a box back home decorated my desk the way they had at the old space.

"Thank you for all of this. Thank you for everything. This is truly amazing."

"And private," he murmured, curling an arm around my waist.

I closed my eyes, devastated by the smallest touch. Weeks had gone by, and I was ready to lose it. I turned to wrap my arms around his neck. I crashed into him, kissing him with fervent passion. He returned my eagerness, backing me up gently to the desk.

Grateful as I was for the space, the world had ceased to exist beyond the two of us in that moment. "I want you, Blake. God, I'm dying wanting you."

"I know." He kissed me, softer tender brushes of his lips over mine. "But let's wait."

I gasped. "Wait?"

"We're getting married in a few days. An army couldn't come between me and making love you to on our wedding night. We've waited this long. What's a few more days?"

I sighed almost painfully, willing the surge of desire to ebb away. A few more days. An eternity when so much time had passed without intimacy. I closed my eyes, relenting. "Okay."

He smiled and tipped my chin up. "I will be making good use of this desk in the future, though. Rest assured."

CHAPTER NINETEEN

The sea rolled in with the tide. Warmth and the promise of change mingled with the ocean air. Turquoise and gray clouds slid across the autumn sky, revealing the clear blue above. A perfect day.

Someone called my name. Alli leaned over the Landon's deck, waving me inside. The giddy smile that marked her features today hadn't changed. The knot of anticipation in my belly grew, threatening to explode every few minutes.

Today was the day. Today I would become Blake's wife. Today we would bind ourselves to one another, for always.

I joined Alli and the other girls. Caterers and family friends buzzed around Blake's parents' house. Alli pulled me into one of the large bedrooms where everyone was getting ready.

Fiona was already dressed, a picture of perfection in her strapless flowing lavender bridesmaid gown. Alli and Simone rotated between distracting me from being nervous and telling me what to do next. Makeup, hair, and smiling for the ever-present photographer capturing our casual moments.

We were light, champagne bubbling through us. Everything about today was surreal. Each moment moved in slow motion but slipped away too quickly. Blake's mother fussed over us. Fiona rushed around after every detail, ensuring perfection for a day that she'd spent so much time helping to plan. Alli doted and directed me, making sure I was everywhere I needed to be. We laughed and fought tears. I wanted to tuck each moment away, so I could remember it forever.

Blake and the boys were nowhere to be found. No one wanted to fess up to where they were hiding out. I missed him, but I honored tradition and resolved to wait. We'd waited so long. I could wait a little longer.

Marie arrived before everything was about to begin. She was stunning, in a shimmery espresso dress that hugged her lithe figure. She came close and hugged me tightly.

"You look beautiful. Thank you for being here," I whispered.

She smiled warmly, tears shimmering in her eyes. "So do you. And there's no place I'd rather be than here with you, baby girl."

"No crying!" Alli barked. "Her makeup is perfect. Hold it together, people."

We both laughed, Alli's order adding some levity to the moment. Marie and I had made our amends. We were both sorry, for our pride and for everything that had pushed us apart. She was still mourning Richard, still in shock that he'd not only betrayed her, but had also been ripped from her life so suddenly. She'd loved him, I had little doubt. The tears she fought each time we met since the shooting told me so.

He'd been at the wrong place at the wrong time, but so had I. I wanted to blame Daniel, but I could have easily blamed myself for naively bringing him into my life months ago, thrusting myself into his dangerous world and not knowing the consequences of my choice. Life had played out, but too much had happened to carry grudges. Richard had lost his life, and I'd almost lost mine. Marie was too important to me, and life had proven too short to put any more distance between us.

"You ready for all this?" she asked.

I laughed. "I think so, yeah."

"I think so too." She smiled. "You're going to be beautiful, Erica. But I'm going to seriously lose it when I see you in your dress."

"Hold that thought," Alli said.

She'd emerged from the adjoining bathroom with a large garment bag containing my wedding dress. The well of happy tears surged behind my eyes again. I took breath after steadying breath, determined not to ruin the makeup she'd spent hours perfecting.

A few minutes later, I stepped into the dress and Marie carefully zipped up the back, sealing the fabric tightly around my chest. There wasn't a spare inch anywhere. I couldn't imagine how the dress could fit me any better. The gown was a light cream with a sweetheart neckline, a thousand tiny little beads embroidered into the lace that overlaid the layer of soft satin beneath. Elegant and understated. Delicate and feminine.

I would become Blake's wife in this dress. I'd say our vows. Our vows... I closed my eyes, imagining all the things I wanted to say to Blake. How much he meant to me, and how that would never change.

Alli gave my shoulders a little squeeze. "I'm dying right now. I hope you realize that."

I laughed. "Why?"

A warm smile lit her eyes. "Okay, I'm insanely jealous, but it all pales in comparison to how totally happy I am for you both. I just can't believe this is really happening. I feel like this is the happiest day of my life, but it's yours."

I nodded quickly, my vision blurring with tears.

"It is a beautiful dress," I admitted. The girl wearing it was a wreck though. Only another hour and I'd be in the clear.

"What can I say? I have awesome taste."

I skimmed my hands down the delicate lace that hugged my waist and tapered off at my thighs. "You do. Thank God you came back to Boston. I'd be hopeless without you."

A knock came at the door, jarring me. Fiona opened the door and frowned at a dapper looking Heath, dressed in a sharp tuxedo. "What are you doing here?"

"Special delivery."

Alli's eyes lit up, as if he'd been the groom and this was the first they'd laid eyes on each other. I wanted to see that day, and I prayed Alli would have it. Heath circled around the door.

"A little gift, from the groom." He winked and set a large flat box on my lap before disappearing out of the girl's den.

Simone squealed a little and came closer as I opened it up. Inside, I uncoiled a decadent string of diamonds. Gasps and awes faded into the background.

"Holy shit," Simone muttered under her breath. "Are those diamonds?"

I swallowed hard. "I'm pretty sure." I couldn't begin to fathom the price of the piece, but I'd never seen anything so beautiful.

I handed it to Simone who fastened the shimmering necklace around my neck. It was breathtakingly beautiful, and matched the other gifts—my ring and bracelets—in such a meaningful way.

A few more minutes of bustling and preparing and we started our way through the house. Beyond the windows facing the ocean and the sprawling yard, I could see the guests and wedding party waiting in the warm October sunshine. I trembled at the sight, excited but in disbelief.

"Erica."

I spun and Elliot approached. Beth was by his side, and Clara and Marissa too, in sweet matching white dresses.

"Oh my goodness, don't you look beautiful," I said.

The girls smiled, excitement lighting up their eyes. Alli bent down, handing them flower petals and our rings, reminding them of the tasks we'd practiced the night before.

Elliot caught my hand, squeezing gently. "You ready?"

I released a nervous breath. *Yes*. Nerves aside, I had never been more ready to be Blake's wife. I wanted to step through the doors and run to him. I wanted to marry him the moment I laid my eyes on him. In my heart, I already had.

I nodded and linked my arm through Elliot's, letting

him escort me the rest of the way.

I walked toward Blake, seeing only him. I was floating, every moment taking me closer to the love of my life. And now, there was no fear in my heart. No doubt, not a shadow of it.

The ceremony passed like a dream. Blake, breathtaking in his tuxedo against the backdrop of the ocean. His family and mine, our friends witnessing what we'd known for so long, that we wanted forever with each other.

There were kisses. There were tears. All I knew was that he was mine. My love for him now was a tattoo written on my heart, for all of time.

★ ★ ★

I leaned my head against Blake's shoulder while the party ensued. The day had been long, but adrenaline kept me awake. The heated tent set up in the Landon's yard was filled with our small party. Laughter and music and talking. Happiness surrounded us.

Elliot's girls were dancing with boundless energy on the dance floor around Blake's parents who looked into each other's eyes with a love that warmed my heart. Blake's mentor, Michael Pope, had come too. We didn't speak of Max, but I could see the pride in his eyes when he congratulated us. He'd been like a second father to Blake, and I could only feel his regret that Max had failed us all with his appalling actions.

Still, nothing could dim the celebration. More people

came than I had expected. Our "small" affair had grown in size in my absence, but in the happy embrace of Blake's extended family and friends, I could not have felt more love and acceptance. I smiled, all the way down to my very sore feet. Today had been nothing short of perfect.

I leaned up, pressing a soft kiss to Blake's cheek.

He looked down, trailing lazy caresses up and down my arm. "Let's take a walk and get some fresh air."

"What about our guests?"

He stared out at the party, which had grown increasingly loud over the past hour as glasses were refilled and the night wore on. Simone was talking loudly and Alli was laughing.

"They're having a blast without us. I've had to share you all day. Now I want you for myself." He brushed his thumb across my cheek. "I don't know about you, but I'm anxious for the honeymoon to start."

I bit my lip, and he flashed me a loving smile.

The thrill of being in his arms again warmed me, filling me with contentment. My entire body seemed to buzz with happiness, elation that I was now Blake's and soon, hopefully soon, I'd be even more his.

"Where are we going?"

"I know just the place."

He winked and caught my hand, leading me out of the tent and down the wooden stairs to the beach below. I glanced back at the wedding party. Simone's voice rang out from her perch on James's lap. He was smiling, looking up at her with adoring eyes. No one was missing us.

The sun had set and the ocean breeze blew cool over

my skin. I held my dress and shoes up with one hand while Blake held my other. We walked, anticipation seeming to steal our words. I looked ahead to the rocky incline that always ended our journey when we walked the beach at his parents' house.

"Where are we going? My feet are killing me."

"It'll be worth it, I promise." His eyes sparkled as if he were holding a secret behind them.

We slowed as the sandy beach turned to pebbles and stone. Blake wrapped his arm around me. I shivered and huddled into the warmth of his embrace. We stared out at the dark horizon. Above us, a soft glow lit the homes scattered along the shoreline.

"I love it here." Next to the Vineyard, Blake's parents' stretch of home on the ocean was nothing short of heaven.

He pointed up to the house perched above the cliff ending at our feet. "What do you think about that one?"

"It's breathtaking." Everything about the home was impressive. While Catherine and Greg's home was more modern, this home had all the charm of a historic house. It sprawled across manicured gardens and a yard overlooking the endless ocean.

He squeezed me closer. "I want to give it you."

I raised my eyebrows. "The house?"

He grinned. "Yes, the house, among other things."

"Please tell me you don't plan to walk in and make them an offer."

He laughed. "No, I don't think so. Come on. Let's take a closer look."

He started ahead of me and turned back for my hand.

I hesitated, trying to imagine how I'd scale the small cliff with my current attire. "I'll ruin my dress."

"Who cares? You only get to wear it once."

"What am I going to do with my shoes?" I lifted them up. He grabbed them and tossed each one high up to the grassy yard of our destination.

"Blake," I laughed. "I'm sure these people don't want us poking around looking in their windows."

"Nonsense. No one's home."

I shook my head and took his hand, making my way up the rocky incline. Blake helped me up onto the yard that plateaued at the top. The dewy grass felt cool on my feet as we walked around the perimeter of the house. He led me to the front door, a grand entryway framed by white columns and ornate lighting.

"Blake!" I uttered a harsh whisper as he tried the door, opening it. Before I could stop him, he scooped me up into his arms, walking me over the threshold.

He lowered me to my feet when we passed through the entryway. A large, bright white kitchen sat to our right and an expansive open living area to the left. I took in what details I could in the almost darkness. Blake tightened his hold around my waist, bringing me up against his chest.

"What do you think?" he whispered, delight glimmering in his beautiful eyes.

"It's beautiful." I ran my finger over his lips. "Like you."

He moaned and lifted me off my feet as he did. "Like you."

I tasted the champagne on his tongue and felt the

giddiness from our amazing day rolling off of him. I'd never seen him so outwardly happy.

"I think you're a little drunk," I teased as he set me back down, a broad smile across his face.

"I'm happy. I'm the happiest man alive right now. I can guarantee it."

I returned his smile, unable to argue. I was beyond happy too. He spun me around and walked me up the stairs.

"Where are you going?"

"I'm giving you the grand tour. You like it so far, right?"

I laughed. "I couldn't dream up a more beautiful home, honestly. There's only one problem."

He looked back at me and arched his eyebrows. "What's that?"

"It's not ours, and you can now add breaking and entering to your list of illegal activities achieved in this lifetime. If you want to go house hunting when we get back from the honeymoon, you officially have my permission. We should go. I have bigger plans for tonight than jail."

"Trust me, so do I." He paused on the landing, pulling me up to him. "I want to show you one more thing. I want you to close your eyes first though."

He lifted me back into his arms, and I sensed we were moving down a long hallway. Night had filled the house, but behind my eyelids I saw light. Panicked that we weren't as alone as I thought we were, I opened my eyes. We'd entered a large bedroom, about three times the size of our current one.

Situated in the center of the room was an enormous four-poster bed draped in a silky blue comforter. On the opposite wall, an ornate fireplace was set into the wall and cast off a warm glow from the fire inside. On its mantle and every available surface, candles burned, lighting the large room. What was all of this?

"Blake." My voice was barely a whisper.

He lowered me to my feet, keeping my body pressed close to his. I looked up into his eyes, sparkling now more than ever. The mischief there had been replaced by something else.

"It's ours. Yours and mine."

My breath left me. "This...?"

"The house. All of it. It's my wedding gift to you."

"A house?" I laughed, incredulous but somehow not at all surprised that Blake had justified the extravagant purchase for our special day.

"Do you like it?" he asked, his expression tentative.

Tears formed in the corners in my eyes. "Blake, it's... My God, it's beautiful. I don't know what to say." A thought occurred to me then that we were literally only steps away from his parents. "Your parents, they know?"

His hesitation vanished with a grin. "Are you kidding me? Catherine was the one who told me as soon as the neighbors were going to put the house on the market. We had an agreement before they could even talk to a realtor."

Wow.

"I can't believe you did this." I was still in disbelief that this enormous, magnificent home would be ours.

Ours. "Are you okay being so close?"

He nodded. "It'll be an adjustment. But I owe it to them in a way. I've spent a lot of time on the fringes, until recently. And I thought it would be good for us to finally be closer to family."

I looked down, toying with the rose that poked out of his jacket pocket. "I love them like they're my own."

He lifted my chin, stroking my cheek gently. "They are yours. We're one family now, you and I. And they love you like a daughter. That will never change."

"I'm the luckiest girl in the world."

He ran a thumb over my trembling lips, lowering slowly to capture them with a kiss. "I'll spend the rest of my life making sure that never changes. I want to give you everything..."

I lifted to my toes, surrendering to the love in his kiss. His hands roamed. He exhaled unsteadily.

"Are you ready to say goodbye to this dress for the night? Because I can't wait another minute to make love to you."

I nodded, breathless and speechless. He caressed down my shoulders.

"So beautiful."

I turned in his arms. He made quick work of the clasp and zipper at the back of my dress. The weighty fabric fell to the floor, pooling at my feet. Behind me, I heard Blake tossing his own garments to the floor. I turned and caught him staring, slack-jawed, hunger in his eyes. I stood before him, in the white lacy underthings I knew he'd love.

He traced the hem of my panties and thumbed over

the scar emerging above it. Out of the dizzying happiness of the day, a small sadness floated over me. He caught my chin, lifting my gaze to meet his.

"No sad eyes tonight. This is the time for the man of the house to make passionate love to his beautiful bride. I may not stop for hours, because I'm starving for you."

Then his hands were everywhere, unhooking the corset and slipping down the delicate white lace panties just the way I'd imagined he would. Lowering to his knees, he lingered, pressing delicate kisses over my belly and just above the patch of hair between my legs.

Slowing over the place on my abdomen where the wound had puckered the skin, he brushed his lips over the dark pink scar that had begun to form. I had tried to ignore the imperfection, averting my eyes whenever they were drawn to it as I was dressing or undressing.

"Don't, Blake..." I covered myself, feeling self-conscious. I tugged at his shoulders, urging him to his feet.

He stood, only to coax me back onto the soft bed and return his attentions to my lower half, kissing, licking. I gasped when he dragged his tongue down the inside of my thigh and back up again. He moved up my body, claiming every expanse of skin with his amazing mouth until I was quivering and on edge.

He captured my face in his hand, all traces of humor having left his expression, our bodies warm with passion and champagne and the candles casting heat and a warm glow across our skin. "Erica...I love you...all of you. Even your scars."

The deep, determined kiss that followed his words

stole my breath. I wasn't sure if I could have formed a word or taken a full breath anyway, the way he was holding me and touching me. I'd missed him so much.

"I told you I was going to kiss every inch of you one night. I'm almost done."

He lifted my knees, hooking them over his shoulders. Then his mouth was over me, lavishing firm, deliberate licks over the hot ache between my thighs. His tongue teased my opening, taunting me with shallow dips into the place where I was already soaked for him.

I gripped his hair tightly. I lifted against him, desperate for more contact against that sensitive spot. My thighs trembled, brushing against his shaven face. With strong hands, he parted me again, baring me for him completely.

I gripped the comforter, bracing myself for the orgasm that loomed and threatened to take me under. I couldn't believe we'd made it this long, but now that we had, I was helpless against the sensations rocketing through me. A few more seconds of dedicated attention under his mouth and I was at the edge. My heart beat wildly. I was starved for him, an exposed nerve, waiting for him to set me off with a spark. Then he did, tonguing me until I could scarcely breathe.

"Blake!"

I screamed his name, frozen around the pleasure he gave me. It had been too long. I shuddered, utterly blissed out, but knowing that we had the whole night.

He rose over me, his toned body warm and protective over mine. I caught my breath, letting him come into focus again. He smiled and kissed me sweetly.

"I missed that," I hummed.

"Me too. You're going to lose count of how many times I make you come tonight. I have to make up for lost time."

A delirious smile curled my lips, contentment washing over me. "I can't wait."

His arms rested on either side of my head as he stared down with a look that felt like wonder. "Erica, do you have any idea how much I love you?"

I swallowed hard. If he loved me a fraction of how much I loved him, I knew. Every sliver of wonder in his stare ricocheted into me, landing squarely on my heart. I feathered my fingertips over the hard lines of his features, awe and desire mingling inside of me.

"I think so. But I'd rather you show me."

He closed his eyes a long moment. Gently he kneed my legs apart. I wrapped my legs around his hips, urging him to me.

Slowly, he slid inside of me, joining us together. I whimpered, growing tense around his body. I cried out softly, trembling with the pleasure of having him inside me again, filling me so perfectly after such an absence.

The first wave of pleasure overtook me. The sheer bliss of our bodies together again almost too much to bear. I came back down, only to feel my desire building again.

"Blake," I whimpered, clinging to him as he took me there, again and again, with deep, steady thrusts.

I'd grown slick around him, my thoughts swirling from the passion in our touch, the energy that exploded between us every time we made love. We had all night like this. We had every night. We had forever.

Blake nuzzled into my hair, inhaling me, kissing me, loving me.

"My wife," he whispered.

A tear fell, sliding down to my ear. Our breath mingled, ragged and in time with each other all at once. We couldn't be any closer. We were one. Nothing could tear us apart.

CHAPTER TWENTY

Over the speakers, airport staff rattled off boarding instructions for the flights around us while we waited for our turn. By morning we'd be in Dublin, the first stop of the month long honeymoon that Blake had promised and planned for us. I sat beside him, focusing on some invisible point in the darkness that had fallen outside.

I'd spent weeks having downtime. Emotionally and physically I had struggled to get back on my feet. But becoming Blake's wife had lit a fire inside of me again. I was ready to start fresh. Jet setting around the world or even just a small part of it was a good start in a new direction.

My phone vibrated in my pocket, distracting me from my daydreaming. James's name appeared and I answered quickly.

"James, hey."

"Hey, I'm super sorry if I'm interrupting your honeymoon. I wasn't sure if you'd left yet."

"I'm at the airport actually. What's up?"

He cleared his throat. "I was wondering if you might have any room for a front-end developer at the new office?"

I hesitated, a little blindsided by the request. "Why? Is everything okay?"

"Not really, no. Everything has gone to shit here. The site… It's gone."

"What?" I looked over at Blake and turned the volume up on the phone so he could hear James.

"Things were transitioning okay with their team. I mean, not great, but Isaac's techies were figuring things out slow but sure. We were moving it to the Perry Media Group servers, and everything went down." He sighed. "They accused me of sabotaging the switch. Obviously I didn't, so I left."

"Do you think we were hacked?" I shook my head. I still spoke about Clozpin as if I had some claim over it. I didn't. I'd lost it.

"Definitely."

"Really? Has anyone taken responsibility since you left?"

He paused, and my thoughts filled in the silence. Threats from the past lurked in the confines of my mind. But how…

"I think it's Trevor."

My heart stopped, Trevor's name echoing in the silence. The ghost that I'd hoped would disappear along with Max when Blake had taken out their copycat site. He was still the one person I could always count on to viciously troll and attack our online assets. He'd been mercifully absent. Could he really be back to haunt us now? I glanced up to Blake, his eyes steely and cold.

"But why? Sophia and Isaac aren't allies. Why would he attack their assets?"

"If this is Trevor's handiwork, I'd be willing to bet he had no idea Isaac is on your bad side. For all he knows, it was a completely amicable sale, and that you're still vested."

I released an exasperated sigh. "I'm surprised they haven't reached out to me…"

"I think they've got their hands full trying to pick up the pieces right now. But with all the bad press and the downtime, it's going to be hard for them. We were small, and when Trevor hit us, we recovered pretty easily. This is different. Everything they've done since the sale has been in the spotlight, because Isaac's been putting this new venture in the limelight from the day you left."

I closed my eyes. I wouldn't have known. I'd been living in near isolation for weeks. Plus, if anyone had gotten wind of this, they likely wouldn't have told me. "This is crazy."

"There's more."

I lifted my eyebrows. "Oh?"

"Whoever hacked their site also hacked email accounts hosted on Perry's server. They've been releasing things."

"Like what?"

"Email transcripts and illicit photos."

I thought I might be sick. Illicit photos?

"Photos of who?" I asked tentatively.

"Isaac with models, along with a hell of a lot of complaints. Did you know he's got a handful of girls threatening him with sexual harassment lawsuits? Sophia basically blackmailed him into acquiring your site along with Alex's business, because she had all this dirt on him. She promised to keep the girls at her agency quiet in exchange for a slice of the ownership of Clozpin."

I ground my teeth. I knew it. I knew she had something on Isaac. I couldn't possibly know what though.

Diversify, my ass. She'd wanted revenge, and she'd gotten it.

"It's turned into a complete PR shit storm for Perry Media," James continued. "I don't want anywhere near it. Chris put out feelers and got recruited to another tech lab here in the city. I was going to do the same, but figured I'd touch base with you first. I wanted to leave with the rest of you, but you know, we're not all married to billionaires."

I laughed softly, flashing a look to Blake. "No, I understand. And I don't blame you. I just couldn't... I couldn't stay and work with her. It would have been hell."

"Yeah, well, I can validate that. When it hasn't been stressful, it's been nothing short of hell."

"Honestly, I'd love to have you back. We're going to be working on some new projects as soon as Blake and I get back. Maybe we can meet up then."

"Sounds like a plan. And sorry for dropping this on you right now. I didn't mean to impose."

"Not at all, James. I'm glad you called. I'll talk to you soon."

We hung up, and I stared at the phone a moment, letting the shock settle over me. I wasn't sure if I was happy or not that Isaac and Sophia had managed to bulldoze my site to the ground. For the most part, I'd come to terms with losing it, but having their deceit and skeletons exposed in the process was undeniably satisfying.

What worried me more was the prospect that Trevor might be up to his old tricks. He'd been after Clozpin before. He was relentless, trying to meddle with Blake's affairs, until I'd confronted him. What could he possibly want from us after all this time and destruction?

"I can't believe it," I finally said, turning to Blake.

"I told you Isaac couldn't be trusted."

"True. And I told you Sophia was a conniving bitch. So I think we're both learning to trust each other's instincts, finally. Do you think Trevor did this?"

Blake stared past me. He appeared cold and emotionless, the way he could become whenever someone like Trevor threatened one of us. "Probably," he said finally.

"What are we going to do?"

He took my hand, holding it tightly. "Not a damn thing right now. Sounds like he has his sights set on Perry, so let him wreak havoc on them for awhile."

"He's not going away, Blake. You have to know that."

The speakers blared again with a new announcement. First class for our flight was boarding.

Blake stood to collect our bags. "Come on. Let's go."

I followed him, my thoughts heavy with the news James had left me with.

We took off out of Logan. The plane banked side to side gracefully, and the city lights came into view below us. For the moment, I convinced myself we were leaving all of our problems behind.

MEREDITH WILD

BLAKE AND ERICA'S STORY CONTINUES
IN THE HACKER SERIES SEQUEL,

HARD LOVE

TO BE RELEASE SPRING/SUMMER 2015

FIND UPDATES AT WWW.MEREDITHWILD.COM

ACKNOWLEDGEMENTS

For years my mother asked me when I was going to write a novel. I would roll my eyes and say something about never possibly having time for that. Three kids, a business that demanded so much of my time and energy, not to mention whatever else life could throw at me made that dream seemingly impossible. Never in my wildest fantasies did I imagine that writing would become such an important part of my life one day. Now that it has, I've become dedicated to keeping it that way as long as I can.

Over the course of penning *Hard Limit*, I had to make some very hard, heart-wrenching decisions. The hardest one of all was the decision to sell my business. Days after completing the manuscript and with a heavy heart, I drove down to Boston to say goodbye to a team I've grown to love, an industry that has taught me so much, and a place at the head of the table that has given me so much purpose for the past ten years.

This book is dedicated to the talented team who've made the business what it is today and who, over the years, have become some of my most loyal friends. Susan, Luc, Kurt, Derek, Yvonne, and Chris, from the bottom of my heart, thank you for your brilliance, for all the laughs, and for making me proud every single day.

This book is also dedicated, in a secondary way, to the people from my entrepreneurial travels who I would rather poke in the eye than look at but who've made lovely character profiles for my villains. And to all of the others who have crossed my path, however briefly, on this intense journey, thank you for whatever lessons and small moments you brought to my life. Every experience has helped make me who I am, and for that, I have no regrets.

While this milestone inspired a lot of emotions in the book, rest assured that I didn't sell my company to a villain and there are no circling hackers waiting for a chance to strike at me and my billionaire boyfriend. I have great faith in the next chapter of my life and that of the business. As real-life Sid always says when something mind-blowing happens...I love the future.

Eternal gratitude goes out to my husband, Jonathan, for speed walking through this incredible life with me. I love our adventures, and I love that we always have each other to enjoy the triumphs and get through the tough stuff together. As always, this book could not have come to fruition without your support, motivation, and single parenting.

I would like to thank my mom, Colleen, for helping keep me grounded, listening to all my venting, and lifting me up when I needed it the most. No surprise really, but I'm super lucky that you're my kind of crazy. We always have each other!

Mia Michelle...my Facebook bestie...my sweet! Thank you for always being there for me, for being real and cheering me on, and for vowing never to publish a tell-all novel based on our Facebook conversations. Seriously though, you are truly one of the most genuine people I know. You have a heart of gold, and I'm so blessed to have found you!

Many thanks to my editor, Helen Hardt. We've come a long way together in a year, and I can't imagine having taken this journey without your help and guidance.

Thanks once more to Remi, for consulting the stars and giving me so much to look forward to as life unfolds.

A big thank you goes out to my new get-things-done angel, Shayla Fereshetian. You have played no small part in saving my sanity these past few weeks. Ask anyone I know—they think your middle name is *awesome*. Be prepared to have your name listed here regularly!

Thanks to my rock star beta readers for your always thoughtful and amazingly prompt feedback. You cannot possibly know how important your input is to me in the process of putting a book into the world. Special thanks to the lovely Megan Cooke. Your twelve-page Word documents complete me!

Huge thanks to my proofers, Amy, Haidee, Liana, Jill, and Claire, for catching whatever I might have missed.

Last, but certainly not least, a big shout out to Team Wild and M89 Underground, my ever-dedicated street team crews, and to all of the beautiful fans and readers out there who have given me so much support and so many kind words. I write my books for you, and I can't wait to share *Hard Love* and many more stories with all of you very soon!

DISCUSSION QUESTIONS

How does stepping into Blake's head for the first time affect how you understand his character? Does his point of view change anything for you with how you view Blake or Erica?

Erica has two men who take on a fatherly role in her life: Elliot and Daniel. Both of these relationships are complicated. How have these different fatherly relationships affected Erica and the decisions she's made?

While they are in the club, Blake and Erica learn a lot about each other as they share a heated and honest moment together. Do you believe that Blake doesn't really want what the club offers? Do you think there is a part of Erica that does?

Erica makes one of the hardest decisions of her life when she decides to sell her business. Would you have made the same decision? In the end, when everything is revealed with the sale, do you think Erica would go back and change her mind about selling if she could?

Daniel ultimately makes the decision to separate himself from Erica in order to protect her and save her from all that surrounds him. In that moment, did you feel for the sacrifice that Daniel was making? Does this moment redeem Daniel at all for all that he's done?

Erica and Blake have both grown and evolved over the course of the series, but remnants of who they've been linger. In what ways do you see the "old" Erica and Blake in the "new" Erica and Blake you find in the present of the book?

Erica and Blake push one another emotionally, physically, and professionally. Do you think there will there ever be a point in their relationship where they no longer push each other, or is that part of the solid foundation that makes them who they are together?

Hard Limit is the fourth book in a series of five. With Blake and Erica's story nearing the end, where do you think the events of the next book will take them? How do you think their relationship will continue to evolve and change as they approach "the end"?

CPSIA information can be obtained at www.ICGtesting.com
Printed in the USA
LVOW07s1119201214

419729LV00004B/35/P